AF207550

Fine

FINE

a novel

AmyLea Murphy

FINE ©2020, AmyLea Murphy

All rights reserved. This book or parts thereof may not be reproduced in
any form, stored in any retrieval system, or transmitted in any form by any
means—electronic, mechanical, photocopy, recording, or otherwise—
without prior written permission of the publisher, except as provided
by United States of America copyright law. For permission requests,
contact: help@finenovel.com

Cover and eBook formatting by The Book Designers, Inc.

Ebook (.ePub) ISBN: 978-1-7352719-1-0
Ebook (.Mobi) ISBN: 978-1-7352719-2-7
Ebook (.PDF) ISBN: 978-1-7352719-3-4
Print Edition ISBN: 978-1-7352719-0-3

Library of Congress Control Number: 2020918359

For information about special discounts available for bulk purchases,
sales promotions, fund-raising, and educational needs
contact the publisher at help@finenovel.com

This is a work of fiction. Names, characters, places, and incidents are
either products of the author's imagination or are used fictitiously.
Any resemblance to actual persons, living or dead, businesses,
companies, events, or locales is entirely coincidental.

More information about this novel can be found at www.FineNovel.com.
Visit the Author's website at www.AmyLeaMurphy.com.

To Greg, Isabelle, Aiden, and Brian
—for being the light.

The most beautiful people are those who have known defeat, known suffering, known struggle, known loss, and have found their way out of the depths.

—*Elisabeth Kübler-Ross*

Buena Vida County
Sherriff's Office

PRESS RELEASE

FOR IMMEDIATE RELEASE: APRIL 21, 2012, 3:00 P.M.

MISSING PERSON

The Buena Vida County Sheriff's Office Criminal Investigations Division is asking for the public's help in locating seventeen-year-old Anna Williams, of Mission Valley Road.

On April 21, 2012, at 11:10 a.m., Buena Vida County Sheriff's Office deputies responded to 13677 Mission Valley Road in Buena Vida to investigate a report of a missing person. According to relatives of Anna Williams, she was last seen by friends and classmates at Macklemore High School around 3:15 p.m. on April 20, 2012.

Currently, our detectives are actively working to locate Anna Williams. Anna is described as a Caucasian female, 5'04", 115 lbs., with brown hair and brown eyes. The vehicle driven by Anna, a 2002 black Honda Civic, was found abandoned at the Macklemore High School Student Parking Lot.

If anyone has information or knows the whereabouts of Anna Williams, please call the Buena Vida County consolidated dispatch center at (657) 555-2504.

Today is Anna's 24th birthday.

Every year, on June 8th, I get out of whatever obligations I have and spend the day at home. I watch movies, eat macaroni and cheese, and listen to the CDs she made me. Sometimes I do something crafty, or even read one of her old books. I always spend Anna's birthday doing the things we used to do together, wallowing in my sorrow and celebrating the best sister anyone could ever have.

But not this year. This year I have to work because my manager, Roger, refused to give me the day off. Apparently, making smoothies is more important than my annual ritual. I would have called in sick, but my mom's been having a fit about me showing responsibility, and this job is the only thing I have going for me right now. So here I am, half-asleep, parking my car in front of The Smoothie Spot.

I check my face in the rearview mirror, taking an extra second to make sure I don't have anything in my teeth, and dig around the backseat for my apron. Once I yank it free from the shopping bags it's trapped under, I force myself to leave the safety and serenity of my Ford Focus.

I pull my unwashed hair into a loose ponytail and tie my apron on before theatrically rushing through the front door. Roger's behind the register and sees me right away. He gives me a dad look, which is ridiculous considering he's only three years older than me. I join him behind the counter hurriedly and flash him a pitiful smile, innocent like a puppy, hoping I can avoid yet another one of his lectures.

"You're late, Katie."

"I know, I know. It's just that today is—"

"I told you the next time you were late, you would be fired," Roger says in his condescending, nasal tone. "You're fired."

"Oh, come on! I'm only fifteen minutes late!"

"You're *always* fifteen minutes late," he sneers.

"Give me a break, Roger."

Two customers come in, moms in gym attire with toddlers on their hip. Roger and I plaster fake smiles on our faces.

"Welcome to The Smoothie Spot. Can we take your order?"

Roger rings them up while I busy myself with the blenders, fuming quietly. He's not really going to fire me, I assure myself. He wouldn't do that to me, not today.

As I pour the pineapple juice into the blender, Roger slithers towards me until he is uncomfortably close. I hear him whisper-yelling in my ear.

"I've given you a break, Katie. Your drawer has been short for the past month, you're rude to customers, and frankly, nobody wants to work with you."

"That's because they're a bunch of self-righteous, spoiled rich kids," I spew as I slam the two smoothies on the counter. "Order ready for yoga moms!"

"And yet those rich kids manage to get here on time and act politely to the customers."

"Look, I'm doing my best. Alright?"

"I seriously hope, for your sake, this isn't your best," he says as he looks me up and down. "You can collect your things."

"You're serious?" I squeal, realizing he's not bluffing this time. "Oh, come on! You have to give me another chance. I promise I'll be here on time from now on. I swear."

"I'm sorry," he says. But he isn't.

My face flushes with humiliation and rage. I storm into the back room and look around for anything that belongs to me, but nothing does. That fact makes me come unglued. For a minute, I consider taking one of the many Starbucks travel mugs from the employee shelf. Thinking better of it, I reach around to untie my apron and charge out towards the registers.

I walk straight up to Roger, pull my apron off and fling it at him. I can feel his embarrassment at being disrespected in front of the middle-aged woman asking about the protein boost. I won't lie—it feels good to see him squirm. Serves him right for ruining Anna's birthday on multiple levels.

"I don't need this stupid job anyway!" I shout as meanly as possible.

I head towards the door and notice the two moms staring at me with their smug, frozen Botox faces. I stare right back at them. Then I march up to the one with her midriff showing and snatch the green smoothie right out of her hand. I take a long sip in front of her as her mouth drops open. *Take that.*

After storming out dramatically, smoothie in hand, I run to my car and somehow manage to peel out of the parking lot before the tears start streaming down my cheeks. They come one after the other, silently. I do my best to ignore them as I drive my Focus in the direction of home—well, my old home.

I reach over to the passenger seat, fumbling around for my purse. It's lost amongst the millions of other things that have piled up on the passenger seat. While trying to keep my eyes on the road, I rummage through water bottles, scrunchies, and a bunch of junk. I yank out my sweatshirt and throw it in back, but as I do, my purse spills all over and I see the Buena Vida Community College flyer my mom gave me come flying out. Just like that, I can hear her voice booming in my head.

> *Katie, it's time you grow up. You are an adult now. I'm sorry, but you need to move out by the end of the summer. You need to figure out a way to afford your own place.*

My stomach drops at the thought of moving out. I'm not ready. I have no idea how to adult. I'm only eighteen. I just graduated high school, and that was a miracle in itself. I have no idea what I'm doing. I can't even keep a job at The Smoothie Spot. How am I going to find a place to live, let alone pay for it? I can feel myself heading towards a big, ugly cry.

No. I will not fall apart right now. I will hold it together. I thrust my hand into the mess and feel around the napkins, tampons, and phone charger until I find what I'm looking for—an old mint container filled with an assortment of pills. I pop it open and feel around for my mom's Xanax, pulling two pills out. Then I wash them down with the green smoothie I confiscated and take a few deep breaths. That's better.

Parked across the street from my old house on Mission Valley Road, I can feel my body calming down. There's something about this house that makes the world seem a little less awful. It's so grand and majestic with its columns flanking the red front door. The yard is meticulously maintained, just like all the neighboring houses, and there are lilies everywhere. Someone's walking a dog along the sidewalk, and I can hear a child laughing in the distance.

I have so many happy memories here. First day of school pictures on the front steps, helping my mom trim the roses in the front planter, and running amok with my sister all summer long. Anna used to make me peanut butter and jelly sandwiches for lunch, and we would eat them beneath the willow tree out front. It was our office— at least, it used to be.

Six years have come and gone since my sister vanished, not that anyone cares. That Friday morning, Anna left for school like always. She took too long in the bathroom and left her phone on the sink. I yelled at her to come get it, but she didn't hear me because her music was too loud. When I got out of the shower, she barged into the bathroom looking for it. I yelled, "A little privacy would be nice!" Twenty minutes later, she was driving to school and I was walking to the bus stop. That was the last time I saw her.

I was only twelve. Being an adolescent in the grips of hormones and social anxiety is hard enough when all you have to worry about is what outfit to wear and whether the cute guy in science class likes you or not. Being twelve when the worst tragedy you can imagine rips through your family—well, it just sucks.

At first, I was waiting for her to come home. Every day after school, I dropped my backpack on the kitchen table and called out her name, expecting her to pop her head out and say, "Hi, Kit Kat." It was just a matter of time before she would reappear, explaining where she was and why it took her so long to get back. I was sure she'd have an epic adventure to share.

Days went by and she never showed up. My stomach twisted in knots as I started to wonder. Where would she have gone? Why wouldn't she have told me where she was going? Was she going to stay gone forever?

These thoughts made me wretched and nauseous, but my mom sent me off to school anyway. I had to sit through class after class, unable to hide the fact that I couldn't care less about chemistry or Shakespeare. Teachers gave me sympathetic looks, but mostly left me alone while they went on lecturing and assigning homework as if it mattered. My friends acted super weird around me too, either avoiding any mention of Anna or offering clueless puppy dog eyes. Not knowing how to act around me, they ended up circling the same conversations about so-and-so's new haircut or the hilarious thing so-and-so did in fifth period. It was all I could do to survive until the bell rang.

At home, things weren't much better. My mom, who wasn't exactly together to start with, fell apart completely. She cried a lot, and when she wasn't crying, she was yelling. I wasn't sure what to do. Anna had always managed my mom's craziness after the divorce. My dad came around for a while, trying to help with putting together flyers and search parties, so he got the brunt of most of her screaming. It didn't last long, and soon he was gone again, leaving Mom and me on our own.

Every now and then, Mom would ask me if I was doing alright. I knew enough to be guarded, but occasionally I would open up. Within minutes, I would end up comforting her. She would carry on for hours, then make me stay up all night watching Hallmark movies—even on a school night. I didn't mind at first, but it became so predictable. She never wanted to talk about my feelings, just hers. Once she got it off her chest, she would go right back to yelling at me over some water glass I left on the coffee table. I realized that she was going to yell whether or not my room was clean or the dishwasher was unloaded, so I stopped doing chores and avoided her questions.

Soon enough, Mom got distracted with moving us into a small apartment where we are today. It's a two-bedroom on the second floor, complete with vaulted ceilings and a tiny white kitchen that looks like it was designed by Joanna Gaines. It's nice, of course, but it's never felt like home without our height marks etched in the hallway. Plus, a balcony with succulents is a sorry replacement for a yard. At least to me, it is.

Soon after we settled in, she became obsessed with getting back into the dating game, as she called it. I suppose she needed to think about something other than Anna. She flitted about from one boyfriend to another, and I was on my own in a strange new place. That's where I've been ever since.

I was just as eager to leave behind the nightmare of Anna's disappearance, to be honest. I spent all of my time at my friend Josie's house trying to play the part of an average teenager. We hung out at Denny's at all hours of the night, dyed our hair every color of the rainbow, and snuck out to smoke up whenever one of us got our hands on a joint. It was better than sitting home alone, haunted by Anna's ghost. Although now I wish I'd spent more time in this old house, close to all those memories of happier times.

I just miss Anna so much. She was everything to me—my big sister, my role model, and my best friend. We were inseparable as kids, spending hours looking for the long-lost Ladybug Queen or building make-believe boats on the swivel chairs in our living room. Anna was obsessed with reenacting movies, so she would make me dress up like Cinderella or Rapunzel and I would repeat whatever lines she fed me. As we got older, we watched movies, did our nails, or talked for hours over an unending game of Uno. I could tell her anything and I knew she would always know just what to say. Anna was my person. I don't know how anyone is supposed to go on with this life without their person.

It's hard to believe that it all happened six years ago. I've lived one-third of my life without Anna, yet I'm still just as lost as I was the moment she went missing. Time stopped the second she didn't come home, and after that, everything became so unreal. It's like I woke up in the middle of a bad dream, but not the kind that sends you screaming and running. The kind where you wander in the desert for days without water or a camel or any hope of being rescued. It's as if I got stuck in limbo or something.

To be honest, it hasn't been all bad. In fact, it was kind of nice. Other than my mom's nagging and a few calls from the attendance office, nobody really cared where I was. If I felt like eating Doritos and binging on *Pretty Little Liars*, I did. If I felt like driving three hours for a grilled cheese, I did. I did whatever I wanted and I said whatever came to mind. I floated in between days and weeks without any reason or purpose. I was fine with it, or at least I was. I'm not sure anymore.

All I know is I miss this house, and I miss my sister.

MISSING

Have you seen me?

Anna Williams has been missing since Friday, April 20th. She was last seen at Macklemore High School. If you have any information about her whereabouts, please call Diane Williams at **(657) 512-2407** or the **Buena Vida Police Department.**

Tap, tap, tap.

I jump out of my skin when I see someone outside my passenger side window, and spill the green smoothie all over my shirt. I frantically wipe off the cold slush while straining to see who it is.

"Katie? Katie, is that you? It's me, Jack. Open up."

It's Jack. I've known Jack Nelson forever. He grew up next door to us, and Anna and I spent every minute playing with him when we were little. We ate graham crackers in our fort and played rescue on our deck. Ever the director, Anna would throw over my ponytail of yarn for Jack, my brave knight, to climb up to save me. His mom used to babysit us a lot, but even after Anna was old enough to look after me, we still spent a lot of time at the Nelsons'.

After we moved out of that house and into the apartment, we didn't see Jack or his family much anymore. Once Jack left for college, I didn't see him at all, except for a handful of awkward encounters during his college breaks. In such a short period of time, I lost my sister and my home. It's strange how everything you thought was rock-solid can disintegrate in a heartbeat.

"Katie Williams!" Jack says, lighting up. "Checking out the old neighborhood, huh?"

"Yep," I say, forcing a smile.

"Man, it's been a long time. How are you?"

"Fine. You?"

"Can't complain. Heading to grad school in August, so I'm hanging out in good old Buena Vida for the summer. What's new with you?"

"Not much," I say. I keep forcing myself to smile, hoping my eyes don't look puffy from crying. I try to resist the urge, but I run my fingers along my eyelids to make sure my mascara isn't smudged.

"You just graduated, right?"

"Yep."

"Cool."

A long, awkward moment ensues as he gets comfortable in the passenger seat of my car. I wonder what he's doing here.

"Why don't you come in for a second? My mom would love to see you."

An image of his mom, Sheila, flashes to mind. Quirky, artsy, and super nurturing. She was forever doting on Jack and treating him like a little prince. My little Jack this and sweet little child that. Her sweetness would have been annoying if it wasn't so genuine. I'm sure she hasn't changed a bit.

"Can't. I gotta get going, actually."

"Where you off to?"

"Umm, I've got to meet a friend."

I feel bad lying to him. I wish I had a friend to meet. My only friend, Josie, is in Europe with her family. She's going to be there until the fall when she leaves me to go to college in Colorado.

"Oh, okay," Jack says, making no effort to get out of my car. "How's your mom, by the way?"

"Diane is still Diane. She's in Hawaii, at least for another couple of days. With Kurt, her trainer," I say, trying not to roll my eyes.

"Ah," he says sympathetically. "Maybe that's a good thing. Today's probably a tough day for her. And you."

The whole world comes to a complete and utter stop. I stare at the dashboard of my car, my eyes glued to the odometer as if that will steady me. I feel like I'm coming undone. How could he have remembered after all of these years?

"Today's Anna's birthday, right?" Jack says, as if I didn't already know exactly what he was talking about.

"Look, this isn't really a good time for me. I have a lot going on, so..."

"You can tell me. We go way back, remember?"

I turn my head to look out the window, determined to avoid crying in front of him. My old house, the house where we were a complete family once, stares back at me. Suddenly it hurts to look at it.

"You can talk to me, Kit Kat."

My old nickname. He remembers that, too. It's too much. I crane my neck even further away so he can't see me cry.

"Hey, hey. It's alright."

I feel his hand on my sleeve.

"Please just go," I say, harsher than I intend.

"I think you might need a friend right now," Jack says kindly.

His kindness is upsetting. I don't want him to be nice to me. I don't want him to pity me. I want him to leave me in peace so I can go back in time to when things made sense.

"I need you to leave, Jack."

"Katie," he pleads.

"I'm serious! If you want to be a friend, get out of the car," I demand.

He doesn't budge. I know he's trying to be nice, but I don't need him or his niceness. I don't need anything or anyone. I don't need my mom on my back about being an adult. I don't need Roger and his obsession with promptness. I don't need any of this. As my indignation surges, I can feel electricity racing through my veins. My face swells with heat and rage.

I put my car in drive and hit the gas, then veer into the road carelessly.

"Wait! What are you doing?" Jack yells, reaching for his seat belt.

I pick up speed as I leave the neighborhood in my rearview mirror, along with the unattended bikes, scooters, and "Drive like your kids live here" signs.

"You had your chance to get out."

"How about we slow down a little?"

"You want to talk? Let's talk. Do you know I'm the same age Anna was when she disappeared? Older, actually."

Jack grips the door's handle as I swerve into the

two-lane road leading downtown.

"She had college to look forward to, marriage, kids, getting out of this God-forsaken town."

"Seriously, can we—"

"I, on the other hand, have no hope of being anything other than an utter disappointment. And the one person who might have been able to help me is gone."

"How about we pull over and talk?"

"Talk about what? About what the hell happened to Anna? I'd love to! Tell me, do you know what happened? Do you know how my sister went from being a straight-A cheerleader to a ghost story? Because I sure don't."

Jack's back is rigid as I change lanes, squeezing between cars who don't feel like letting me in. I turn to face him.

"Everyone acts like it never happened, like it didn't forever change EVERYTHING!"

I turn back around, and a garbage truck seems to have appeared out of nowhere. I slam on the brakes to avoid hitting him, but I'm going too fast. There's a car on my left, so I jerk the wheel towards the right. We hurl down an embankment, our bodies flopping around like rag dolls as my car bumps and bounces to a stop.

The engine idles quietly, but everything else is still. Nothing seems to have changed. I lift my head from the steering wheel. It hurts. My whole body hurts, actually. I look over at Jack, suddenly remembering that he is with me. He's frozen stiff, his eyes wide as he looks out the windshield. I notice that his lip is bleeding. I suddenly feel terrible.

He slowly turns his head to look at me. For the first time, I notice how pretty his greenish-blue eyes are. They're like twin oceans swallowing me whole. The way he's looking at me makes me feel exposed, like he can see right through me. It hurts to think about what he must see, what he must be thinking. He's probably thinking that I'm a total mess, that he should never have gotten in my car. Maybe he's wishing he never knew me. I bet he's probably wondering what happened to the little girl he used to know. I know I am.

Diane Williams

Anna has been missing since yesterday afternoon. She was last seen at school. Her car is still there. I'm worried sick. PLEASE, if you know anything, call me or contact the police directly. Please copy and share with everyone you know.

Like · Comment · April 21, 2012 · 🌐

👍 49 people like this.

 Write a comment ...

I'm not sure what I thought a police station would look like, but this isn't it. The pinewood panels in the lobby are so outdated, but the vanilla walls of this tiny room are even worse. And it smells musty, like an old library. I think the metal folding chair I'm sitting on is the same one I sat in during elementary school assemblies. If I look underneath, I bet there's gum stuck to the bottom.

I shouldn't complain, though. I'm lucky to be here as an invited guest, rather than a criminal. After the stunt I pulled, I suppose I could have been put behind bars. They could have charged me with vehicular manslaughter or reckless driving or something like that. Thankfully, no one got hurt and the Nelsons are too nice to press charges.

The Nelsons, Sheila in particular, are so nice that they invited me to stay at their house for a couple of days while my mom is gone. Sheila insisted I stay so she could make sure I didn't have a concussion. She's something else, but in a good way. In addition to feeding me and letting me camp out on her couch, she also arranged for me to talk to her best friend, Karen.

Karen is a psychologist or therapist or whatever. I saw one of those right after Anna went missing, but I hated every minute of it. What business did a total stranger have asking me questions about my family? She didn't know them. My mom was paying a stranger to care about me, and that just seemed wrong. I'm still not a fan of the whole therapy thing, but the problem is, I don't have many friends to lean on. They've all moved on, except Josie, but now she's far away and hard to reach. So I gave in. The next thing I knew, Karen and I were having a little chat in Sheila's study.

She was nice enough, I guess. She didn't know about Anna, which was a nice change. It felt good to tell someone about Anna, someone who didn't know the whole story already. I went through some of my favorite memories and then, only because she wasn't pushy, I dipped my toe into the whole disappearance thing. Thankfully, she didn't give me those doe eyes or look away uncomfortably. She just listened. The problem was I didn't know what to say about what happened to Anna because I didn't know. I didn't know anything.

"It's like walking down the street, expecting that the road is going to keep going, but then suddenly the ground disappears and you're suspended in midair, looking down into a giant abyss," I told her.

She asked if I could talk to my parents or other people about Anna, but I laughed. Probably too loudly. My parents haven't brought up Anna's name in at least two years. Even before they started acting like she never existed, they would avoid me every time I asked about her. Dad would rush off the phone or suddenly want to take me out for ice cream. Meanwhile, Mom would say something snippy before leaving the room offended. Josie's the only one I dare talk with about Anna anymore, but she's out having the time of her life in London or Paris or someplace wonderfully far from here.

I started talking about what I did remember, although it wasn't much. I said they did a full investigation, but I wasn't sure what they found. Weeks later, it didn't matter anymore. The case was basically closed. That stupid officer who said he'd find her never brought her home. They didn't have any answers, either, at least none of the answers I needed—otherwise, Anna would be with me right now.

After our therapy session, I talked to Jack about Anna. It was the first time in a very long time that we even broached the issue, and it was the first time we ever talked about what might have happened. He's the one who suggested I take a look at the police file myself.

I thought he was crazy at first. For starters, I'm not a detective. How would I even understand what they wrote down? They probably used code words like "51-50" or "Charlie Bravo 911" or something. And what if the file didn't exist anymore? Maybe they get rid of files after a certain number of years.

Plus, I wasn't so sure it was a good idea to resurrect the past. For as long as I can remember, everyone has pushed me to move on. My friends, my teachers, everyone wanted me to forget what happened and get on with things.

"There's nothing back there for us," my mom used to say.

But then I started wondering if maybe the file would answer some of my questions, the questions my parents won't go near. I just know there's more to what happened than what I've been told. There must be. If I could just see what the police uncovered all those years ago, maybe I could finally make sense of it.

Then I started thinking that, if nothing else, maybe I could catch a glimpse of my sister one more time. I'd give anything to be able to feel close to her again. If I could only bring her back to life for just a second, just long enough to remember how it felt to be with her, maybe that would be enough. Maybe then I could start figuring out how to get out of limbo and start to live in this world again.

As soon as I decided it was worth asking about, Jack immediately offered to help. I had no idea how to go about it, and he had time on his hands before starting graduate school, so I took him up on it. I didn't actually think it would be possible to track down the file, and even then, I didn't think they'd give it to me.

Leave it to Jack Nelson to make the impossible possible. Within two days, he managed to get in touch with the detective who investigated my sister's case, who said I could see his working file anytime I wanted. I was shocked. I wasn't expecting it to be a possibility. Then I was scared of what I might find out. I immediately told Jack to forget the whole thing.

But when I went back to my apartment, I practically choked on the stillness. Being at the Nelsons was like being part of a family again, and I hated leaving it behind. I turned the electric kettle on for tea, but it didn't compare to Sheila's whistling teapot. I didn't have biscotti or loose-leaf tea or misshapen ceramic mugs made in pottery class. Even the jazz playlist on my phone seemed inadequate in comparison. It was more than that, though. In the quiet of our lonely apartment, I couldn't hide from my thoughts. I couldn't deny my curiosity. After a long, restless night, I called Jack and told him I changed my mind.

When I entered through the double doors this afternoon, Officer Christiansen was already waiting for me in the lobby.

"You must be Miss Katie Williams," he said with annoying formality.

"Yeah, I'm Katie," I said, refusing to apologize for being late.

"I'm Officer Christiansen," he said with his hand outstretched to me. "You probably don't remember me, but I—"

Remember? Of course, I remembered. I can still see him standing in my sister's room with a cardboard box in hand, callously scanning her stuff and tossing her personal things into his stupid box. How could I forget the man who told me he was going to find my sister, but didn't?

"I remember you," I said curtly.

He rambled on about being surprised to hear from me and how happy he was to help me in any way. Blah, blah, blah. Then he finally led me to this hot, stuffy room. He pointed to a giant box, not unlike the one I saw him holding all those years ago, and told me that everything I needed was in there. After showing me his office, the bathroom, and the vending machines, he finally left me alone.

Now I'm seated in this metal folding chair, listening to the air conditioner creak and moan, and trying to remember why I wanted to come here. The room is stuffy and the fluorescent lights are obnoxiously bright. I let my fingers find Anna's dragonfly pendant, the one I've worn around my neck since she vanished.

When I first open the box and pull out the accordion file, the flyer Mom and I made falls out along with a copy of her post begging everyone to help find Anna. I remember duct-taping those flyers to trees and power poles all over town. I still have one shoved in a drawer at home somewhere, although I haven't looked at it in years. Seeing it now, a lifeless piece of paper among a stack of lifeless papers, seems strange. Unreal, even. Like it belongs to another person's life story, not mine.

The file is so unofficial looking, and it looks like it was pulled out of an accountant's or lawyer's filing cabinet. I stare down at my sister's name—printed in black and white, all caps. I feel my heart beating in my chest. Who am I kidding? I'm probably not going to find anything helpful in this thing. It's just a bunch of paper, some stupid words written down in a hurry; words that didn't change anything back then and likely won't change anything now. I have half a mind to walk out and forget the whole thing.

But I'm not going anywhere. As hard as it may be, I have to do this. I have to see what's inside this file. It's the only window I have into a moment, and a person, that has vanished.

FILE CONTROL NO. 23167
MISSING PERSON – ANNA WILLIAMS

Note to File completed by Officer Christiansen on April 21, 2012, 4:42 p.m.

IDENTIFYING INFORMATION

- Name: Anna Williams
- DOB: June 8, 1995
- Ht/Wt: 5'4" — 115 pounds
- Brown Hair, Brown Eyes
- Place Last Seen: Macklemore High School, Buena Vida, CA
- Date Last Seen: April 20, 2012, approximately 3:15 p.m.
- Home Address: 13677 Mission Valley Road, Buena Vida, CA
- Known medical conditions: n/a
- Known medications: n/a

SCOPE OF INVESTIGATION

On April 21, 2012, at 11:10 a.m., Diane Williams called the Buena Vida police station to report her daughter, Anna Williams, missing. In California, a missing person is someone whose whereabouts are unknown to the reporting party. This includes any child who may have run away, been taken involuntarily, or may be in need of assistance. It includes a child illegally taken, held, or hidden by a parent or non-parent family member.

Children and young adults make up 85-90% of all persons reported missing. Statistics show that children under the age of eighteen who go missing are typically found to be in one of four case types: 1) 86% are endangered runaways (at risk for child sex trafficking as well as drug abuse, homelessness, etc.), 2) 10% are abducted by family members, 3) 1% are abducted by non-family members, and 4) 3% are lost, injured, or otherwise missing. Given the danger Anna Williams could be in, it is imperative that this investigation be conducted with speed, accuracy, and integrity.

As an initial matter, a "Be on the Look Out" (Bolo) bulletin was broadcast due to Anna's minor status and the fact that she may be at risk of harm. A Missing Person's Report was filled out and sent electronically to the Attorney General's Office. Anna Williams has been entered into the FBI's National Crime Information Center and the Department of Justice's Missing Persons System. Anna's disappearance has also been reported to the National Center for Missing and Exploited Children and the Polly Klaas Foundation. At this time, no Amber Alert has been issued because law enforcement does not have sufficient information to believe that Anna is in imminent danger of serious bodily injury or death by an abductor.

Anna Williams's cell phone has been tracked, but it appears to have been powered down while at Macklemore High School since it was last pinpointed at that location at 1:24 p.m. on April 20th. Inquiries have been made to all area hospitals, homeless shelters, coroner's offices, and prisons with no leads.

At this stage, we are collecting all necessary information and details from friends and relatives. We will visit places Anna Williams has been known to frequent, inquire about health or medical conditions, sources of money, and events that could be linked with her disappearance. We will collect DNA samples for subsequent forensic examination, review security camera footage, and perform a thorough search of Anna's home and personal belongings. The department will also enlist the help of the media.

Furthermore, I plan to conduct interviews with all relevant sources and will begin those interviews straightaway. The contents of each interview will be transcribed and recorded for inclusion within this file. All evidence collected throughout the investigation will eventually be marked and entered into a log. In the interest of expediting the investigation, these administrative tasks will not occur until time allows.

To that end, I have informed the administration of Macklemore High School of my intention to arrive first thing Monday morning to interview administrators, teachers, and students who might have any relevant information regarding Anna.

PRELIMINARY INFORMATION RECEIVED FROM MOTHER, DIANE WILLIAMS, AT INTAKE

Anna Williams is a seventeen-year-old honor student at Macklemore High. According to her mother, Diane Williams, Anna was last seen by friends and classmates at the end of the school day on Friday afternoon, although no one has yet come forward to say that they saw her in the school parking lot or near her car. When Anna did not come home by nine and was unresponsive to her mother's calls and text messages, Diane drove around town looking for Anna. She discovered her 2002 Honda Civic still parked in the school's student lot. Diane then phoned friends and neighbors to find out if Anna had stayed overnight somewhere or maybe snuck out to a late-night party. She checked to see if she had posted anything on Facebook, Twitter, and Instagram about her whereabouts, but there has been no activity on her social media accounts since late Thursday night. When she still had no idea where Anna was by Saturday morning, Diane called the station and filed a missing person's report.

INTERVIEW WITH DIANE WILLIAMS

Sunday, April 22, 2012, 9:30 a.m.
Transcribed from Digital Recording

JC: Officer John Christiansen

DW: Diane Williams

KW: Katie Williams

JC: Begin recording. Thank you for
        meeting again, Ms. Williams.

DW: Of course. Do you need a different
        photograph? I pulled out some newer
        ones in case you needed them. I also
        put her hairbrush and toothbrush
        into a zip lock bag like you asked.
        If there is anything else, please let
        me know. Whatever you need to ask me,
        whatever you need to know to find my
        baby and bring her home, just ask.
        I'll do anything.

JC: Thank you, Ms. Williams. I'll try to
        make this as painless as possible.

DW: Painless might be a bit much to aim
        for, don't you think?

JC: Point taken.

DW: Can I offer you something to drink? I
        could get you a cup of coffee. I also
        have some tea if you prefer.

JC: No, thank you. Okay, can you start by

telling me what Anna is like, what she does, who she hangs out with, and anything that seems relevant?

DW: Well, I already gave you her birthday and eye color and all that yesterday. I told you she is a great student, didn't I? She's smart as a whip and headed for any college she wants. She has a 4.0 GPA and she took extra college classes over the summer. That's my girl, always plugging away at her future. That is—

[Voice cracks]

DW: —if she would just come home.

JC: I understand. This is an awful situation to be in, Ms. Williams, but we can't waste any time worrying about Anna. What we need to do is focus on finding her. What else can you tell me?

DW: Let's see, she's active with student council at her high school. Anna and another girl thought it would be fun to run for president and vice president, and they won. So now my Anna is vice president, which means she's part of the meetings and helps organize events like sports rallies and dances. It's great for her college applications, too.

JC: Who is this other girl?

DW: Oh, her name is Piper Abbot. She is definitely an outgoing kind of girl, and

very pretty. I guess she's probably one
of Anna's more popular friends—which
is why I assumed Anna was off doing
something with Piper Friday night. She
met her through cheerleading. I wasn't
thrilled when Anna tried out for the
squad, but she did it anyway. I've
always told her that it's better to be
a woman of substance than a ditsy girl
cheering for the boys. I mean, what
did all those feminists fight for? Then
again, I was a cheerleader, so who am I
to say anything!

[Nervous laughter, sound of pencil scratching
on paper]

DW: The thing is, my Anna always makes
good decisions. She participated
in the mock trial competition her
sophomore year and was part of the
Give Back club, although this year
she quit all that. She said she
wanted something different.

JC: Did she give you any indication as to
why she wanted to change things?

DW: I'm sure it's just the flimsy theatrics
of being a teenager. One day they're
obsessed with a boy band and the
next day it's a childhood pastime to
be scoffed at. I tell you, teenage
hormones cause a lot of havoc.

JC: Did she talk with you about any of this?

DW: No, not really. She just said she
needed a change.

JC: Did she have any problems with these activities or the people in them?

DW: I don't think so. She never mentioned anything.

[Phone rings in the background]

DW: Let me see if that's Anna. Hold on just a second.

[Footsteps, clattering sounds, hushed whispers]

DW: No, it wasn't her. Just a friend of mine. Everyone's worried sick about Anna.

JC: Alright, then. Let's get back to the questions. How about friends? Do you know who Anna's friends are?

DW: Well, I told you about Piper Abbot. Anna and Maddie Le used to be close. I don't know if they had a falling out or something. I just know she doesn't come around much anymore.

JC: Can you think of anyone else?

DW: She knows the girls on the squad and kids in her classes, but I can't think of anyone particularly close with Anna. Jack and Anna are friends—he's the boy next door. Let me think... Once in a while she will bring up some of the kids she works with at Sub Station. I just don't know their names offhand. Hmm...

[Pause]

DW: I'm sure there are more, but I can't

think of any right now. I'm just so
tired and worried. I think the stress
is getting to me.

[Deep sigh from Ms. Williams]

JC: What about boyfriends?

DW: I'm actually... oh, you mean Anna.
          Well, there was Jacob Hunt. It
          happened so fast, though, that if I
          blinked I would have missed it.

JC: Can you tell me about him?

DW: He's a very cute boy. He plays
          football and I guess that's how they
          met. It seemed like an unexpected
          match to me, but what do I know?

JC: Does she spend time with any other boys?

DW: She spends a lot of time with Jack, but
          not romantically. He's a nice boy and
          comes from a good family. Very smart,
          too. I wish she would get involved with a
          boy like that, rather than Jacob. Nothing
          against Jacob, of course. It's just that
          Anna's father was the life of the party
          when I met him, and I've learned the
          hard way that the fun doesn't last.

JC: Anyone else?

DW: No. She keeps her crushes to herself,
          mostly.

JC: How about Anna's sister?

DW: Oh, Katie? If anyone would know about
          Anna's secret crushes, it would be
          Katie. They're really close.

JC: How old is Katie?

DW: Twelve.

JC: Where is she right now?

DW: She's at a friend's house right now.
        With everything going on, I thought
        it might be better for her to be with
        friends.

JC: I'm going to need to ask her some
        questions.

DW: Of course! What was I thinking? I'll
        text her right now.

        [Clicking sounds, beeps]

DW: Done.

JC: Is Anna usually safe and cautious?

DW: Yes, she is definitely a safe girl. We've
        been through all the scenarios together.
        She knows not to go alone to certain
        places and to use her common sense.

JC: Does she have a curfew?

DW: She has a 12:00 a.m. curfew and has never
        missed it. Officer, she's a smart girl and
        wouldn't put herself in harm's way.

JC: Alright. Let me see. What about her
        father? Is he around?

DW: No. Since our divorce, Keith has been
        pretty much out of the picture.

JC: How long have you been divorced?

DW: The divorce was final about a year ago,
        but we split up almost three years back.
        Anna was thirteen and Katie was nine.

JC: What is your custody arrangement?

DW: He's supposed to take Anna and her sister, Katie, every other weekend. He isn't consistent at all. Sometimes he'll pick them up both times a month, other times he won't see them at all.

JC: Why not?

DW: He blames his job, as usual. He travels a lot, but that's just an excuse. Personally, I think he's too hungover to bother with his daughters, but that isn't my problem anymore. All I can do is protect my girls. I don't sugarcoat it. I tell them straight that their father is not dependable. He may be fun for a while, but you can't count on him. Of course, they will have to learn that the hard way.

[Dramatic sigh]

DW: I sure did.

JC: When is the last time he saw the girls?

DW: Let me think. He came and got them back in February. I remember Anna was upset because there was going to be a Valentine's Day event put on by student council and she really wanted to be there, but it was on his weekend. So she had to go off with him and miss the whole thing. I told him she was going to resent him for it. He made this big fuss about having so little time to spend with her and wanting

Valentine's Day to be special. You
can't tell that man anything.

JC: Was that the last time he saw Anna?

DW: As far as I know. He had an excuse
        for both weekends in March, as well as
        the first weekend of his in April. She
        doesn't want anything to do with him.

JC: They don't have a good relationship?

DW: They used to, but that was when she
        was much younger. He doesn't know how
        to relate to a teenage girl. He is
        clueless. Just clueless.

    [Footsteps in the background]

JC: Did Anna ever express any fear about
        him?

DW: No. He's a complete loser, but he's nobody
        to fear. He's an alcoholic, you know.

    [Sound of liquid pouring into a cup]

DW: Are you sure I can't offer you some
        coffee?

JC: No, thank you. You said your
        ex-husband is an alcoholic?

DW: Oh, yeah. He started drinking years
        ago, but it was casual. We all drank,
        but he started drinking more than
        just on the weekends. He was having a
        Seven and Seven in the evenings before
        dinner during the week. It seemed to
        make him happy and less edgy for a
        while, but then he'd have a second
        round. That's when he became agitated

and every little thing upset him.

JC: Did you have a lot of arguments?

DW: Constantly. He would pick a fight with
        me about everything. I think Anna
        was afraid of him when he had too
        many drinks because he became loud
        and belligerent.

JC: Did he ever hit you?

DW: No.

JC: Did he ever hit the children?

DW: No, never.

JC: Do you think it is possible that he
        could have taken Anna?

DW: No!

[Puff of laughter]

DW: He barely takes them under a court-
        sanctioned custody agreement!

JC: But you said he was insistent upon
        taking Anna around Valentine's Day

DW: Yes, but it was rare for him to make
        a stink about it. I also told you
        that he hadn't seen the girls for
        months at a time, too.

JC: Alright. Well, how about your
        relationship with Anna?

DW: What do you mean?

JC: How is your relationship with her?

DW: Fine. It's as good as any mother and
        daughter relationship, I suppose.

JC: Has she shown any signs of distress?

DW: What do you mean?

JC: Has she been upset about anything?
        Any angry outbursts or concerning
        behaviors?

DW: No, just the usual complaints about
        chores and that kind of thing.
        It's not easy being a single-parent
        household, so we all pitch in. Plus, I
        believe she needs to learn how to live
        on her own. I can't coddle her for -

[Ping sounds from a cell phone, brief pause]

DW: She knows I only want what's best
        for her. One day she'll thank me for
        preparing her for the real world.

JC: Does she confide in you about what's
        happening in her life?

DW: I'm always asking her how she's doing,
        and she shares a few things here and
        there, but you know how teenagers can
        be. They just shut you—

[Sound of phone pinging]

JC: Do you need to check your phone?

DW: Do you mind? It could be Anna.

JC: Please.

[Lapse of time, spurt of laughter from Ms.
Williams]

JC: Everything alright?

DW: Oh, yes. I'm sorry. It's just a friend of
        mine checking in. He knows how torn up

I am right now. Anyway, where were we?

JC: We were talking about your relationship with Anna and how—

DW: Oh, yes. We have a great relationship. We're very close.

JC: Did you and Anna have any disagreements lately?

DW: Not that I can recall. Wait a minute, there was a bit of a rub last week. She asked about getting some extra cash for gas money, but I had to break it to her that she's responsible for earning gas money. I paid for the car and I pay the insurance, so the deal is she pays for gas.

JC: Okay, how did she—

DW: That's why she has a job. So I told her no and reminded her of our agreement, but we didn't argue over it. She obviously wasn't happy about it given the sulky face I got, which is why I asked her if she was upset. She said she was fine and went to work.

JC: I don't know how to broach this, Ms. Williams, but I need to ask. Is there any reason to think that Anna might have taken her own life?

DW: God, no! How could you even ask that question? Anna is a wonderful girl with every reason in the world to live. She has a great life now and a great life ahead of her. There is no way that's even possible.

JC: I'm sorry, ma'am. I have to be
        thorough in this investigation.

DW: Okay, okay. I'm just saying that she
        would never do such a thing to me.
        She has no reason in the world to do
        something like that.

JC: Do you think she may have run away?

DW: Run away? Run away where? Where's she
        going to go without her car? She has no
        money. I don't think she has ever ridden
        a bus in her life. She has no skills to
        get a real job or take care of herself.
        Why would she run away? No. There is no
        way this is her doing in any way, shape,
        or form. Someone has taken her, and
        you better find that piece of garbage
        immediately. She is in danger and I
        don't want to waste another minute
        running our mouths about something that
        is irrelevant to bringing her home.

JC: I apologize for upsetting you, Ms.
        Williams. I know how hard this must
        be for you. In investigating the
        disappearance of a minor, we need to
        consider any and all potential leads.
        Given her age, we can't rule out the
        possibility that she ran away.

DW: Well, she didn't. I told you. She didn't
        even pack a bag. I checked. Nothing is
        missing except her backpack, phone, and
        keys— - all the usual things she takes
        with her to school.

JC: Is there anyone you can think of that

would want to hurt Anna?

DW: I can't think of anyone who would
want to hurt my sweet girl. Anna is
my angel.

[Sniffling, crying sounds.]

JC: Alright, let's move on. Is it possible
for me to take a look in her room?

[Deep breath]

DW: Sure, I'll show you. Follow me. It's
probably a mess, but I've given up
trying to make her clean it. I'm
constantly nagging her, which I hate.
I am not a nag. She makes me a nag.

[Footsteps, door creaking]

JC: It looks pretty clean to me.

DW: Well, I guess it isn't too bad in
here. At the moment. She probably
shoved everything into her closet or
under the bed.

[Shuffling sounds]

DW: Wow. I haven't really looked around
in here for a while. She's changed
things around a bit. She has all
these quotations on her wall now.
Oh, and her music. She always has
something playing in here. I don't
know how she can get her homework
done with all that noise, but
somehow, she does it.

JC: Is pink her favorite color?

DW: No, why? Oh, the walls. These pink walls

do seem odd now. I suppose I should have
asked her if she wanted to paint in
here. I mean, she is seventeen.

[Silence, muffled background sounds]

DW: I suppose she could have redecorated,
        but I'm not sure what she would have
        wanted. I do know it wouldn't have
        been pink. It's always dark colors
        with her lately, rarely anything
        bright and pretty.

JC: She never asked to paint or change
        things around?

DW: No. Fashion and décor are much more
        in my wheelhouse than Anna's. I could
        have done a lot in here, but... well...
        I guess I kind of missed the fact
        that she grew up. I can't believe I'm
        old enough to have a daughter who is
        almost eighteen and will be applying
        to colleges soon. It went so fast.

JC: Which colleges is she interested in?

DW: She hasn't decided on anything in
        particular yet. I don't think she will
        want to be too far from me. We're a
        really close family, especially after the
        divorce, so we need to stick together.

JC: She must have something in mind. Isn't
        the time to apply coming up soon?

DW: You sound like her teachers. She's
        always nagging me to visit campuses.
        I told her we could do that over the
        summer, but I am not dragging us all

over the state of California in order to
see every school ever made. Just a few.

JC: Is this a piggy bank?

DW: Yes, she got that years ago.

[Soft reminiscent 'hmmm']

DW: She used to store up all of her money
        in it until it was bursting, then
        she would come to me and ask to go
        shopping. Of course, I was more than
        willing to take her! It's empty now.

[Sigh]

DW: It's not easy for kids to save money
        and not spend it right up, but Anna was
        always very smart and mature for her age.
        She knows the value of saving money.

JC: Does she have a checking or savings
        account—one she has access to?

DW: Yes, I opened one for her a couple
        of years ago. She deposits her check
        from Sub Station and any money she
        gets from occasional babysitting jobs
        or birthday gifts. She's got a good
        amount saved in there now, maybe
        $1200 or so.

JC: Ms. Williams, do you have access to
        her accounts?

DW: Yes, I had to be on the account with her.

JC: Can you check her balance right now?

DW: Sure, let me pull it up on my phone.

[Several seconds of silence]

JC: Is this her diary?

DW: What? Oh, that notebook?

JC: Yes.

DW: I don't know. Maybe.

JC: Can I take a look?

DW: Sure.

[Shuffling sounds]

JC: This appears to be a diary or
        journal of some sort.

DW: Oh, well, I'm not too surprised. She's
        probably got lots of teenage drama
        spilling out on the pages of it.

[Lapse in time, riffling of pages]

JC: This could be useful. I'm going
        to take it as evidence, with your
        permission, of course.

DW: Whatever you need.

JC: I'll also need any electronic devices
        like laptops, tablets, phones, etc.

DW: I'll see what I can find after I check
        her account. I know she had her phone
        with her when she went to school
        Friday, so unless it was recovered
        from her car, it isn't here.

JC: That's ok. We have ways to get
        that information if you give me
        authorization.

DW: Yes, of course. You have my
        permission. You can do whatever is
        necessary to find Anna.

JC: Okay. If you don't mind, I'm going to
         look around for a few minutes.

DW: That's fine.

   [Scuffling sounds]

DW: What? I don't understand. Officer,
         her account hasn't been touched. She
         hasn't made a deposit for months. Hang
         on a second. The last deposit was back
         in January... No — no, wait. That was
         the last withdrawal. She took out
         $50 on the 10th. The last deposit...
         let me see... December? That makes no
         sense. What has she been doing with
         her paycheck from Sub Station?

JC: Ms. Williams, how much money did she
         make at Sub Station? I mean, what was
         her paycheck generally?

DW: Well, she worked one day after
         school and one or two weekend days,
         depending. So it was anywhere between
         $90 and $140 a week. I think. Yeah,
         that sounds about right.

JC: Has she worked consistently since
         December?

DW: Yes. She knows I won't tolerate her
         calling in sick unless she is on
         death's doorstep. She needs to learn
         responsibility and accountability.

JC: So we are talking about, let me
         see... Since January, that would be
         at least $1200, maybe close to $2000,
         that hasn't been deposited?

DW: That sounds right.

JC: Maybe she was saving it for something
       and bought it with cash. Has she talked
       about wanting to buy anything lately?

DW: She did have a new dress and shoes
       come in the mail the other day. She
       has been going out a lot more, too.
       Still, that wouldn't add up to $2000.

JC: Well, if none of her paychecks went
       into her bank account, she has either
       spent it or stashed it.

DW: I highly doubt she spent it—at least
       not on clothes.

JC: What else does she usually buy with
       her money?

DW: Gas... coffee... music. Her music isn't
       that expensive. I know because she uses
       my credit card to download songs and
       then pays me for it. It seems hard to
       believe she spent all that money and
       has nothing to show for it. Maybe she
       hid the cash somewhere in her room.
       Oh God, maybe she is in some serious
       trouble that I don't know about...

JC: Do you know if Anna has experimented
       with drugs?

DW: No. Anna has never done any drugs. If
       there is anything I am positive of,
       it's that she would never do drugs.

       [Laughing]

DW: I'm sorry, it's just funny because

Anna is the poster child for the
anti-drug campaign. Just the thought
of her even trying weed is hilarious.

JC: You might be surprised... Do you keep
alcohol or drugs in the house?

DW: Drugs, no. Of course, not. I do have
a liquor cabinet.

JC: Have you noticed any of it missing?
Is there any missing now?

DW: I've never noticed. Let me look.

[Footsteps heard, lapse in time]

DW: Nothing is missing. Everything is there.

JC: Did you check to see if there is
actually alcohol in the bottles?

DW: As opposed to what?

JC: Water. Apple juice. Anything that
looks like alcohol, but isn't.

[Ms. Williams sighs, footsteps heard
again, lapse in time]

DW: No, it's all there. I told you she
isn't the type.

JC: Okay. We just need to be thorough.

[Click of door latch, sound of keys jingling]

JC: Okay. Uh, Ms. Williams, is someone
here? I thought I heard a door close
just now.

DW: It's probably Katie. Katie?

[Rustling sounds]

KW: Mom?

I look up, blinking hard. I can hear the sound of muffled voices outside my door, talking about last night's episode of *American Ninja Warrior*. It makes me want to scream at them. I guess it's normal for other people to go to work and talk about their shared love of climbing cargo nets and warped walls. It's not like *they're* trapped in a time machine to the past. Unfortunately for me, I'm someplace that only exists in my memory.

When Anna didn't come home that Friday after school, my mom was convinced that she was out partying. She was furious that Anna had gone out without telling her first. She probably said as much, but it was the loud slamming of kitchen cabinets that gave it away. I just stayed clear of her until Josie called, and then I ran off to her house to spend the night. When I woke up, there were dozens of texts from my mom asking about Anna and ordering me to come home.

That probably would have made other kids panic, but not me. My mom is notorious for sending a billion unnecessary texts with the same sense of urgency as a severe weather alert. I had learned not to pay much attention. It wasn't until I turned the corner onto our street and saw the police car in our driveway that I knew something was wrong. I stood at the edge of our walkway, frozen in my pajama pants. I think part of me knew that going inside would change everything.

Those first moments were like the opening scene of a horror movie when you're on the edge of your seat, waiting for someone to pop out with an ax or something. Except nothing scary ever happens right away, so you end up jumping out of your skin at least a dozen times before the moment finally comes. And the rest of the time you're holding your breath in anticipation. I feel like I've been holding my breath since I was twelve, waiting for someone to tell me that it's finally safe to breathe again.

This is heavy.

I think that's enough for today. I had no idea it would take so long to read through all these papers. I'm not exactly a Rhodes Scholar and I never took those speed reading classes, so obviously this is going to take a little more time than I thought. Maybe it's better that way. I'll go home, eat some dinner, and binge on some Netflix. I've got the apartment to myself until Mom gets back and complete control of the remote for a few more days. Maybe I'll order Thai.

I close the file, making sure to put a Post-it Note on the page to mark where I am. I've waited six years to see what's in here, so what's one more day? I grab my purse and sneak out, making sure Christiansen doesn't see me. Then I promise myself I'll come back tomorrow.

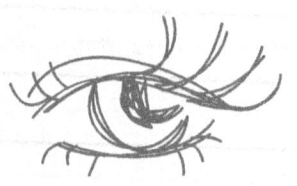

ANNA'S DIARY

June 2, 2011

"How are you?"

The answer to this question is so nauseatingly predictable. My programmed response is to light up with a great big smiling "Good." Sometimes it might be "Great" or "Pretty good." I use "Okay" if I can't muster a smile at all. I might say "No complaints here" if I'm annoyed by the transparency of the question poser and therefore feel the need to channel my grandpa ironically. My classic, however, is "Fine." That one fits best when what's being said isn't as important as what's <u>not</u> being said. Fine is neither good nor bad. It is acceptable, satisfactory, or adequate. It's fine. Period. End of discussion.

Of course, my response is always quickly followed by a reciprocal "How are you?" which can be modified with an extra-long "ouuuuu" or extra-high "ou," depending upon how important it is to make the other person believe my sincerity. It is simply good manners to respond quickly and in kind. Plus, it keeps people focused on what they really care about—themselves.

Although I have mastered the art of handling this ridiculously mind-numbing interaction, I do wish people would just stop asking the question at all. There are a number of other suitable expressions

to throw at one another in passing, so why use one that actually necessitates a response that is almost always a lie? We could say "Nice seeing you" or "Hey there" or even stick to a solid head nod. It seems to me we should say what we mean, and if we mean, "I see you," then say that. Don't start a conversation that requires a response from me if you aren't going to care about what my answer actually is. That, Miss Manners, is actually rude.

My mom says it to everyone. "How are you?" to the bank teller. "How are you?" to the store clerk. "How are you?" to Maddie's mom at school events. Every time she says it, it slides off her tongue like honey. She opens her mouth and these three syrupy words cover the room with sweetness. She puts on her face of concern and even cocks her head ever so slightly to the side to show genuine interest in the person. Her big brown eyes become saucers of care that are distracting, if not unnerving, because of their rarity. I think other people find it comforting and reassuring to believe that someone out there might really care about how they're doing, even if it is a random lady they run into once in a while. They must, because they start gushing about their lives and end up beaming at my mom as she leaves them almost in tears, offering over her shoulder that

"This too shall pass" or "What doesn't kill you makes you stronger" or "Take care of yourself, now."

Sometimes she asks me that dreaded question after school, and I slip and answer truthfully, forgetting how this dance always goes. "How are you?" she'll say with her artificial sweetener voice and big, interrogating eyes. Just like those store clerks, I'll end up falling into her trap and my mouth will start running. Before long, my inner-most feelings are displayed before her like the discards on the front lawn of a yard sale and I am looking to her for something, although I'm not sure what. I just know it isn't a cliché, especially one that rolls off her tongue as she's walking away from me like a window-shopper that just isn't very interested in what I have to offer.

But that's my mom. Other people are not as pleasing as she is on the outside. They usually just cut you off before you begin. I don't think I've ever gone more than two sentences without one of three tactics being used to end the awkward encounter. Some like to cut you off and say something irrelevant like "That's nice, dear" or "Cool" and then move on. Others listen as if they're cornered by Eeyore, nervously fidgeting while their eyes dart around for the nearest exit. My favorites are those who have their excuses planned out in advance. It's like they've been burned by someone being honest and have rehearsed how to politely avoid these interactions. These people are quick to interrupt your sob story to say, "Oh, I'd love to hear more, but I have to run" or "I'm so sorry I won't be able to hear the rest, but I need to be somewhere." If they're really good, they'll make sure it's okay with you by stating, not asking, "You understand, right?" and then insist on catching up soon. Soon, by the way, is code for never.

When it comes to people asking "How are you," I have learned that pretending to care is part of being polite, as is pretending to not notice that people don't care. Everyone loves it when teenagers are polite. So I play along now. I say "fine" a lot and then give the other person the opportunity to do the same. Adults love me. I'm easy for them because they don't have to wade into the depths of my feelings, which go way too deep for me as it is. I understand that. I wouldn't jump into the deep end of me either if I had a choice.

What I don't understand is why these same adults become completely confused when all these teenagers who are presumably "fine" don't act that way. Parents are constantly wondering why their kids don't open up to them about how they feel. School counselors are perplexed by the number of kids failing, having meaningless sex, or even hooked on heroin. Teachers wonder why they can't seem to reach some of their students with all the usual tactics. They look at us like we're a report card for how they're doing. They want us to reflect their hard work, like finely crafted sculptures they can point to as the result of their own doing.

None of these self-professed experts in adolescence, at least none of the ones I know, seem to care about the fact that we are actually people with our own feelings, thoughts, and reasons for doing what we do. My internal chaos may not make sense to them, or even me, but these voices reside inside me, nevertheless. I have to deal with them every day, and I can't just stuff them in my locker or under my pillow so that no one sees them. I have to carry them with me. I have to hide them from the popular kids, the guy I like, and my teachers who only know me to be compliant and attentive. I have to deny them to myself when I'm home for fear that I'll forget to be the dutiful daughter and say something to make my life harder than it already is.

We all do it. We all hide our crazy behind lifeless smiles. We fake interest in other people and offer knee-jerk responses. We play the roles that have been thrust upon us and never deviate from the script. We act like everything is fine because it is expected, it is preferable, and it is easier. For everyone.

<u>INTERVIEW WITH SISTER, KATIE WILLIAMS</u>

Sunday, April 22, 2012, 10:48 a.m.
Transcribed from Digital Recording

JC: Officer John Christiansen

KW: Katie Williams

DW: Diane Williams

JC:	Begin Recording. Interview with Katie Williams, Anna's younger sister.
KW:	Mom, what's going on?
DW:	Officer Christiansen is here to ask us some questions.
KW:	Oh, did you find my sister?
JC:	Not yet, Katie. I'm trying to find out more information so that I can do just that.
	[Sniffling sounds]
DW:	It's alright, Katie, don't cry. Anna will be home soon, you'll see. That's why this nice officer is here—to help us.
JC:	Katie, is it okay if I ask you a couple of questions about your sister?
KW:	Okay.
JC:	What can you tell me about Anna?
KW:	Anna is the best sister anyone could have. She cooks me dinner, helps me with my homework, gives me advice about friends—that kind of thing.
JC:	What kind of things does she like?

KW: She loves music. I like to try on her
        clothes while she plays different
        songs for me. Anna just introduced me
        to Spotify and basically changed my
        life.

JC: What other things do you do together?

KW: We watch movies or laugh at stuff
        online. Why?

JC: I don't know Anna like you do, so I
        really need you to help me understand
        her better. That way I can figure out
        how to find her. You understand?

KW: Yes.

JC: Good. Now, has Anna ever talked about
        wanting to get away from here?

KW: I don't know. She always tells me
        that one day we're both going to go
        someplace bigger and better than
        Buena Vida.

     [Snapping sounds]

JC: Does she talk about going anywhere
        specific?

KW: Not really. But she talks about
        traveling a lot.

     [Snapping sounds]

JC: Has your sister seemed unhappy
        lately?

KW: Uh, yeah. She's been really moody.
        She usually lets me hang out in her
        room, but now she's always yelling
        about privacy.

JC: Has she behaved in any unusual ways?
        (Snapping sounds)

KW: Umm. Like what?

DW: Katie! Stop fooling around with

that stupid hair tie and answer the
Officer's questions. And don't say
'umm.' It makes you sound dumb.

KW: Sorry. What was the question again?

JC: What else can you tell me about your
sister? What does she like to do?

KW: She likes to watch movies, usually
some dopey romance. Anna loves
musicals, too. She made me watch all
kinds of old shows where they tap
dance and stare at each other for
ten minutes at a time. She loves that
kind of thing. I told her she should
do theater or something. She laughed
and said only nerds do theater, and
she really had to change her image.

JC: Why did she have to change her
image?

KW: I don't know. She just said she was
sending out the wrong vibes.

JC: Do you have any idea why she felt
that way?

KW: I think her and Maddie were kind
of like nobodies. Maddie wears
everything on the outside, like her
hair being blue and her clothes being
one of her own crazy designs. Anna is
the opposite. She has all her weird
stuff inside, like her obsession with
musicals and old movies. Did you know
she likes to knit? How old lady is
that? She does, though. She makes all
sorts of cool stuff. Anyway, no one
knows that about her. On the outside,
she is just plain old Anna.

JC: How come you think she keeps her
   artsy side to herself?

KW: Her idea of being creative is not
   exactly cool. At least not in Buena
   Vida. That's why she wanted to be
   cool, I guess. To fit in or maybe not
   stick out so much.

JC: What kind of things does she do?

KW: I don't know. She goes to parties
   now. She buys nail polish and makeup
   and lets Piper try to transform her
   into some Hollister model. She almost
   let her dye her hair blond, but I
   knew she wouldn't do it because she
   doesn't actually care about any of
   it. She just does it to impress the
   girls on the squad—or my mom.

DW: Katie!

KW: Sorry, Mom, but it's true.

DW: That is not true. Your sister knows I
   accept her for who she is, warts and
   all.

KW: Whatever.

DW: Don't you take that tone with me.

JC: Ms. Williams, please. Let her answer
   in her own way.

[Sigh from Ms. Williams]

JC: Katie, please go on. Tell me more
   about what Anna is really like.

KW: Umm, well. Anna likes boys, but she
   can't go near them without freaking
   out. She writes sad poetry and will
   stay in her room reading books all
   weekend if she isn't out with Piper.

[Pause]

KW: She keeps saying she wants to figure out who she is, but I think she just doesn't like who she is. She doesn't feel like she fits in anywhere.

JC: Do you think that's why she joined cheerleading and became vice president of the student council?

KW: Probably. She doesn't share stuff with me anymore, at least not like before. I used to be able to get some information from Instagram, but the only things she posts there are sanitized for parents. She knows I check it too, so she doesn't post anything interesting. She's all closed off now. She just shuts her door and keeps to herself. Sometimes I hear her crying and I try to get in, but she says, 'Go away' and 'Get lost.'

DW: I didn't know that, honey. How come you never said anything to me?

KW: Please, Mom. You know why.

DW: That is it, young lady. I will not have you sassing me in front of Officer Christiansen.

KW: Sorry.

JC: Please, Ms. Williams. I would like to know the answer.

[Snapping sounds]

JC: Katie?

[Long pause]

KW: Well, you're never around for starters, Mom. You're always too busy with whatever you're doing to even

notice us. You hardly ever ask how
we are. You definitely never listen to
the answer. You just do your thing
and leave me and Anna on our own.

DW: Oh, Katie. That is a bit dramatic,
don't you think? I'm sure you're just
feeling upset about your sister and
taking it out on me. Now, I don't
deserve that. I am a good mother
and you know it. This isn't the
time for your 'tween' attitude. We
need to find your sister. So stop
all this nonsense and let's get back
to answering Officer Christiansen's
questions. Please proceed, Officer.

JC: Katie, do you think Anna feels like
she doesn't have anyone to talk to?

KW: Umm.

JC: You can speak freely, Katie. Your
mother understands that all of these
questions are very important if we
are going to be able to find Anna. We
need to know what Anna is feeling,
because Anna is the one who is
missing. Your mother will understand,
won't you, Ms. Williams?

DW: It's just all this worry is getting
to me and... Well, of course. Yes,
please answer the question, Katie.

KW: Umm, I don't know if she talked to
anyone. Maddie and her definitely aren't
talking much these days. Maybe she
talked to the girls on her cheerleading
squad or something. Sometimes we go
next door to the Nelsons'.

JC: What do you do next door?

KW: Mrs. Nelson usually gives us
         something homemade to eat and
         we play video games or watch TV.
         Anna talks to Jack about homework
         sometimes. He's a Brainiac.

JC: Does Anna talk to Jack about other
         things besides homework?

KW: I don't know. Maybe? I just know she
         never talks to Mom and she no longer
         talks to me. Dad is definitely not an
         option. I can't think of anyone else
         she would talk to.

JC: What about your dad, Katie? How do
         you think Anna feels about him?

KW: Pissed off.

DW: Katie, you better watch your
         language.

KW: Sorry.

JC: Why is she pissed off?

KW: I don't know. She just hates him
         lately. Apparently, they used to be
         best buddies, at least that's what
         Dad always says. He's always asking
         me about Anna, trying to get me to
         tell him something. I can't help him,
         though, because she doesn't talk
         about him. She just says I should
         stay away from him, too. I don't know
         why she's like that. All he ever does
         is try to make her happy, but she's
         so mad all the time.

JC: How does your dad treat you?
         [Loud HA sound from Ms. Williams]

DW: I think we already covered that,

72

Officer. Loser.

JC: Ms. Williams, I am going to have to
ask you to stop interrupting. If you
can't let Katie answer the questions
without interjecting, I will have to
interview her in the other room.

DW: There's no need for that. I apologize.
My emotions are just getting the
better of me. Please continue.

JC: Katie, do you remember the question?

KW: Yes. The thing is, he doesn't really
notice me. I'm non-existent, compared
to Anna, anyway. He never comes
around, and when he does, he tries to
do fun things with us. But it always
feels weird because Anna is always
clammed up.

JC: Is she afraid of him?

KW: Not really. She can talk back to him,
and he won't do anything about it. He
just lets her sass him.

JC: Do you remember when this started?

KW: Well, she got all bent out of shape
when I went to the mall with him
for Christmas shopping. I was
buying her a present, so obviously
I couldn't have her take me. Plus,
I thought Dad and I could have
some alone time to get to know
each other better. I miss having
my dad around. I think maybe she
was jealous or something. Maybe she
misses him, too. Maybe me being with
him makes her think about the old
days or something. I don't know.

JC: Did you spend the holidays with your dad?

KW: We went to his place for a couple days after Christmas. He got a tree with presents and decorations. He tried really hard, making a turkey and everything.

JC: What else can you tell me about Anna, Katie?

KW: I don't know. I think I told you all I know. She loves the smell of matches. She never uses a candle lighter because she likes the smell matches make. She's got a crush on Channing Tatum, even though she'll say Harry Styles if you ask her. Um, I don't know what else to say.

JC: Okay, Katie. You did good. If something else comes to you, tell your mom or you can give me a call directly. Here's my card.

KW: Okay.

JC: Listen, Ms. Williams, I think I have enough information for the time being.

DW: Wait, don't forget her laptop.

JC: Thank you.

DW: Do you want me to put it in a bag for you?

JC: No, thank you. I'll handle it.

DW: Alright.

[Crying sounds, sniffling]

DW: I guess I just can't stand watching you put her things into those clear bags and labeling them that way. It's so—

JC: I understand how difficult this must
        be for you.
DW: I don't think you can possibly
        understand.
    [Sniffling]
KW: It's okay, Mom.
JC: I want you to know that we are doing
        everything we can to find Anna. I
        promise I will do everything in my
        power to bring her home safe and
        sound.
DW: I appreciate that. I do. I guess it's
        just becoming so real that she isn't
        here.
JC: You know what? I think it would
        be helpful if you could make some
        posters with a lot of different
        pictures of Anna to post online and
        around the area. Do you think you
        could do that?
DW: Yes, that's a great idea. Right,
        Katie?
KW: Sure.
DW: We can start right away.
JC: Great. I'll be in touch with any
        new information. In the meantime,
        however, if you think of anything
        that will help us, please call me.
DW: Thank you so much, Officer
        Christiansen. Please just bring my
        Anna back. I don't know what I'll do
        if you don't.
JC: I will do my best, Ms. Williams. You
        have my word.
KW: Officer?

JC: Yes, Katie?

KW: You know how to find my sister, right?

JC: I am going to do everything I can to
          find her. In the meantime, try not to
          worry. Everything is going to be fine.
          Just keep me posted if you think of
          something that might help us figure
          out what Anna might have done after
          school on Friday. Also, inform me
          immediately if she makes any contact
          with you or anyone else. Okay?

KW: Okay.

DW: Of course. You have our full
          cooperation, Officer. Anything we can
          do to get Anna back home safe.

JC: Thank you, Ms. Williams. Katie. I'll
          be in touch.

"Liar," I mumble to myself, feeling a deep sense of hatred well up inside of me.

"Do you always talk to yourself?"

Startled, I whip my head around to see Christiansen, with his pants on fire, standing in the doorway with a cup of coffee in his hand. I don't know how long he's been there.

"Do you always spy on people?" I ask flippantly, my eyes narrowing.

"Do you still fidget with your hair tie?" he retorts, thinking himself rather clever for an old man.

I suddenly notice that I'm snapping the hairband on my wrist. I stop immediately and cover my wrist with my other hand, embarrassed.

"I didn't see you leave yesterday."

"I had some things to do," I lie.

He laughs good-naturedly, which irritates me, and then sets the paper cup in front of me.

"Well, since you're at it bright and early this morning, I thought you might like some hot coffee."

"Thanks," I say reluctantly. "I guess."

The coffee looks weak. I can see the bottom of the cup, for crying out loud.

"I know these files can be really hard to read. There's a lot of formalities to follow—regulations and policies. If you have any trouble decoding any of it, let me know. Looks like I'm going to be around here for a few days doing paperwork anyway, so it won't be a bother."

"Okay, thanks." I feel like he wants me to say something else, but that's all I've got.

"Alright. Well, let me know if you need anything."

I say nothing. I know Johnny on the Spot is trying to be nice, but I'm onto him. He's the guy who was charged with finding my sister. He's the one who told me that everything was going to be fine. Now he feels guilty for failing, and he's trying to butter me up so I don't sue him or something. Can I even sue a detective for being bad at his job? Whatever. The point is I am not forgiving him no matter how many stale cups of coffee he brings me.

"I will," I finally say, hoping to get rid of him. He lingers for a minute, so I feel compelled to make him leave. "You can go now."

"Alright." He backs out of the doorway slowly. "Well, you know where to find me."

When he is finally gone, I take a sip of his gas station coffee. It's bad—just like I thought. It doesn't stop me from drinking it, though.

I can't believe that guy. He's just as sneaky as he used to be. Of course, I'm not the same impressionable kid I was back then. Any twelve-year-old kid in my position would have been intimidated by a police detective asking questions about their missing sister while standing in her bedroom. I am older and wiser now. I'm not so easily fooled.

Although, come to think of it, it's hard to remember who I was before that morning. Maybe I was just an ordinary girl. The only problem I had then was being the kid of divorced parents. A lot of kids get messed up over that, but it never really bothered me too much. The truth is, my parents being split up was always normal to me. Plus, Anna was always there to make it all okay.

When she went missing, that's when the world lost its color. I didn't really care about the things I used to care about, and I stopped hanging out with most of my friends. Everything they talked about seemed like trivial nonsense, like boys and clothes and makeup. My friends and their giggling made me irate because it felt like a luxury none of us deserved. Josie was the only one I could tolerate.

I wonder who I would have become if none of this had happened. I probably would have been a pleasant, well-adjusted girl. I probably would have listened when my mom said to do my homework. She did say stuff like that, didn't she? Well, if nothing else, I might have been the kind of girl who can talk politely to a police officer. But it *did* happen, and now I am jaded and dysfunctional. Whatever. I'm still not letting that guy off the hook. He was the one who should have found her and brought her back.

Great. Now I'm all agitated. I reach into my bag and pull out my mint container. I sift through the Advil and Sudafed until I find the Xanax, then pop two into my mouth. Defiantly, I wash the pill down with Christiansen's stale coffee. Here's to day two.

<u>FILE CONTROL NO. 23167</u>
<u>MISSING PERSON – ANNA WILLIAMS</u>
Note to File completed by Officer Christiansen on April 22, 2012, 12:05 p.m.

PERSONAL BELONGINGS TO BE LOCATED AND REVIEWED

- Contents of Anna's room, including any personal information that could shed light on potential motives, suspects, etc.
- Contents of Anna's school locker
- Electronic Media including text messages, email messages, browsing history, and any and all available social media content

POTENTIAL SOURCES IDENTIFIED FOR INTERVIEWS

- Other Persons Residing at the Home: mother Diane Williams, sister Katie Williams
- Known Family Members: father Keith Williams, maternal aunt Maria (resides out of state with her husband and two children), grandmother Rose Williams
- Friends and Neighbors: Nelson family (next-door neighbors including a son, Jack, who is Anna's age), Maddie Le (close childhood friend), Jacob Hunt (classmate and potential boyfriend), Piper Abbot (friend), kids involved with Anna in extra-curricular activities, co-workers at the sandwich shop where Anna worked
- School Sources: Teachers yet to be identified, school guidance counselor, principal

Monday

August 20, 2011

I don't want to be the girl everyone overlooks anymore. I don't want people to stand in front of me, forget my name, and pretend I don't exist. I'm tired of being wallpaper. I want to be noticed. I want to matter.

But I don't. I don't matter to my mom or my dad. I don't matter to my teachers, my neighbors, or the bagger at Safeway who sees me every week and still can't seem to remember me. Every week he says to me, "Oh, hey, you go to Macklemore, right?" Yes, dumbass. I go to Macklemore. We sat next to each other in second grade, played soccer on the same team when we were eight, and just finished a whole year of Spanish with Señora Martinez together. Thanks for taking a moment to acknowledge my existence. Let's do this again next week, shall we?

I've heard the preaching about being true to yourself, spent periods discussing the brave authenticity of creative geniuses, and watched a thousand movies where the misunderstood nerd comes out on top. I've read the trendy fashion advice of "bea-YOU-tiful" scattered across the merchandise of every boutique in town.

Bea-YOU-tiful

I would love to be myself, my truest self. I would. But then there are these rules and mandates about how you are supposed to behave in order to matter.

These rules of what is and isn't okay are so exhausting. And they're enforced with teasing, exclusion, and outright cruelty. There are invisible traps laid everywhere, so that when I try to bea-ME-tiful, I am shamed within an inch of my life until I return to my well-worn seat of mediocrity that exists under the radar. It would probably be easier if I was my true self, because attaining the exact level of mediocrity that keeps you safe is almost impossible. The rules are always changing.

Be a good girl, but naughty is more likable. Listen to your parents, but don't be a nerd. Get good grades, but don't get all high and mighty about it and don't act like you have to work hard for them. Please your teachers, but don't let anyone find out that they like you. Go to college, but only the right one. Don't be promiscuous, but don't be a prude either. Don't drink or do drugs, unless you're at a party where it's offered, because if you refuse you'll be labeled as naive or lame. Actually, go ahead and do them, just don't get hooked or wind up screwing your life up because of them. Get a tattoo or piercing, unless it's too overdone like tramp stamps or tribal designs. Oh, and make sure you find a unique spot not already made popular—or just follow the most recent popular trend. Don't wear provocative clothes if you want to be believed about being date raped, but by all means, look hot. In fact, look as fake as possible. Be thin, and by thin, I mean a size zero or two or four. If you are particularly tall and involved in sports, then you can get away with a six. Be popular, but not so popular that you threaten the already existing social order because, well, you do want to survive through graduation. Don't be the girl next door, unless you are doing it ironically, because it leads to the same dead end as "the friend zone." Of course, good girls are respected and bad girls get reputations.

So unless you've been gifted with extraordinary wealth, good looks, family connections, a magnetic personality, or some other acceptable trait that makes it even possible to follow these mandates for high school survival, it's best to throw in the towel entirely by joining the chess club and hiding out in room 16 during lunch... or find a way to fade into the wallpaper of social life. I have somehow become wallpaper—the kind nobody notices hanging out in the background.

Even Maddie doesn't notice me anymore. I don't mean to be ungrateful, because I love her. She knows I do. We both love music and art and there's no one else in the world I would trust with all my secrets. But she always assumes I like the same things as her—or hate the same things. She can be really mean, like when she says "Don't be a lemming" just because I like some Taylor Swift song.

Truth is, I've always been kind of intimidated by her. She's really pushy about what she likes. Bridesmaids was hands down the best movie of the summer and anyone who doesn't like Hunger Games is an idiot. I guess I'm an idiot. And don't get me started on her fashion ideas... Crackle nail polish is epic. Colored denim is not going to last. Feathers are the single worst fashion mistake of 2011. She is so extra sometimes.

I go along with what she wants because I don't want to hurt her feelings or make her mad. I tend to follow her lead, but doesn't that make me a lemming, too? Aren't I just choosing to follow my best friend instead of some popular trend she thinks is stupid? Maybe I would like a chance at being popular. Maybe I would like to fit in. What's so wrong with that?

Maddie would say everything is wrong with that. Popular kids will never care about me. They only want more followers on Instagram. They need an entourage of friends so they can feel important, and who wants to be just another disposable? I don't. Still, I am pretty disposable as it is... so what is there to lose?

My mom is always telling me that I need to pay more attention to my looks and start wearing better clothes. "Be a swan, Anna, not an ugly duckling." Maybe she's right. Maybe that is part of my problem. Maybe people don't see me because I'm too plain. Or maybe it's because I'm not putting myself out there enough. Other people might not know how great I am because I haven't been brave enough to risk the humiliation and show them. Maybe if I did, they would actually notice me.

It's funny how my mom always talks

about becoming a swan. She just assumes that the swan is an older, more beautiful version of the ugly duckling. I don't think she realizes that the swan wasn't ugly. It didn't look like the other fuzzy, yellow ducks because it wasn't a duck at all. The ducks were too stupid to realize that and told her she was ugly for a duck. The swan didn't do anything to change their minds. She didn't go out and transform into something entirely different to make the others like her. All she did was grow up and find other swans who appreciated her beauty.

I think what she means is I need to be a dragonfly. I need to transform myself into something beautiful, graceful, and luminous. Basically, stop being me—at least on the outside. I need to be colorful and glittery like a dragonfly's iridescent wings that shimmer like fairy dust in the sun. Now that I think about it, I guess dragonflies are pretty cool the way they transform us at the same time. They dart about on the wind in all their whimsical splendor and convince us all to set them apart from the rest of the insects out there. And we oblige by putting them in a class above, along with butterflies and Luna moths. We don't shriek when we see them or call pest control, even though they are still bugs.

When school starts next week, I am going to shake things up. I'm going to try new things and be a new person. I can't believe I'm going to say this, but I was thinking about trying out for cheerleading. I know. Ridiculous, right? Still, you have to give it to cheerleaders. They are always so freaking happy. They're colorful and glittery. Plus, everyone sees them because they're right up in front of the crowd shouting all the time.

I want to be seen, and if I have to dress like a Bratz doll to do it, then fine. I can glide on some obnoxious pink lip gloss and squeeze into some short skirt if that makes people notice that I'm alive. If that's how the world works, why fight it?

I need a little makeover first. Maddie is always trying to get me to wear more makeup and let her style my hair, so hopefully she can help me. She's much better at this kind of thing than I am. If I hate it, I can always change back. There is no law on having to act and look the same forever. If Maddie can have purple hair, I can experiment a little too. I can spread my wings and see what the view looks like from somewhere else.

I have to give it a try, even if it ends up being a total disaster. I can't stay the way I am now. I just can't spend the rest of my life feeling like I might as well not even be here.

I take a sip of cold coffee and lean back against the rigid metal of this uncomfortable chair. It creaks. I can't believe I forgot Anna kept a diary. I wonder where it is now, or if these photocopied pages are all that's left of it.

Man, reading it is like being with her again. Almost. I can hear the lilt in her voice, the way she would trail off at the end of a sentence, and even her mothering tone. If I close my eyes, I can almost picture her hand gestures and facial expressions. She was so animated when she talked, so vibrant. God, I miss her.

She had a way of putting the world in perspective. She was my Toto in the *Wizard of Oz*, pulling back the curtain to reveal the man behind the wizard. Every person has a man and a wizard, she used to say. Most of us only see the wizard. I never understood that as a kid, especially as a girl navigating the strange world of middle school, but she would always say that when she tried to explain to me why one of my friends was acting one way or another. If anyone could see past the superficial, it was Anna. How could she have been so twisted up about popularity and all that? Why did she even care?

Anna used to act like my mom was so dumb, like she could care less about whatever she said. She would shake her head at me, roll her eyes, and imitate my mom's theatrics until I busted up laughing. I had no idea the things my mom said actually bothered her. I definitely never thought it bothered her enough to make her change herself.

I've never let my mom get the best of me. Unlike Anna, I've never been able to bend to her will. I just don't have it in me to let her yell at me without yelling back. That's why I avoid her. It's easier than trying to hold my tongue. I'm so glad she's still in Hawaii until Friday. I don't think I'd be able to lie to her about what I'm doing, and if she finds out, she'll be mad. I don't think I could handle fighting with her. Not while I'm digging through this file.

INTERVIEW WITH FATHER, KEITH WILLIAMS
(VIA TELEPHONE)

Sunday, April 22, 2012, 12:35 p.m.
Transcribed from Digital Recording

JC: Officer John Christiansen

KW: Keith Williams

JC: Begin recording. Interview with Keith Williams, Anna's father, via telephone. Hello, Mr. Williams?

KW: Yes?

JC: My name is Officer Christiansen and I am the detective working—

KW: Yes, yes, I know. My ex-wife told me you would be calling. I can't believe this is happening. Have you found her?

JC: No, sir. We haven't found her yet.

KW: Oh, God. I've been on location in Maine, but I'm working on getting the first flight back home as we speak. It's killing me to be this far away when my little girl needs me. I just can't believe this is happening.

JC: Mr. Williams, we are doing all we can. Part of my job is to talk to everyone who knows Anna so I can start piecing together what might have happened. I need to ask you a few questions.

KW: Of course, of course. Shoot.

JC: First, can you hear me alright?

KW: Yes, this is a great connection. Go ahead.

JC: You are in Maine, you said? How long have you been there?

KW: A couple of weeks now, but like I said, I'm trying to fly back to California immediately.

JC: Alright, when was the last time you saw Anna?

KW: Man, it's been a couple of months. I'm supposed to come get the girls every other weekend, but that doesn't always happen. I've been busy getting back on my feet professionally.

JC: What do you mean?

KW: Well, I've been in recovery for alcohol abuse. I used to be one of the best cinematographers out there, but that all went to crap when my personal life exploded. Now I'm finally getting back into work, and that, unfortunately, requires travel.

JC: You've always traveled for work, then?

KW: Oh, yeah. When the girls were little, I would be gone for a couple months on a project and then home for a month or even just a few weeks. Diane knew what she was getting into. She used to go on location with me before we were married and loved it, but things changed when Anna was born. I think Diane felt trapped at home.

[Heavy sigh]

KW: When I was home, though, I was totally a hands-on dad. We went to the beach, to the park, out for burgers. I even got Anna a pink tool belt to wear when she helped me around the house. We had a lot of fun together. When I'd come home, she'd barrel down the hallway and plow me over to say hi. We were real close. Diane hated that.

JC: What do you mean?

KW: I mean she acted like I was supposed to spend every single moment with her and only her. If I took Anna out for the day, she would say I was spending too much time with her. If I bought Anna a gift, but nothing for her, she'd get upset. At some point, I would do it on purpose just to piss her off.

JC: Did you buy things for Katie, too?

KW: Oh yeah, but mostly as she got bigger. Babies are not really my thing.

[Mr. Williams clears his throat]

KW: Or Diane's, come to think of it. That's probably why we started

fighting the moment Anna was born. I
figured Diane would relax if she got
the big house she always wanted in
a neighborhood with other families
to help her out, but it didn't make
a difference. We kept fighting in the
new house. She would accuse me of—

JC: Accuse you of what?

KW: Everything. Anything.

[Burst of laughter from Mr. Williams]

KW: Cheating on her, having another
        family somewhere else, being a sex
        addict, doing drugs, spoiling Anna,
        flirting with her friends—you name
        it. She would go on and on. That's
        seriously the reason I started
        drinking. I know it is so cliché, but
        that woman drove me to drink.

JC: So you're a pretty serious alcoholic?

KW: It wasn't a big deal at first, just
        a beer here or there, a Seven and
        Seven, maybe a glass of whiskey. I
        thought I was handling it, but I just
        kept pouring another one whenever I
        couldn't deal. Before I knew it, I
        couldn't get through the day without
        it. I didn't want to face the fact
        that my marriage was falling apart,
        and I didn't want to be the dad who
        walked out, either. I lived that as
        a kid and swore I would never do the
        same. I guess it was easier to hide
        out in the bottle.

[Deep exhale]

KW: Obviously, I was wrong. By the time I climbed out, it was like a tornado had blown through my life.

JC: I get it. In all my years on the force, I have never seen an alcoholic or addict make it out unscathed.

KW: Ain't that the damn truth?

JC: When did you get sober?

KW: Not until after we split. It took more than a year to really commit to it, but I finally did. Losing my family and almost losing my career was bottom for me.

[Sniffling sounds, coughing]

JC: What about when she was older? You didn't divorce until she was thirteen or so, right?

KW: Yeah, she was almost fourteen. Honestly, she kind of stopped being daddy's girl around nine or ten.

JC: Why?

KW: Diane and I were always fighting, I was drinking, Anna was getting older. I told you.

[Background noise, muffled voices]

KW: Hang on a second... okay, sorry about that.

JC: Has Diane communicated anything to you about Anna?

KW: Not really, no.

JC: Diane said you haven't seen Anna
        since February, is that true?

KW: Sounds about right.

JC: She also said Anna hasn't wanted to
        see you.

KW: Diane's always trash-talking me in
        front of Anna and Katie. It's hard
        enough when I don't live with them,
        but then to have their mother putting
        me down every two seconds, it's no
        wonder she doesn't want to see me.
        Diane's a real piece of work.

JC: So your divorce did not go smoothly,
        I take it.

KW: No, it did not. I still don't
        understand how she cheats on me, but
        still manages to get custody and
        most of my paycheck. I'm living in
        the Valley so I can afford her lavish
        lifestyle, the kids, and my own
        place. So not only do I not get to
        see my girls very often, but it's now
        even harder to get there.

JC: Did you know Anna was mad at you?

KW: I don't know if I'd say she was mad.
        She's just been moody, and I'm the
        lucky recipient of her moods.

JC: Do you know why she's been mad, or
        moody, as you say?

        [Silence]

KW: I'm sure she's been fed some kind of
lies from Diane about what a jerk
I am. It doesn't matter what I say,
because the girls believe their
mother no matter what.

JC: Okay. Do you generally bring the girls
to your apartment when you have them?

KW: Yes. Diane is constantly giving me a
guilt trip about how Anna needs to
be with her friends and do stuff at
school, but that's just her way of
taking more of my time with them away.
I only have two weekends a month.

JC: So do you think Diane is the reason
you and Anna are not in a good place
right now?

KW: Of course. She is constantly
undermining me.

JC: Do you know if Anna drinks alcohol?

KW: I don't know.

JC: Does she do drugs?

KW: I don't know.

JC: Has she been in any trouble?

KW: No.

JC: Is there anyone who might want to
hurt her?

KW: Oh, God. I never thought of that.
Could someone have taken her? Did she
go off with some guy she shouldn't
have? She's just a baby. Oh, God.

JC: Mr. Williams, please don't jump to

any conclusions. We haven't ruled
out foul play, but we haven't any
evidence pointing to that either.
All these questions are intended to
shed some light on what was going
on with Anna at the time of her
disappearance. That way, we can
determine how to find her.

KW: Alright, alright. I'm sorry. I'm just
getting a bit crazed over the whole
thing. You read about this stuff
happening and you feel bad for a
second, but then you move on because
it's just too horrible. You never think
it's going to happen to your family.
You never think it's even possible. I
have so many amends to make, but Anna
deserves a lifetime of them.

JC: Can you remember anything that
you or your ex-wife may have done
to upset her in some way, even
accidentally? Something that might
make her want to run away?

KW: No. Absolutely not. I love my
daughter. She knows that.

JC: This isn't about you loving your
daughter, Mr. Williams. It's
about finding her. I need to know
everything.

KW: If I know something, I'll tell you.
She's my daughter, for Christ's sake.

JC: Okay. Does she have a boyfriend that
you know about?

KW: No.

JC: Okay. What can you tell me about her relationship with Katie?

KW: Oh, they love each other. Those girls are what Diane and I did right. Anna looks out for Katie and Katie just adores her. That's part of the problem. It's like Anna is mad at me, so Katie feels like she has to be mad too.

JC: So Katie has been upset with you as well?

KW: Not really, but if Anna doesn't come for the weekend, Katie won't either. Then if Anna acts sulky and upset, Katie sides with her. Sometimes she tries to run interference, but most of the time she's on Anna's side.

JC: Okay. I think I've asked all of my questions at this point. If you think of anything else, you need to call me. This is my cell number, and you can reach me on it anytime, day or night.

KW: Okay, Officer. I will.

JC: In the meantime, do we have permission to search your apartment for anything that might help us find Anna?

KW: Yes, of course. My ex-wife, Diane, should have a spare key.

JC: Thank you, Mr. Williams. I'll be in touch.

KW: Okay. Thank you. Bye.

I slip out of the office and walk towards the vending machine. It's way past lunch, but I can't stop reading now. Sliding my dollar bills into the ancient machine feels retro, but not in a cool way. I have to smooth out the wrinkles several times before it finally accepts my money. I push the numbers and letters until a granola bar and a bag of M&Ms drops down. I snatch them out of the tray at the bottom, then disappear back into the office, deciding against purchasing a Diet Coke. I don't have all day.

Ripping open the bag of candy, I empty a handful into my mouth. I love chocolate, although not as much as Anna used to love it. M&Ms, especially. My mom put them in dishes around the house during the holidays. She only bought the ones colored to match the seasonal décor, never the ordinary rainbow ones. Pastel pinks and blues for Easter, bright reds and greens for Christmas. No matter what color they were, they didn't last long around Anna and me. We ate them by the handful.

It's crazy, but I remember everything about that last Christmas we spent together. I made her open our gifts to each other on Christmas Eve because I just couldn't wait any longer. We opened them in her room without my mom knowing, then re-wrapped them all to open again the next day. It was nice, just the two of us. She had knitted me a teal scarf and bought me the Vans I had been drooling over for a month. Of course, she made a CD, too. She did that every year.

Afterwards, we listened to Christmas music on the radio station until we fell asleep. I liked the stillness of being together, the comfort of not having to talk. I wish I could have that time back. I would talk with her all night long, pestering her with all of my questions that I foolishly thought there would be time to answer later on.

For as far back as I can remember, I've longed to have my dad in my life. Even when he was around in elementary school, he was always off filming for weeks at a time. When he was home, he was always more interested in hanging out with Anna.

That Christmas, I thought I had finally gotten him to take an interest in me. He took me shopping so I could pick up gifts for my mom and Anna. I got my mom her favorite perfume, and I got Anna a t-shirt that read, "My brain is 80% song lyrics," and a hardcover copy of *Pride and Prejudice*. I thought I nailed it, until I came home to Anna being mad. It was like she was jealous that I finally got to enjoy the good stuff with our dad. For once, he took me out instead of Anna. I couldn't understand why she wasn't happy for me.

My dad has always been a big drinker, but he tried stopping over and over again. That Christmas, he was sober and happy being around us. He actually came to pick me up when he said he would, he didn't make us have lunch at the bar so he could keep his glass full, and he asked me about school. It was the best Christmas present he could have given me. Way better than the emoji pillow he wrapped up that year.

My dad's sobriety disappeared with Anna. He acts like he's changed, but he hasn't. I'm not fooled by the same old story about how he's going to meetings and really taking it seriously. I talked to him a few weeks ago and he was blitzed. He slurred through the whole conversation and kept mumbling, "Yeah, I know," but he wasn't connecting any dots. He keeps saying he'll sort things out so we can spend time together, but he never does. He just cleans up long enough to get through a job and then slides right back into it.

I know losing Anna was too much for him. They shared this strange bond that I couldn't break into, no matter what I did. It was like Anna held some magic power over him, but she didn't want it. I never understood it. I would have gladly been daddy's little girl, but he's never been interested in me. I'm not sure what hurts more—that he loved her more when she was around, or that he still doesn't love me now that she isn't.

FILE CONTROL NO. 23167
MISSING PERSON – ANNA WILLIAMS
Note to File completed by Officer Christiansen on April 22, 2012, 3:40 p.m.

PREMISES SEARCH – PRIMARY RESIDENCE

The home where Anna lives is a spacious, well-kept, two-story house in an affluent neighborhood. The outside is immaculately landscaped, much like the other houses in the subdivision. A thorough search of the house revealed nothing of interest. The house is very clean and well-kept with family photos on the wall. There is a liquor cabinet with some wine, vodka, and rum. Ms. Williams noted that nothing appeared to be missing. No drugs or other paraphernalia were located in the house.

Anna's room looks like the room of a small child with pink walls, porcelain figurines on the shelves, and stuffed animals suspended in nets in the corner. Her drawers and her closet are filled with clothes, none of which seem to be missing. The books, tablet, and other items in her room appear to be in their proper place. Her bed was made. No alcohol, drugs, or paraphernalia were found in her bedroom.

After talking with her mother, Diane Williams, we have learned that Anna has never tried to run away before, nor has she ever threatened to do so. Diane has not noticed any serious signs of distress or suicidal tendencies. Her mother also firmly believes that Anna has never experimented with alcohol or drugs, and we found no evidence to the contrary.

EVIDENCE

After a full search of Anna's home and bedroom, I collected

the items listed below as evidence.

Evidence collected from Diane Williams's house:

- Fingerprints
- Toothbrush
- Hairbrush
- Laptop
- Diary with sporadic entries dating back to June 2011 with the last entry on April 19, 2012
- Calendar
- Undated letter
- Quotations taped to Anna's wall
- Prom Flyer
- Shoebox filled with mementos, including greeting cards, photos, and trinkets.

PREMISES SEARCH – FATHER'S APARTMENT

Officers conducted a search of the father's two-bedroom apartment after being given express authorization. The apartment is located approximately thirty minutes from Anna's primary residence in Buena Vida. It is sparsely outfitted, containing mostly furniture and electronics, but well-maintained. No alcohol or drugs were found in the apartment.

The bedroom where Anna and her sister stay when they visit Mr. Williams contains two bunk beds, a desk and chair, a television, and two beanbag chairs. There were very few personal items of Anna's present, with the exception of some clothes in the closet and some beauty products in the medicine cabinet.

Fingerprints were collected, as well as a hairbrush kept in the bathroom. No other evidence was obtained from the premises.

FINE

Keith Williams's Handwritten Messages Inside Greeting
Cards Found in Anna's Bedroom on April 22, 2012

ENVELOPE POSTMARKED JUNE 8, 2011

You may almost be a woman, Anna, but you will
forever be my little monkey. Happy 17th.
Love, Dad

HANDWRITTEN DATE OF FEBRUARY 14, 2011

No matter how mad
you get, I still love you.
Happy Valentine's Day.
Love, Dad

Undated Letter From Anna Williams to Katie Williams
Found in Anna Williams's Bedroom on April 22, 2012

A NOTE FROM ANNA....

I'm sorry, Kit Kat. I really am.
I know I overreacted over the whole
Christmas shopping thing. I get that you
wanted to go shopping to surprise me and
Mom, which is so sweet of you. Forgive me?
XOXO

October 11, 2011

I haven't written in here forever. I haven't had any time! I've been so busy with cheerleading and student council that I'm hardly ever home anymore. I didn't even have a chance to write about joining the squad or the election or anything. My entire life has changed so much in just a couple of months! It's crazy.

Anyway... I can't believe I'm a cheerleader. Piper  and I have been hanging out a lot—she's on the squad and super popular and pretty. She's so great. She talked me into running for student council and we won! I think things are finally turning around for me, which led to the thing I really want to write about...

I got a tattoo! Seriously. Me. I got a tattoo... and I love it. I thought I would immediately regret it, but I don't. All the time I spent worrying about whether or not I should get one was such a waste. It's a beautiful dragonfly with green and blue wings. It's just a small one on my left ribcage so no one will ever know it's there. It's just my little secret.

I've thought about getting one for a long time, but I never had the nerve. I've always been too unsure of myself. My whole life, I have been so cautious and scared. I've always felt like there's something wrong with me, and if I'm not really careful, everyone will discover how stupid and awful I really am. So I made sure no one noticed me, but now I'm realizing that was a mistake. I was becoming a ghost.

Since I joined the squad, people are starting to notice me and talk to me. People remember my name and invite me to parties. They ask me to be in their selfies and post my face along with theirs on Instagram. They like being around me. It's the best feeling ever.

I know, I know... they haven't known me that long. At least, that's what Maddie said the last time we talked. They may be newer friends, but they are still friends. We hang out all the time and I am always laughing. I'm there for them whenever they need to talk or cry—and I'm sure, in time, I will be able to confide in them too. I'm sure this is just the beginning.

That's why I had to write about it. I want to make this feeling of hopefulness more permanent. I don't want to forget how it feels to be vibrant and full of potential. That's why I got a dragonfly. It's a reminder that we all can break free from whatever holds us back... and fly!

And that's just what I plan to do.

Wait a minute. Anna, my straight and narrow sister, got a tattoo? She never even mentioned that she wanted one. I mean, we talked about a lot of things, including tattoos, and not once did she ever even hint about getting one herself. The most she ever offered was advice on where NOT to place a tattoo. I heard Maddie talk about it on occasion, contemplating whether to put it on her ankle or behind her ear, but Anna seemingly had no interest. That is, until New Anna came along and split her personality down the middle.

My hand instantly reaches for the pendant around my neck. I can't believe this. She wore this dragonfly necklace all the time, but she never once showed me the dragonfly on her body. Was she embarrassed about it? Did she think she would seem like a bad influence on me? Why would she hide it?

Then again, why would she hide how invisible she felt? She could have talked to me. I would have understood. I would have set her straight. If I knew she was feeling stupid and awful, and like she was wallpaper, I would have shown her how wrong she was. She wasn't invisible, because I saw her. And I thought she was perfect.

INTERVIEW WITH NEIGHBOR, SHEILA NELSON

Sunday, April 22, 2012, 5:24 p.m.
Transcribed from Digital Recording

JC: Officer John Christiansen

SN: Sheila Nelson

JC: Begin recording. Thank you for
        meeting with me, Mrs. Nelson.

SN: You can call me Sheila.

JC: Okay, Sheila. Let's get started.

SN: Oh, yes. Of course. I'm sorry Jack
        isn't back. I texted him and called,
        but he hasn't gotten back to me yet.

JC: Where is he?

SN: He and some friends went out looking
        for Anna. They met here around
        lunchtime and compiled a list of
        all the places she might be and then
        split up to look for her.

JC: With any luck, maybe they have
        already found her.

SN: I sure hope so.

JC: In the meantime, I need to continue
        my investigation. I can meet with
        him at school tomorrow if he doesn't
        return in time. I have other students
        to question.

SN: Alright, then. Go ahead and ask me
        whatever you need to.

JC: Okay. How long—

SN: I'm sorry to interrupt, but can I
        offer you a drink of water, a cup of
        coffee, tea, or something to eat? I
        feel terrible not offering when you
        first got here.

JC: No, thank you. I am short on time, so
        I would like to get straight to it.

SN: Of course. I'm just a little nervous.
        I've never experienced anything like
        this before.

JC: I understand. Please relax and we'll
        simply have a conversation. Okay?

SN: Okay.

JC: How long have you known the Williams
        family?

SN: Well, we've lived next door for, let
        me see... ten, no eleven years. Yes,
        eleven. We've been in this house
        since Jack was a baby, but the
        Williamses moved in when Anna was in
        first grade. I remember because the
        kids were in the same class and rode
        the bus to and from school together.
        I helped out Diane a lot back then
        since Katie was only a baby.

JC: Would you say that you are close with
        the Williams family?

SN: Sure. We have lived next door for all

this time. You get to know someone
pretty well after a while.

JC: What can you tell me about their
family life?

SN: Let me think. Diane is really
nice, very outgoing. Her house
is immaculate, too. I have never
understood how she keeps it so tidy.
Even when the girls were little,
she kept things so clean that her
house felt more like a model home
to be visited. She is just that kind
of person. I, on the other hand,
am obviously not gifted with that
talent, as you can see from the looks
of this place.

[Stilted laughter from Mrs. Nelson]

SN: Anyway, the girls are great. Anna is
a really good kid. She is kind and
helpful. Every time I see her, she
asks how I'm doing and has the best
manners. She really is mature for her
age, I think. Almost like a little
adult, really. I suppose that's why
she's like a second mom to Katie.
Katie, being five years younger, has
always looked up to Anna. She tagged
along after her and Jack all the time
when they were little. It was the
cutest thing. Anna made her lunches,
took her to the park down the street,
watched her ride her bike, tied her
shoes for her... all that kind of

stuff. Peas in a pod, I call them.

[Coughing sounds]

SN: I'm talking too much, aren't I? I tend to babble when I get nervous. My husband is always telling me to just—

JC: You're doing fine, Mrs. Nelson. Now, what can you tell me about Mr. Williams?

SN: Oh, Keith? Well, Keith was—is—a nice man. When the kids were little, our families would get together a lot. We would bring a dish and bottle of wine over and let the kids run wild while we all caught up with each other. My husband, Eric, got on well with Keith. They talked about sports and motorcycles, all the usual men topics, I guess.

JC: Can you tell me anything about their divorce?

SN: We were shocked when we heard about them separating. It was terrible, actually. We heard it from Jack first, who had heard it from Anna. I don't like to bring up someone else's dirty laundry, but you should probably know that... Oh, I feel awful saying this to you, but it seems like you should know.

JC: What?

SN: Well, I'll just say it. Anna apparently caught Diane with another

man, which was upsetting for everyone
involved, as you can imagine.

JC: So Anna was a witness to her mother's
infidelity?

SN: Yes. Poor thing, having to see
something like. I guess it was just
one of those circumstances when two
people fall out of love, but they
sure fell out of it hard. I figure
we all go through tough patches in
marriage, and this was theirs.

JC: I understand that. I've been married
for twelve years myself.

SN: Oh, that's nice. Do you have
children?

JC: Yes, two girls, two and five.

SN: Oh, those are such sweet ages.

JC: Yes, well... anyway, please proceed.

SN: Diane told me later that she had been
upset with Keith for years. I think it
had a lot to do with his drinking and
all the traveling he did with work.
I remember talking to Eric about it,
wondering what went wrong. Eric said
Keith never mentioned a word to him
about Diane. He didn't talk about
their relationship or anything, so
I don't know what Keith thought. I
suppose men of our generation weren't
raised to talk about their feelings,
which is a shame.

JC: Then they divorced?

SN: Yes. I think it took a couple of
        years for the divorce to finalize,
        especially since they fought over
        everything. They couldn't agree on
        who should keep the stemware or the
        linens. One point of contention was
        the grill, which is ridiculous since
        Diane doesn't even know how to use
        it. I think I told her that once, but
        she shrugged it off. It was definitely
        not an amicable divorce.

JC: How did the girls appear to handle
        the divorce?

SN: Oh, they handled it so gracefully.
        Anna was very supportive of her
        mother, always trying to make her
        life a little easier. She kept up on
        the house chores, made dinner, and
        watched one bad movie after another
        on the sofa next to Diane well
        after Katie had gone to bed. She was
        understanding and very grown-up when
        it came to the infidelity. She never
        brought it up. She just seemed to
        roll with it.

        [Doorbell ringing in the background]

SN: Let me just see who that is.

        [Sound of footsteps, faint utterance of
        thank you, and door closing]

SN: Sorry about that. Just FedEx dropping
        something off. They're out awfully
        late today. I'm sorry. Where did we
        leave off?

JC: I was asking about how Anna and her sister handled their parents' divorce.

SN: That's right. The girls handled it really well. I guess we all handle things so differently in this life. My son Jack would not have been as understanding, I can promise you that. He'd be in therapy for years.

[Nervous laughter]

SN: He isn't in therapy now, of course. I just mean that if—

JC: I understand what you meant, Mrs. Nelson.

SN: The thing is, ever since he was little, I have tried to protect him from the world. I double-checked Halloween candy, only let him ride his bike where I could see him, and never let him watch adult movies until he was at least twelve. Now I'm not sure if it was a good idea after all.

JC: What do you mean?

SN: You'll see, Officer. When your girls get older, you'll see what I mean. My Jack feels like the world has turned upside down on him. He went from being a happy-go-lucky little boy to a moody man-child. I can't even begin to make sense of what happened to the Williams family back then, or now, and I have no idea how to put any of this in understandable terms to a

kid who is too old to be appeased by
saying "It's adult stuff."

[Lapse in time]

JC: Mrs. Nelson?

SN: Yes, I'm sorry. I guess revisiting
this whole issue makes me wonder.

JC: What do you mean?

SN: I just wonder how much Anna was
carrying around on her shoulders.

[Pause]

SN: Thinking of it all these years
later, it had to be a lot to process
at her age. Still, if anyone could
handle it, Anna could. She handled
everything that came her way. I
think that's why her disappearance is
so upsetting to all of us. She really
is just a nice kid with so much going
for her. It would be a shame if...

[Sniffling sounds]

SN: Well, there is no use going there.
She will come home. I know it.
Whatever has happened, she will make
it home alright.

JC: Tell me, how does Anna feel about her
father?

SN: I'm not sure. He picks her up for the
occasional weekend, and they seem to
get along fine. I don't know much more
than what Diane tells me, which is
basically that Keith is a deadbeat dad

who can't bother to spend time with his own children. I take her opinion with a grain of salt, of course. I've seen Keith spend time with the girls when they were younger, and he seems to genuinely love them. He was always doting on Anna, especially. Daddy's girl, I guess.

JC: When did that change?

SN: I think it was just before they split up. Third grade, maybe? That sounds about right.

JC: Have you ever talked with Anna about any of this—the divorce, her mother's affair, or her father?

SN: I try to let her know that I'm there, but I don't want to be pushy and pry into her private business.

[Silence]

SN: Although, sometimes she lingers on the porch, almost as if she doesn't want to go home. Maybe she was trying to tell me something.

JC: What do you think she's trying to tell you?

SN: I don't know. Be honest, Officer Christiansen, do you think any of this has something to do with why she is missing? Do you think she ran away? Do you think she was so upset she would have hurt herself? Oh, tell me that can't be the case.

JC: Mrs. Nelson, I am in the middle of the investigation, and all the information you are giving me will hopefully point us in the right direction. Now, is there anything else you feel it would be important to share with me?

SN: No, not really.

JC: Okay. Thank you for your time, Mrs. Nelson. If you think of—

SN: Wait. This probably isn't relevant, but I did notice something. Eric and I were out on date night a few weeks back, and we ran into Anna that night. She was with a bunch of other kids that I didn't recognize. Usually, I know most of the kids by now since Anna and Jack are the same age and have grown up side by side. These kids weren't familiar to me, and they were dressed kind of... um... how do I put this? They had tattoos and piercings all over. Their hair was dyed all kinds of colors and cut in haphazard ways. Do you know the type?

JC: Yes, I can picture it.

SN: Well, she was with part of that crowd, dressed all in black. We barely recognized her and by the time we did, we had already walked past them. I meant to mention it to Diane, but I know Anna works down there so I thought maybe they were work friends.

Still, I didn't think it was like Anna
to hang out with that kind of group.

JC: You said you didn't know any of these
kids?

SN: No. I've never seen them at a school
function or anything.

JC: Where did you say you saw them?

SN: Downtown on High Street. I know it's
kind of run-down over there, but
they're bringing so much life back to
the area. They put in this artist's
boutique that has beautiful spun
glass and other trinkets. I have one
right here on the coffee table. See—

[Thud]

SN: Oh, how clumsy of me. I'm just a
bundle of nerves I guess. Good thing
it didn't break.

JC: It's nice.

SN: I like it. Anyway, Eric likes to
have dinner at this little hole-in-
the-wall Italian place, which he
loves because it's decent and decent
Italian food is impossible to find
around here. Of course, he's from
New York, so his standards are a bit
high. Anyway, we usually have dinner
and then stroll down the sidewalk a
bit to check out what's new at the
boutique. Plus, we love the idea of
revitalizing downtown. I'm sorry, I
am totally off-topic. This is not

important. Anyway, that's where we
saw her. Do you know the area?

JC: I'm familiar with it. Actually, we
have a lot of calls down there.

SN: Oh? Should I be worried about going
there?

JC: Um, no. I mean, you and your husband
are adults and you can exercise good
judgment. Just stay on High Street.
Don't get sidetracked on one of those
side streets.

SN: Why, Officer? What kind of things go
on down there?

JC: A lot of drugs, for starters. Just in
the past two months, we cracked down
on two meth dealers.

SN: Oh, I didn't know that.

JC: Well, drugs are everywhere.

SN: I guess I just didn't think that here
in Buena Vida—

JC: Buena Vida is not a bubble. We aren't
insulated from reality here.

SN: I know that. I just thought... Well,
anyway.

JC: Tell me, did Anna seem happy when you
saw her? Did she appear to be there
of her own volition?

SN: Yes, she was laughing and talking.

JC: Okay. Anything else?

SN: Not that I can think of.

JC: Okay. I appreciate your time, Mrs. Nelson. I better get going.

SN: Of course. You obviously have a lot to do. I'll walk you out.

JC: Alright. If you think of anything else, here's my card. Call me anytime.

SN: I will. I definitely will.

What?! This has got to be a joke.

I jump up from my seat and pace around the small room. It's difficult to maneuver past the desk and the filing cabinets, but my feet need to move to expel the shock.

I just can't believe it. I can't believe Anna walked in on my mom cheating with some other guy. Gross, gross, double gross. I wish I could unread that part. No wonder my mom didn't want me knowing stuff.

To be honest, it doesn't surprise me that Mom cheated. She's always been a flirt. And with Dad hardly around... Still, how could she be so careless to let Anna find her with someone? She must have been reckless on purpose, maybe hoping my dad would be the one to catch her. I wouldn't put that past her. I can't imagine she wanted us to find out at all, let alone the way Anna did. Oh, man, what if I had been the one who interrupted them? Gross.

I can't even imagine how Anna felt. She must have freaked. I know I'm freaked out reading it for the first time at eighteen, so I can only guess that for Anna, it was ten times worse. No child wants to even think about their parents having sex. Seeing them in action would require some serious eye bleach. And that's your parents—not your mom and some strange guy. That had to mess her up.

I sit back down and flip through the pages until I find Sheila Nelson's interview. I glance over it again. I bet that's what Sheila was thinking. She was wondering if stumbling in on them messed up Anna in some way.

Okay, okay. I need to slow down. Maybe I never knew about this because everyone wanted to protect me. I was what, eight or ten? Of course, they wouldn't tell a little kid about something like this. But what about now? I'm an adult now. My mom probably wants to spare herself the embarrassment, but what about my dad? After all these years of hating my mom, how did he never let it slip? And what about neighbors and friends? This is the kind of juicy gossip that eventually gets out.

I guess it doesn't matter. I know now. Although, now I'm not sure I want to know. I mean, so what if my family has a lot of secrets? What family doesn't? I never tell anyone about my dad's drinking. I talk him up to kids at school because he has a cool job making films. I score points when I tell people the movies he's worked on. I don't want to lose all those points by sharing the fact that he never comes around because he's too wasted. I keep his secret because I love him... and I don't want to be judged for what he does. I know I'm not the only one who does that. I'm sure lots of families do the same thing. Right?

I think it's time for that Diet Coke now.

FILE CONTROL NO. 23167
MISSING PERSON – ANNA WILLIAMS
Note to File completed by Officer Christiansen on April 22, 2012, 7:23 p.m.

POTENTIAL LEADS

Potential Categories of Missing Persons and their Applicability to Anna Williams –
At this time, only four of the categories can be ruled out.

- Lost – possible
- Parent/Family Abduction – (ruled out)
- Runaway – possible
- Stranger Abduction – possible
- Suspicious circumstances – possible
- Unknown Missing – possible
- Voluntary Missing Adult – n/a (ruled out)
- Catastrophic Missing – n/a (ruled out)
- Dependent Adult – n/a (ruled out)

WITNESSES

Immediate Family Members
Diane, the mother, has primary custody of Anna and her sister. She does not work outside of the home, but leads an active personal life. She has been separated/divorced from the father, Keith Williams, for three years and does not have a positive relationship with him. During her interview, she appeared very controlling over her daughter Katie and overly concerned about her reputation as a

good mother. However, she appeared to be visibly upset about her daughter's disappearance.

She describes Anna as a smart, hard-working girl with a normal home life. She has not noticed any behavioral changes in Anna, except for a shift in her extracurricular interests. Most notably, Anna has become active in student government and cheerleading as of this year.

Katie, Anna's twelve-year-old sister, is very close to Anna. She said Anna has been very moody and emotional lately, demanding more privacy than usual. She also notes that Anna is not close with her mother and has a strained relationship with her father. She was noticeably distraught.

Keith Williams, Anna's father, is a recovering alcoholic who has a long history of extensive usage but is working to repair his life and his relationships. He has not seen Anna in the past several months due to her unexplained anger towards him, which has been an issue since December. Mr. Williams blames his ex-wife, Diane, for purposely undermining his relationship with Anna and her sister.

Sheila Nelson, Anna's next-door neighbor, described Anna as a nice girl who was very helpful to her family. She divulged more about the Williams family history, which raises some concern for Anna's emotional state. She also expressed concern about Anna hanging around unfamiliar peers in a questionable part of town, but the area has been confirmed to be where her part-time job was located.

Other Relatives

We have reached out to other relatives of Anna Williams identified throughout the investigation.

Her paternal grandmother, Rose Williams, is in a nursing facility about an hour north of Buena Vida, and a brief telephone interview was conducted with her. Although she suffers from dementia and couldn't respond to most of my questions, she spoke highly of Anna as a sweet, smart girl. No useful information was gained. Anna's father, Keith, is the only child of Rose and Henry Williams, Henry having passed away in 2005.

Her maternal aunt, Maria Randolph, was also contacted by telephone. She lives in Missouri with her husband and two young children. She said she has very little contact with Anna or the rest of the family because of a falling out with her mother, Diane Williams. The two families essentially parted ways after the death of Anna's maternal grandmother, Marie Jenkins, in 2005. It is unclear what the reason for the parting is, although discord over a small inheritance is a likely cause. Anna's paternal grandfather passed when her mother was a child.

There are no other known family members.

NOTE

Both parents seem legitimately distraught over their daughter's disappearance, and at present, they do not appear to have been involved in any foul play. Family members noted that Anna seemed moody, but no one considered her behavior to be of any concern. Nevertheless, the family has a history of divorce, alcoholism, and bad relations. Anna has expressed concern over her identity and self-expression, as well as an overall feeling of not fitting in. Taken together with Anna's failure to deposit her paychecks and the little I've been able to learn from her diary, these factors support a theory of Anna being a typical teenage runaway. Statistically, that is the most likely reason for her disappearance.

If she is a runaway, we must assume she is at risk. She may be on the streets, without parental supervision, and vulnerable to a variety of harms. Since we are still in the acute phase of this investigation, it is crucial to move quickly. We've added Anna to all available databases and sent alerts to every relevant authority. If we haven't located her by Monday evening, the odds of finding her are drastically reduced.

Of course, we are not ruling out any other theory at this time.

December 19, 2012

My father is such a jerk. It's like he has no idea why I'm mad at him. He acts like he's this perfect dad now, always trying to win us over with movies and trips to the mall. Like that is going to fix anything. Did he forget? I mean, did he actually forget, or did he think I would?

I wish I could forget. It would be so much easier if I could. It's not like I haven't tried. I have. I do everything I can to forget all the pain I feel inside. I run, I write, and I stay busy. But I can't forget it.

My dad has this angry side to him, this quick temper. It usually only comes out when he's drinking. That's when he and Mom fought the worst. I can still hear them yelling and slamming doors, and it makes my stomach tighten into a knot even now. When they finally tired of yelling, Mom would collapse on their bed and my dad would come to my room. He said I always made him feel better. I wanted him to feel better. I also figured if he felt better, then Mom would feel better, and we all would feel a whole lot better. So I was more than willing to make him feel good—even if—well, I somehow thought I was helping. I thought I was stopping the fighting.

Today he called to make sure we were coming to his place after Christmas. He always talks these things out with me because he and Mom can't say more than three words without screaming. I told him I didn't really want to go, but he said I was coming whether I liked it or not. For some reason, the way he said it was scary, like when he used to drink. So I started wondering if he was back to it again. I got off the phone right away.

As soon as I hung up, I started shaking and my jaw would not stop chattering. I cried and sobbed and heaved for twenty minutes like I was possessed by something or someone else. When I tried to get myself out of it, I ended up hitting myself in the head over and over again. I finally stopped, but I left bruises on my forehead, just under my hairline. I actually bruised myself. What is wrong with me?

I can't keep pretending like everything is fine all the time, especially if I am going to have to see him every two weeks and act normal for Katie's sake. But why does Katie's well-being depend so much on me?

I guess I should give my dad a break. Apparently, alcoholism is a disease, so I guess I can't be mad at him for being sick. Although, it seems like a disease he chose to contract. Still,

I guess I have to be more understanding. He is trying really hard to talk with us and ask questions. Plus, I know that he loves me. He tells me that all the time. I am probably too hard on him. People make mistakes, right? I make mistakes all the time. What kind of person am I if I want others to forgive me, but I won't forgive my own father? I just wish I didn't have to carry this around all by myself.

FINE

INTERVIEW WITH FATHER, KEITH WILLIAMS
(VIA TELEPHONE)

Sunday, April 22, 2012, 9:00 p.m.
Transcribed from Digital Recording

JC: Officer John Christiansen

KW: Keith Williams

JC: Interview with Keith Williams via telephone. Begin recording.

KW: Hello?

JC: Mr. Williams, this is Officer Christiansen with the Buena Vida Sherriff's Office. We spoke this morning—

KW: Yes, what is it? Is she back?

JC: Not yet. I'm calling because I have a couple more questions for you.

KW: Alright, shoot.

JC: In one of Anna's diary entries, she talks about you having done something to her. Do you know what she is referring to?

KW: No.

JC: You don't have any idea?

[Pause]

KW: Not really.

JC: She writes about you being drunk and
screwing up, that she's not over what
you did.

KW: I've never hurt Anna.

JC: What about when you were drinking?
Could she be referring to a time when—

KW: Look, I don't know what she is
talking about.

JC: You can't think of any situation,
even something small?

KW: No. Seriously. I haven't a clue.

JC: She said she yelled at you on the
phone about a visit around Christmas.

KW: I remember that.

JC: She describes having an episode right
after that call where she became
dazed and rocked herself back and
forth, then hit her head to the point
of bruising it.

KW: I had no idea.

JC: What happened around Christmas? Your
daughter Katie mentioned that you
had a nice Christmas with the girls,
but only afterwards did Anna become
upset with you.

KW: I don't know. All I know is
everything is fine one day and
then she is raging mad the next—a
lot like her mother. I see her so
infrequently that it's hard to know
what's going on in her head.

JC: Did you talk on the phone about
       something in particular?

KW: Not really. I called to confirm our
       weekend together after she hadn't
       responded to my texts.

JC: Did she bring anything up at that time?

KW: No, she just said she didn't want to
       come. I told her it was our time and
       that mattered more than whatever else
       she wanted to do. She was upset, but
       that's just one of those parenting
       things you have to do. She can't call
       the shots all the time. She's getting
       older and, in a year or so, I won't
       have any time to spend with her. I
       need to protect all the time I do
       have with my girls. So I do.

JC: Your daughter Katie said Anna was
       upset that you spent time alone with
       Katie. Why would Anna be upset by
       that?

KW: I don't know. I'm not a mind reader.

JC: Is there something from the past that
       may be upsetting Anna now?

KW: Officer, I told you I don't know. I
       can't figure it out myself. If I knew
       something, anything at all, I would
       tell you. I want my daughter found. I
       love her.

   [Mr. Williams's voice cracks and trails off]

JC: I understand how hard this must be
       for you, Mr. Williams.

[Lapse of time]

KW: For so long, she was the only bright
light in my life, other than Katie.
She's most of the reason I'm in AA,
trying to work the program. I drank
because I was pretty low, depressed
really. I lost every shred of
confidence and pretty much gave up
on myself. Anna, even though she was
a little girl, was the one who was
there for me. I know I shouldn't have
relied on her so much now, but when
you are drowning, —I guess you just
grab onto anything that keeps you
afloat.

JC: How exactly did you use Anna to keep
you afloat?

KW: Like I said, Anna was my little
sidekick. She would watch a game with
me or fix stuff around the house.
We'd go out on adventures and stuff.
Sometimes if Diane and I were at it,
she would come slip her arms around
me and tell me everything was going
to be okay.

[Sigh]

KW: I hate to think of how I used to be.
I was messed up, I won't lie. I was
drinking to the point of blacking
out. I couldn't always remember most
of what happened. I'm ashamed to admit
it, but that went on for a year at
least. What I do remember isn't pretty.

FINE

JC: What do you—

KW: But I'm straight now. I'm sober and
        I'm going to stay that way.

JC: Did you black out often?

KW: I don't know. It happened often
        enough, I guess.

JC: Is it possible something happened
        during one of those times?

KW: Are you accusing me of something,
        Officer?

JC: I'm asking you why your daughter is—

KW: For Christ's sake! My little girl
        is missing. God knows what kind of
        trouble she's in, and here you are
        throwing outrageous accusations at me.

JC: Is she trying to protect you?

KW: No! She doesn't need to protect me.
        Officer, you're out of line.

JC: That's all I have for now

Stop. Stop right there. No. Uh uh. No way. I am not reading what I think I'm reading.

I always wondered what her problem was with dad. He was always so sweet to her, which made me so jealous. She was his little monkey, his favorite helper. I remember him taking her off to the hardware store, dressed in her pink overalls, while I had to stay behind with mom. Every time, I cried and whined about being left behind. I wanted to go with him. I wanted to be his helper. But he never chose me.

Why? Why did he like Anna so much? Why did he favor her the way he did?

I don't understand what she's saying. She clearly could not have been implying that he... I mean, he would never... There's no way. My dad is a drunk, not a pervert.

Anna was probably just mad about being the grown-up in our house. Anna has always been the responsible adult in the Williams house. She was the one who took care of me when my parents were fighting, and when they weren't. She used to make me macaroni and cheese and then read to me with a flashlight under the covers. If my mom forgot to make lunches, Anna did it. If my dad didn't come to get us for the weekend, Anna would let me make brownies or start a pillow fight. Being a little kid, I never realized how much she did until she wasn't around to do it anymore.

Of course, she was mad! But she kept it all to herself. Sheila was right—she needed to talk to someone. She needed to let all this out. I don't understand how she carried this around with her all the time without losing her mind. I would have let my parents have it. I *have* let my parents have it.

But she's more than mad. She was crying and sobbing after she hung up with my dad. She hit herself in the head repeatedly. I'm not an expert or anything, but people don't normally harm themselves unless they have a reason.

I jump out of my seat, and as I do, the folding chair bangs into the desk loudly. I start pacing, mindlessly snapping the hair tie on my wrist. Three steps to the left. Three steps to the right. Three steps to the left.

I have to call my dad. I have to ask him about all this. I mean, what is Anna talking about? First, she's his little helper who makes him feel better. Then she is angry and hanging up on him. Then she's hitting herself. Why would she be writing all this?

Hold on a minute. I need to calm down. I mean, this must be some kind of misunderstanding. I've clearly seen too many movies. This is real life. These are my people. I am obviously reading way too much into this. This is why my mom didn't want me to read through the file. It's incomplete and confusing and points too many fingers in too many directions.

Still, maybe I should call my dad. I want to know what was going on with Anna. I need to know. My mom is clearly not going to open up anytime soon, but maybe my dad will. Maybe we can put everything out on the table and finally figure out how to have a relationship after all these years.

Probably not. My attempts have always failed in the past. If I bring up anything sensitive, he shuts it down. At first, he will be offended and make me feel like I did something wrong for bringing up a sore subject. He'll say something to put himself down and make me feel sorry for him. I'll eventually give in when he tells me he loves me. We both know that's my Achilles heel. Then he'll change the subject.

Still, I feel like he knows something.

Screw it. I grab my purse and slip out of the office. I offer a nod to the woman at the front desk and walk through the front doors. It's getting late, and the lights in the parking lot are already on. I get in my car and sit in the driver's seat. After a couple of deep breaths, I dial my dad's number. My stomach churns as I wait for him to answer.

"Keith Williams."

"Dad?"

"Katie, is that you?" he asks, surprised.

"Yes," I say, hearing how strained my voice sounds.

"What's the matter?"

"Umm, I need to ask you a few things."

"Whoa, there," my dad skids on the brakes, "what is this about?"

I can't tell if he's been drinking or not. He's pretty good at covering it up. I'm hoping he's slightly buzzed because he won't be able to lie as easily.

"Umm. Well. I've been looking at Anna's police file, and there are all these—"

"You're what?" he demands.

"I've been looking at—"

"I heard you, I heard you," he stammers.

"Oh," I say, confused.

"You shouldn't be doing that, Katie."

"Why not? Don't you miss her?"

My dad breathes heavily into the receiver.

"Of course, I miss her." His voice softens. "Katie, there are some things you can't change, no matter how much you want to."

"Anything in particular you wish you could change?" I ask pointedly.

"What are you talking about?"

I take a deep breath. It's now or never.

"What happened between you and Anna?"

"For Christ's sake, Katie. Are you kidding me right now? You read a few nasty words about me in a police file and you're suddenly ready to accuse me of something?"

"No, no, no. Of course, not. I'm just trying to figure out... you know..."

"I'm not having this conversation with you, Katie. There's no point in it."

"But we've never had this conversation. And there are so many secrets in our family, so many things I didn't know."

"All families are complicated, kiddo. Everyone has secrets."

"Like Mom's affair?"

My words stun him for a moment. I can hear him thinking through his breaths.

"There are reasons we don't talk about certain things. So before you start opening doors that are purposely closed, you might want to think about the consequences of doing so."

"Consequences?"

"People don't need to hurt anymore. We've been through enough. Just move on from all this, Katie. Put your energy into something else, something that isn't a dead end."

"But Dad, I—"

"I mean it, Katie."

I'm fuming, but there's nothing left to say. Well, nothing except this.

"Why don't you love me the way you loved Anna?"

It takes a second for my dad to answer. A very long second.

"I do love you, Katie."

"Yes, but not like her."

I hear him sigh into the phone, heavy and defeated.

"Katie, a lot has happened over the years and it's taken a toll on all of us. I know I haven't been the dad you wanted, but I did the best I could. It wasn't enough—I get it. I screwed up miserably and I'm sorry. But I do love you."

We hang up and I beat myself up for calling him. I'd foolishly hoped that this time he would open up about Anna and everything that happened in the past, but I knew better. I know how this goes.

I stare out into the darkened parking lot, my hands gripped around the steering wheel. I don't know why I thought looking at her file would help. It's just taking me back to a place I would rather forget. It's creating doubts and suspicions that I never had until now. Maybe I don't want to know anymore. I thought I did, but now I'm not so sure I can handle it.

I reach for my keys and start the car. I'm going home.

January 10, 2012

I don't get it. I'm supposed to be having the time of my life right now. I'm supposed to be happy. But I'm not.

Maybe I'm mentally ill. Maybe I have a disorder and that's why I feel so awful. Maybe I'm bipolar or manic-depressive. Maybe I'm schizophrenic—this is the age it would start to come out, right? I could just be sad, but that isn't a big enough word. I'd say melancholy, but it's worse than that. Morose, maybe? That sounds like a word for my English teacher. She'd love it if I slipped that word into one of my English essays.

I hate school. I really do. I hate all the teachers, none of whom even notice I am alive. I hate the constant push to be perfect. No one gets excited when I get an A, but they give me crinkled eyebrows at a B. All I do is study anymore. I work and work, but for what? What's the point of all this?

I hate all the kids, too. I'm not like everyone else, I guess. Everyone seems to fit into these groups of friends, but I don't. I'm not like Maddie, who can just be her weird self even though everyone is whispering behind her back about how strange she is. I love her, but it's hard being talked about all the time. I heard kids talking about her the other day and it was horrible. They were making fun of her hair, her clothes, and pretty much everything that makes Maddie, Maddie.

I wanted to stand up to them and say," Shut up!" I wanted to scream that they have no idea what a great person she is and how talented she is, but I didn't. I said nothing. That's the problem with me. Most of the time, I feel one thing, but I can't let it out. Instead, I just want to disappear. I want to evaporate into particles that float in the air.

But I can't do that either. I have to be happy and positive all the time. What do cheerleaders have to be upset about, right? I mean, we have it all. I'm now popular with most of the kids, I have a built-in network of people to hang out with, and my phone is constantly buzzing with messages, tweets, and Instagram pics. Piper keeps trying to fix me up on a date with some cute guy. What more could I want? I've been so lonely, and now that I have all this, I should be happy.

I was actually happy for a while. I really was. The girls were so welcoming and fun to be around. Everyone said hi to me in the halls and I really thought I mattered. But suddenly I feel like I could send an entirely different girl, dressed up like me, and none of the girls would notice. They would carry on the exact same way.

Sometimes I feel like I might fit in with the smart kids at school, like Jack, but they have their own tight-knit circles that don't feel very inclusive. They're pretty full of themselves, too. They act like they're all going to be working at Google, producing films, or spearheading a non-profit one day. I love that on one hand, but it's annoying. They're so smug. Plus, they stress me out by asking all these questions about college applications and discussing the hierarchy of schools. Each one of them has this innate knowledge, apparently, about how the college you choose will dictate the rest of your life. I don't need that pressure, thank you. And that's all they seem to talk about anymore.

I feel like I fit in with the kids at Sub Station far better. They're a totally different group, way edgier than Maddie could ever be. I like them, though. They say what they think and they're honest, which is nice for a change. Still, I'm not like them either. I'm worried about college, and some of them are worried about how they're going to pay rent or how much they can contribute to their family's income. One of them has a kid. I know they look at me like a rich girl who doesn't really need to work, but I do.

All I know is I should be happy. But I'm not.

<u>FILE CONTROL NO. 23167</u>
<u>MISSING PERSON – ANNA WILLIAMS</u>
Note to File completed by Officer Christiansen on April 23, 2012, 6:45 a.m.

SEARCH RESULTS FOR ELECTRONIC ITEMS

Officers in our department have reviewed the electronic devices recovered from Anna Williams's home. Her cell phone is the only device still not located. Some text messages, emails, and her call history have been obtained from the phone company with proper authorization. Officers are currently reviewing the data for relevant content and, as of this report, have found the following:

<u>Phone Calls:</u>   Calls were made and received from known contacts, all of whom have been identified and questioned. Other calls from four unknown cellular numbers were received in the weeks before her disappearance (including the morning Anna disappeared), but further investigation did not reveal the identity of the caller. They appear to be prepaid phones, otherwise known as burners.

<u>Messages:</u>   Social messages with friends, mother, and sister. Since Anna's phone has not been recovered, we have requested friends, family, etc. to provide any and all text messages sent to or from Anna in the past six months.

Instagram: Various posts and pictures, frequently used.

Facebook: Select, infrequent posts relating to school, cheerleading, and family.

Snapchat: Anna seems to have used this app for most of her private communications. Typical of most teenagers who want to maintain privacy. Relevant content is included in this file.

Email: Emails sent and received for school purposes and occasionally social reasons. Not much of import, except a few exchanges with Jack Nelson.

Relevant electronic media content will be included in this file as necessary.

"Do you always eat like that?" I ask Jack, who is sitting across from me and devouring a burger at my favorite burger joint. It's a shack, barely visible from the street and not much to look at inside. But it has the best burgers and is only a couple blocks from the police station.

"What?" he asks with ketchup on his chin.

"Like you're starving," I say as I pick at my salad.

Jack laughs while rubbing a napkin between his hands. Then he flexes his bicep and says, "How do you think I fuel this machine of mine?"

I'm glad I'm here. After yesterday's deep dive into the past, I wasn't sure I could go back today. I still might not. It's so much nicer being with Jack. His eyes are so warm, and he has these adorable dimples when he smiles. He has always been a sweet guy, but I never realized he was cute. Funny too. I feel like I can be myself around him, and I don't think it's because I've known him forever. I bet he makes everyone feel that way.

"So, how's it going? What did you find out?"

"Not much, really. I've only read through a couple of

her diary entries and some interviews."

"You okay?"

"Yeah, it's just harder than I thought. Reading those transcripts is like getting in a time machine. It's jogging my memory about a lot of stuff, but there are still so many things I forgot. And way more things I never knew." I roll my eyes, trying to dismiss the image of my mom with some nasty guy.

"It was a long time ago, and you were pretty young."

"I guess," I say, sulking. "Did you know she had a tattoo?"

"Yeah," he smiles. "A dragonfly."

"Why would she tell you and not me?" I wonder, reaching for my pendant.

"You know she was always really protective of you."

"Apparently," I pout. "It seems like she protected me from a lot of things."

Jack's eyes widen. "Like what?"

"Nothing." I try to keep my mouth shut, but it's pointless. "Did you know my mom cheated on my dad? And that Anna walked in on her and some guy?"

"Umm."

"Oh my God! You knew that, too?"

"I'm sorry," Jack says kindly. Obviously, he has no idea how to respond.

"Don't be. It's fine."

I'm humiliated. Not only do I have a big mouth, but now the most normal and well-adjusted person I know has a front-row seat to my dysfunctional family.

"Have you talked to your mom about any of this?"

"No. She's not back yet, and I don't want to say anything over the phone. She'll just hang up," I say, my stomach churning at the thought of it. "Anyway, I need to focus
on finding out what happened. All this other stuff is just
a distraction."

"Well, maybe not," Jack offers. "Maybe it's part of the
puzzle you want to solve."

"I guess," I say, agitated that he can disarm me so easily.

"I get it. It's hard going back there."

Jack slides back in his chair and crosses his arms. I
recognize the pain in his face. It flickers across his eyes
for just a moment, but it's unmistakable. It's such an odd
kind of ache that it's impossible to miss in another person
once you've felt it yourself. I feel awful. In all these years,
it never occurred to me that Jack would have suffered
in the same way. To be honest, I never even considered
that someone else could be hurting over Anna. I was too
obsessed with me.

"It's strange. When it first happened, I used to think
about it all the time. I would go over everything—every
conversation we had—and obsess over what I could be
missing. I knew it was bad when my mom had her therapist friend Karen come over for a little chat," Jack says,
winking at me.

"And here I was thinking I was special," I quip.

"You are. You think my mom guilts Karen into offering free therapy to just anyone?"

"Great. I really am a charity case."

"Oh, don't worry," Jack smiles, "she'll charge you the
next time."

I start pushing around the salad on my plate, wondering why I didn't order a burger. I guess I was trying to seem like the kind of girl he would like, one who doesn't eat.

"I just couldn't wrap my head around it."

"You ever come up with any theories?" I ask tentatively, not sure if I want to know.

"Nothing more than the usual talk around town."

I sigh, recalling the endless chatter that circulated among people. We live in the safest town on Earth, not to mention the most uninteresting. Nothing bad happens in Buena Vida, let alone something like this, especially to a cheerleader and a straight-A student. Anna's disappearance was quite the scandal, which delighted the town gossips to no end.

You know what I heard? I heard she had an online relationship with some older man… a real sleaze who came to pick her up after school. Hmm mmm, that's why teaching kids about internet safety is so important.

Gasp! I didn't hear that. I was under the impression this was some kind of suicide pact or something and it didn't go according to plan. Or a Thirteen Reasons Why or something.

Well, kids these days are under a lot of pressure. Parents push their kids too hard, and colleges are getting to be outrageous with their admissions requirements.

Wait. Wasn't she involved with drugs? I heard she was meeting a dealer or something.

No, no. She's just a runaway. Poor thing ran off thinking she could do better and found herself in trouble.

That's ridiculous. You're all wrong. Someone took her. I've heard there's been a lot of suspicious characters lurking around here. We really need to take a harder stance on crime, get more police out there.

I hated hearing people whisper about Anna. At least they mostly did it behind my back, only to zip their lips when I turned around. It became a game to me, glaring at people until their faces turned red with shame as they put together the fact that I was "the girl's sister." Sometimes, I'd interrupt their hushed conversations with an exaggerated rumor about Anna that was even more sensational— that would really shut them up. But only for a second. Then they would start up again, painting a picture of my sister I didn't want to see.

"I don't know why people always assumed she was some kind of mental case. Like she just cracked under the pressure. There was nothing wrong with her. I mean, if Anna was screwed up in the head, then every teenage girl in the world is."

"I guess it's hard to know what's going on in someone else's head," Jack says gingerly.

"She's my sister, Jack. I would have known if she was losing her mind."

Jack avoids my narrowed eyes.

"Oh, I get it. So you think she had a nervous breakdown and ran off? You think she would have—"

"I didn't say that."

"You didn't have to," I sputter, glaring at him. How could he possibly side with those gossiping jerks, thinking that my sister had anything to do with her disappearance? I thought he was on my side.

"Why does that make you so mad?" he asks.

"Because she wouldn't have left me on purpose!" I blurt out angrily.

Jack shifts in his seat. I suppose I look as uncomfortable as I feel. Maybe I shouldn't have opened this can of worms in the first place.

"Well," Jack reconsiders. "I always thought it was odd that her car was still in the parking lot. I don't see why she would have left it if she was planning to run away."

I breathe a sigh of relief.

"Exactly. I'm sure there must be something in the file about what happened when school got out. Security footage or something. Speaking of which, I should probably head over there now. I was hoping to get through it all before my mom gets back Friday."

"Do you want me to come with you?" Jack asks. "I can read some of it, take some notes, or whatever."

"Thanks, Jack." I want to take him up on his offer, but I can't. "I think I have to do this alone."

"Okay."

I sip my Diet Coke slowly, hoping I can drag out my time with Jack a bit longer. I don't know what it is about him. Maybe it's because we shared our childhood or because he knew Anna. Whatever it is, I feel like I want to orbit around him.

Before long, I'm back in the boring office annex. This time around, I notice the cracked ceiling tiles above me. I think I can picture a handful of old police movies that were probably filmed in this very room. This whole place feels old and forsaken, much like the files it houses. It sure doesn't feel like happy endings are found here.

I immediately miss Jack and wish I was with him instead. Maybe I should have let him come with me. It would be helpful to have someone else go through this with me. Even if he just sat here, it would be nice to have some company.

No, I tell myself, I need to do this alone.

INTERVIEW WITH MACKLEMORE HIGH
PRINCIPAL COURTNEY EGGERS

Monday, April 23, 2012, 7:30 a.m.
Transcribed from Digital Recording

JC: Officer John Christiansen

CE: Courtney Eggers

JC: Begin Recording. Thank you for taking the time to meet this morning, Principal Eggers.

CE: Yes, of course.

JC: Let's get started.

CE: I understand you are here to investigate Anna Williams's disappearance, and I want you to know that we are ready and willing to help you in any way we can.

JC: Thank you.

CE: Do the officers searching the school need anything else? Our custodians are prepared to show them around and give them access to any area they need to see.

JC: Thank you. I appreciate your cooperation. These cases are very time-sensitive, and I need to cover as much ground as possible today.

CE: Yes, of course.

JC: Now, I would like to ask just a few
        questions of you and then interview
        some members of your staff and some
        of the students.

CE: I'll make sure they are available for
        you.

JC: That would be very much appreciated.

CE: Do you have a list of people you are
        planning to interview, or do you want
        some help in identifying teachers or
        students that know Anna?

JC: Actually, I have a few people already
        identified. Here is the list of names.
        If there are others you think would
        have relevant information, I'll need
        to speak with them as well.

CE: I'll get this list to our Vice
        Principal, Fiona, and have her
        prepare them to meet with you after
        we are finished. Excuse me for one
        minute.

[Shuffling sounds, hushed whispers in the
background]

CE: Thanks for waiting. Let's begin,
        shall we?

JC: Great. Can you share with me any and
        all information you have about Anna
        Williams?

CE: I reviewed her file this morning.
        She is a top-notch student with
        mostly honors classes. In fact,
        she's on target for being in the top

twenty, maybe even fifteen, of her
graduating class. So her academics
are fantastic. She has no record of
any disciplinary actions, not even a
detention. I've never seen her in my
office, other than to discuss student
council matters.

JC: How did she seem during those
        encounters?

CE: Fine. She was friendly and polite,
        which was how she always seemed.
        She seemed excited about prom and
        did a lot of the planning for it.
        However, she didn't take the lead
        in discussing it. Shy, maybe. Piper
        Abbot, president of the student
        council, did most of the talking, but
        Anna was right there in the mix and
        seemingly in good spirits.

JC: Have you had any feedback from
        teachers regarding Anna?

CE: Well, our education system is run
        on a tight schedule. We expect a
        lot of our teachers and students.
        The teachers need to produce
        students that are capable of going
        onto the next chapter of their
        academic careers. They are charged
        with instilling knowledge in their
        students so that they are prepared
        for their futures. Our teachers have
        large classes, which is not within
        our ability to change at this time.

As a result, they are responsible for doing a great deal. The students, therefore, must learn responsibility and take action on their own.

JC: I get it, but—

CE: This is a critical skill, especially now that kids are growing up with an overabundance of parental involvement, and we want them to be able to succeed on their own in college or in whatever vocation they pursue. All that being said, you can see how teachers are not capable of being completely tuned in to one particular student at a given time.

JC: I understand your point, but what I'm—

CE: That isn't to say that the students aren't given adequate instruction, but it does mean that teachers are not able to connect with every student as much or as often as they may like.

JC: I get it. My question is, have any teachers offered specific feedback about Anna?

[Pause]

CE: No, not really. I called an emergency faculty meeting this morning and spoke with them about Anna. We take this very seriously, especially since she was last seen here at school.

We pride ourselves in maintaining a safe campus, so the idea that someone could have potentially kidnapped one of our students while they were on school grounds is a very big problem.

JC: We do not know what the reason is for her disappearance yet.

CE: I realize that, Officer Christiansen, but you can understand that even the prospect of that kind of criminal activity occurring at our school is just not acceptable. The negative press has not gone unnoticed by the school board and the community at large.

[Phone ringing in the background, brief tapping sounds]

CE: Sorry about that. Where were we?

JC: I was asking what you knew about Anna Williams.

CE: Yes, that's right. I did speak with some of her teachers. They did not notice any change in her behavior. Her grades have remained stable for the most part, with some low marks on her physics exams. Her English teacher noted that she received a C for a term paper, which was lower than her normal marks and caused Anna to have a discussion with her after class. Other than that, she hasn't fallen below a 4.0 GPA. If there is anything more specific the

teachers can add, I am sure they will
be willing to discuss it with you
today.

[Knock on the door]

CE: Excuse me, Principal Eggers. I just
wanted to ask if Officer Christiansen
would like to meet with students in
the teacher's lounge.

CE: Officer?

JC: That will be fine. Thank you.

CE: Thank you, Fiona. I'll make sure
Officer Christiansen finds his way to
the lounge.

CE: Alright. Sorry for the interruption.

[Sound of door clicking shut]

CE: I can have the teachers meet with you
in their rooms afterwards, unless you
would rather meet with them first.

JC: No, that's fine. Thank you.

CE: You are welcome.

JC: It seems that Anna may be under a lot
of stress at school—

CE: Well, there is always a bit of stress
involved. The last two years of
high school are pivotal for many
students. These young people must
start preparing for the adjustment
into adulthood, and we do them no
favors by holding their hands too
much. Stress is a logical result
of this kind of change. I think

most students are able to handle
the challenges without any undue
hardship. However, there are always
those who have a more difficult time.
That is why we have our guidance
counselor here to help them navigate
these ever-changing waters.

JC: Do students take advantage of
talking to the guidance counselor?

CE: I believe they do. We make it a
point to remind them periodically of
Ms. Burgess's office hours, as well
as having her update them with all
kinds of news through flyers and on
our website. She has her own column,
where she discusses pertinent issues
facing teens. Her articles contain
a lot of critical information about
things like application deadlines,
managing stress, and living a
balanced and healthy lifestyle.

JC: I definitely need to speak with Ms.
Burgess today, if possible.

CE: Of course. I'll take you to her office
when we are finished—before you begin
student interviews.

JC: That will work. Now, can you tell me
if there are security cameras in the
student parking lot?

CE: No, there are none at this time—
although that is clearly going to
change. There is one camera by the
last row of classrooms that does

capture the walkway from the lot onto
campus. I have arranged to have that
footage handed over to your team.

JC: Thank you. Is the parking lot secured
        by a fence or a lock?

CE: The lot is not accessible by car from
        the street except through the main
        gate. That gate is unlocked at 5:45
        a.m. and locked at 5:00 p.m. unless
        there is an event going on.

JC: Was there an event on Friday?

CE: No.

JC: So cars had access to the lot from
        5:45 a.m. to 5:00 p.m. on Friday.

CE: Yes, but they have to have a student
        pass to park there. Our security
        guard monitors the lot regularly.

JC: Did he monitor the lot on Friday
        afternoon? Can I speak to him?

CE: Our security guard is a woman.

JC: Oh, my mistake.

CE: She does not monitor the lot during
        dismissal because she is needed at
        the front of the school. At that
        time, there is a lot of activity in
        front due to the buses, cars picking
        up students, and the walkers. The
        back lot is generally very quiet.
        Also, if there were any parking
        violations, I would have been
        alerted already.

JC: Can pedestrians walk into the student
        parking lot?

CE: They would have to climb over the
        fence, but it has been done before.

JC: Okay. Is there anything else you
        would like to share that might help
        us in our investigation?

CE: Unfortunately, no.

        [Heavy sigh from Principal Eggers]

CE: I wish I knew how something like
        this could have happened. You hear
        about school shootings and parental
        abductions often enough, but it's a
        whole different matter when a student
        just disappears into thin air. It
        creates a degree of uncertainty and
        fear that's hard to manage as an
        administration. I have had so many
        phone calls from parents asking about
        our security measures, questioning
        whether a stranger could gain access
        to students in the parking lot,
        and so on. I can understand their
        concern and, frankly, I don't know
        how to answer them. We do everything
        we can to maintain a safe learning
        environment, but when things like
        this happen... It's just tragic.

JC: We don't yet know—

CE: Honestly, I couldn't sleep last
        night. I have a ten-year-old
        daughter, and I can't imagine how I

would feel as a parent if this were
happening to my child. To be a school
administrator, charged with—among
other things—ensuring student safety,
I cannot help but feel that I failed
somehow.

JC: Principal Eggers, we do not know
whether or not Anna was abducted
at all, let alone whether she was
abducted from the school parking lot.

CE: With all due respect, Officer
Christiansen, Anna was last seen
here. She never made it home after
school and her car is still here.
I may not be a detective, but it
sure seems like a lot of signs are
pointing in the same direction.
After all, she's a good student with
a bright future ahead of her. She's
a cheerleader and vice president
of the student body. Kids like that
don't just run away. There must be
something we could have done to have
prevented this.

JC: Safety can always be improved upon,
I suppose. Can you tell me who is
the last teacher Anna would have
seen on Friday?

CE: Let me see.

    [Shuffling sounds]

CE: She had history with Herbert Jones.

JC: I may need to speak with him.

CE: I'll have it arranged.

JC: Principal Eggers, is there anything
        else you want to say with regard to
        Anna?

CE: No, not at this time.

JC: Well, if you think of anything,
        please don't hesitate to call me.

CE: Of, course.

JC: Thank you for your cooperation.

Man, Christiansen. I could have told you she wouldn't be helpful. I mean, she's a principal. She's trained to say only what she wants you to hear.

My phone lights up and I look down at the caller ID. Oh, great. Speaking of unhelpful women.

"Hey, Mom."

"When were you going to get around to telling me about your accident?" she demands.

"How did you find out?"

"That's not the point, Katie," my mom says incredulously. "You could have killed Jack Nelson. You're lucky you two walked away with nothing but scratches."

"I know, Mom. I'm really sorry."

"Oh, you will be. You know my insurance rates are going to skyrocket because of this. And if you think I'm paying for..."

"I said I'm sorry. What else do you want me to say?"

My mom fumes quietly on the other end of the phone.

"Well, I'm glad you're okay."

We are both quiet for a moment. I know it's my turn to

ask her about Hawaii and Kyle. I'm sure she's dying to tell me about the beautiful view they have from their bungalow, or maybe she's about to tell me he popped the question at the top of a volcano or something. But I should probably tell her about the file.

"Mom?"

Just say it, Katie. Tell her you are looking through the file. Tell her what you read about Anna walking in on her.

"What?"

I can't do it. I just can't. At least not over the phone.

"Are you and Kyle having a good time?"

My mom's relief rushes over me. We both relax into a conversation about her tropical adventures. The sound of her voice is comforting, but her words are wholly insufficient. I suddenly start wondering if this is the best she can do. Maybe this is all she has ever been capable of. What a depressing thought…

"All right, then. Kyle is waiting for me, so I'm going to have to let you go. We can catch up more when I get home. In the meantime, please keep up around the house, and I'll see you in a couple of days."

I want her to stay on the phone with me. I want her to fill in these pages with colorful details that help paint a picture I can finally understand. But I know it will only make her angry, like I am going over her head somehow. She's told me everything I need to know—at least everything she thinks I need to know.

"See you soon," I say, holding myself back from telling her to have a great time.

"Love you," she says.

"Love you, too."

I feel like Anna's loneliness has seeped out from the pages and grabbed hold of me, dragging me into the hopelessness of it all. My mom has a knack for bringing that emotion out of her daughters, I guess. I glance up at the clock right as it turns four o'clock. I flip through the file and realize I have a long way to go. I better pack up and leave it for tomorrow. I've got a lot to do around the apartment before my mom gets back.

January 14, 2011

Today sucked. No reason, really. It just
sucked. I'm glad I'm home and no one else is
here. I'm not up to being the good daughter or
the responsible sister. I just want to sleep. And
sleep. And sleep. Maybe forever.

That sounds suicidal, but I'm not. I mean,
not really. Well, the thing is I think about it
from time to time. I think about driving my car
straight into a median on the highway. I'm a
teenager, so I'm sure people would assume I was
texting while driving. Maybe they would blame
my inexperience in driving. They would find
some way to believe it was an accident because,
surely, I would have no reason to end my life
on purpose. I don't have any red flags flying
about me—no rehab stints or trouble with the
law. I don't even have a diagnosis, unless "drama
queen" counts.

I bet no one would miss me anyway. They
would probably act like it for the first few weeks
to get sympathy and attention, but they really
wouldn't miss me after a month or two. "Anna who?
Oh, that girl who drove her car into the tree?
Such a shame... anyway, how are things?"

I think I would rather go quietly, anyway. If I could will myself to die in my sleep, I would. That would be the most peaceful way, but I can't bear the thought of Katie finding me. She would be the one to discover my cold, stiff body beneath the covers. I wouldn't do that to her. I would rather slip off somewhere far away where no one would find me. I would take a few too many pills or jump into a river someplace where no one would think to look. People disappear all the time. I would just disappear forever and fly away with the angels.

I wonder what the angels would do. Would they come down from Heaven and intervene? Would they save me or let me die? Is it their job or mine to keep me alive? When we were little, we went to church, but it didn't stick. It did teach me a few prayers and introduced me to the Holy Spirit and Saints, which I talk to from time to time. They don't really answer, of course, so I don't quite see the point in that. Still, it helps to know a few names just in case. I'm not a huge fan of church anyway. Church didn't stop my dad from drinking and it didn't save my parents' marriage. It didn't make us a happy family. Maybe we were too far gone for church, or maybe church was also too concerned with how things look to notice that things in the Williams house were not as they should have been.

I shake my head and brush away the tears that are about to run down my face. It's too early in the morning to start crying. I peer out the crack in the door to see if anyone is in the hallway. I really hope Christiansen doesn't decide to pop in with a cup of bad coffee right now. I don't want anyone, especially him, seeing me like this.

What in the hell made Anna write all those things in her diary? She's fantasizing about overdosing or drowning or whatever. I can't even believe what I'm reading. That is not the Anna I knew.

The Anna I knew was always making me smile. If I had a bad day, she would barge into my room and sing her own crazy rendition of "Don't Worry Be Happy" until I cracked a smile. If that didn't work, she'd clobber me with a pillow until I got mad enough to fight back. Then she would run down the stairs, weaving in and out of the kitchen and living room, with me chasing behind with a pillow raised over my head. If all that failed, she would pull out a box of brownie mix, and we'd bake.

I remember lying in her bed one night, well after my

mom thought we were asleep, talking. I was upset because I didn't get the memo about how you can't play with dolls once you turn a certain age or else everyone will make fun of you. Earlier that day, my friend had come over for a playdate, and I'd suggested we play with Barbies. Big mistake.

"Ella says playing with dolls is babyish."

"Well. Ella's stupid."

I laughed, then she laughed. That was all it took to feel better.

I knew Anna was sad sometimes, especially in the months before she went missing, but it never seemed as bad as what she wrote in her diary. I just don't understand. How could she have kept this much hidden from me? We talked for hours about song lyrics or the benefits (and misery) of cutting sugar from our diets entirely. We talked about plastic surgery, celebrities, and which one of our friends was likely to get married first. We talked about all kinds of stuff, but not once did Anna even hint about being so miserable. I'm starting to feel like I didn't know my sister at all.

INTERVIEW WITH MACKLEMORE HIGH GUIDANCE COUNSELOR GINA BURGESS

Monday, April 22, 2012, 7:52 a.m.
Transcribed from Digital Recording

JC: Officer John Christiansen

GB: Gina Burgess

JC: Begin recording. Thank you for meeting with me, Ms. Burgess.

GB: Sure thing. Anything I can do to help.

JC: I understand that Anna was in your office just a month ago. Can you tell me what you both discussed?

GB: Anna had made an appointment to talk over college applications and plans. We encourage all the students to come in for an appointment this time of year, given the mounting pressure of college applications and SATs. It can be very overwhelming.

JC: I can imagine.

GB: These days, the financial aid issue is always a hot topic, as well as the pros and cons of junior college. Then there are the kids who have no interest in college at all, and the kids who are barely going to

graduate. So this time of year, we
want to check in with all of them. As
it turns out, maybe twenty to thirty
percent of the kids make their way
into my office. Anna was one of them.

[Sudden blast of muffled music playing]

JC: I see. What did Anna talk to you
        about?

GB: Let me check my notes. Hmmm. Oh,
        yeah. That's right. She was asking
        all the normal questions about
        deadlines and scholarships.

JC: Did she say anything specific about
        colleges she was considering?

GB: We talked about Stanford, UCLA,
        USC, Loyola Marymount—all four-year
        colleges with quite a price tag—as
        well as a handful of solid junior
        colleges that had high rates of
        transfers to four-year universities.
        I asked her about possible choices,
        but she shrugged it off. She said she
        didn't know just yet and wanted to
        keep her options open.

JC: Did she bring up the option of not
        attending a university right away?

GB: No. Honestly, those who aren't going
        to college at all are often already
        considering specific occupations—
        hair stylists, firefighters, plumbers,
        electricians, etc. I make sure that
        all students who come in here not

knowing what trade to pursue are given several questionnaires and surveys to determine their strengths and abilities, which usually helps them start figuring out what steps are next for them. It is important to direct these students early, because usually they need to pursue training of some sort, even if it isn't at a university.

JC: Yes, but did Anna—

GB: Anna is highly intelligent and at the top of her class. She is definitely on track to be accepted at many universities, all of which will help her start whatever career she determines is best for her. She has a good head on her shoulders and knows that not attending college would be a waste.

JC: So Anna is planning to apply to a four-year university?

GB: I'm sure she is.

JC: But she didn't say which one. Is it possible she may be thinking about junior college?

GB: It's possible, but not likely. Some students may be more inclined to attend community college, but they often languish there if they aren't self-motivated. Plus, many kids are just there to buy a few extra years before deciding where to go next.

Anna could decide on community college for financial and geographic reasons, but she will not be there long. She's a university kid.

JC: Is it possible she's considering taking a year off before going to college? Maybe traveling?

GB: It's possible, but I seriously doubt it.

JC: Why? Did she say something to make you think that?

GB: Well, not exactly. She was pretty quiet that day, but just look through her file. She's the kind of kid who goes to college right away. If she wasn't, she wouldn't be taking extra classes over the summer or focusing so hard. Her record speaks for itself.

JC: She was quiet, you said?

GB: Yes.

JC: Was that normal for her?

GB: I guess. I don't really know.

JC: Do you think she was struggling with college decisions?

GB: No. Anna is very bright, her grades are good, and her extracurricular activities are diverse enough to satisfy most college admissions officers. She really has a lot of wonderful opportunities. It's nice to have kids like Anna who have their heads on straight and are putting in the legwork. It's even better when the parents are supportive, but not overbearing, like Anna's mom.

JC: Do you remember if she brought up anything else?

GB: Well, as I said, I think she expressed interest in the financial aspect of things. She said that her mom was a single mom and that she needed to find a way to reduce the cost of college.

JC: So she was worried about affording college?

GB: Yes. I gave her all kinds of information on scholarships, grants, and loans. I told her, depending upon her interests, there are lots of scholarships out there.

JC: Did she mention her father?

GB: No, I don't think he's around. If he is, he definitely isn't in a position to pay for Anna's college. At least that's what I understood.

JC: Did she ask any other questions?

GB: Not really.

[Muffled sound of music continues, but louder]

GB: Do you hear that? I swear I hear my phone ringing... Anyway.

JC: Did you ask her any questions

regarding why she was quiet?
Maybe about whether something was
bothering her?

GB: I didn't think much of it. If kids
are quiet, it's probably because
thinking about the future is
overwhelming. I still don't know what
I want to be when I grow up! Yet, I'm
here being paid to tell these kids
how to proceed with their lives. The
irony that I am only six years ahead
of them doesn't escape me, by the
way. But that is not the point.

JC: Did she bring up anything else,
perhaps a boyfriend or friend...
something unrelated to college
applications?

GB: Not that I can remember.

JC: So you weren't worried that she was
acting out of character?

GB: No, not really. Anna isn't the kind
of kid I worry about. It's the kids
who don't have good families and need
more support that I have to really
focus on reaching, although they
are usually on a mission to self-
destruct.

JC: You don't think Anna's one of those?

GB: No.

[Shuffling sounds, banging sounds, papers
crinkling]

GB: Sorry, I'm just looking for my phone.

I swear I heard it ringing.

JC: That's fine, I guess. Do you want me to wait?

GB: No, no, no. I'm sorry, Officer. Please go ahead.

JC: Okay. So, to be clear, you didn't talk to her about anything personal?

GB: No. That wasn't the purpose of our meeting. She'd signed up for one of the slots dedicated to preparing for after graduation.

[More shuffling sounds, sigh from Officer Christiansen]

GB: Aha! It was my phone. I knew I heard it ringing... sorry, I'll silence it. Please continue.

JC: So are you saying that you didn't ask Anna anything about her personal life because she didn't sign up for that kind of meeting?

GB: Well, that's not exactly—

JC: But you didn't inquire about anything other than her college plans? And she didn't mention boyfriends, bullying, stress—

GB: We didn't have time. As a guidance counselor, I am here for kids in all capacities. They can come to me with any problem they're having, and I'll be there for them. I can address any issue, ranging from drugs and

alcohol to sex and self-esteem. I
attend continuing education classes
to stay current on what kids are
facing. I mean, I was there myself
not too long ago. I'm up on bullying,
social media problems, eating
disorders, gender identity issues,
and everything that has ever been
highlighted on the evening news.

JC: That's great, but I—

GB: The real problem, however, is that no
one comes through the door to seek
my advice. They're all too cool to do
that. When they do manage to cross
the threshold, I try my best and
hope that I've offered them enough
optimism and resources that they
feel better when they leave my office.
The reality is I focus on future
planning and college applications
more than anything else. That and
problem behavior. So, no. We didn't
get into anything other than college.
She knows we could have made an
appointment to address a particular
issue—if she wanted.

JC: Did she make any of those
appointments with you?

GB: Not that I know of.

[Lapse in time]

JC: Did she talk about how she was
handling the pressure?

GB: No. I asked how she was doing and she
       said she was fine.

JC: Did she look okay to you?

GB: Sure. She's thin, but then again, all
       the girls seem to be thin these days.
       I guess it is just the pressure of
       society to be thin and perfect all
       the time. Such a shame to put so
       much pressure on the way girls look.
       Anyway, she's a cheerleader, too, and
       that tends to have a thinning effect.

JC: Did she appear to be on drugs or
       otherwise altered?

GB: Not really.

JC: Did she seem well-rested?

GB: Sure. She seemed just fine.

JC: Alright. Is there anything else you
       want to add that may help us find
       Anna?

GB: I wish I had something else to say.
       I do. I wish she would have opened
       up to me about whatever was going on
       with her. I could have helped her.
       I can't bear the thought of her not
       being found, let alone the why and
       how of it all. She's only seventeen.
       How bad can any seventeen-year-old's
       life be?

JC: You were seventeen not too long ago.

GB: Well, it couldn't have been that
       bad. After high school, the

responsibilities of life only
increase. Soon they'll have career
pressure, job insecurity, rent, and
all sorts of demands on them. Trust
me, I know. That's if they aren't
already married with kids and a
house. This is the easy time.

JC: Maybe it isn't the easy time for
everyone.

GB: Well, no. That's not what I mean.
I just mean that her problems are
small now, and we can help her solve
whatever is bothering her. She's only
seventeen. She doesn't have adult
problems. It only gets messier and
more complicated as you get older.
That's all I mean.

JC: With all due respect, Ms. Burgess,
problems are problems. If she's
struggling with something, it might
not be as benign as you think.

GB: But she's so young. How bad can it
be? I just can't imagine what would
make someone give up on life when
they have so many more years ahead of
them to make it better.

JC: We don't know whether—

GB: I know. I'm fixating on that specific
outcome. Maybe she didn't take her
own life. Maybe some psycho took her.
All kinds of other tragedies are
just as likely, but this one really
strikes a chord in me.

[Chair squeaks, slight pause]

GB: So many teenagers end up taking their
     own lives, and it's just terrible.
     Just last month, a boy in my mother's
     town filled his backpack with bricks
     and walked straight into the ocean.
     No one knew why. They still don't.
     They have so many years ahead of
     them to make the life they want to
     live. They don't have the ability to
     see how impermanent life is at this
     point. Things change so fast, and
     often they can change for the better.
     If she was suffering, I wish I could
     have helped her. That's all.

JC: I understand completely, Ms. Burgess.

GB: I do hope you find her. I hope
     that whatever happened to her, she
     survives it and comes home.

JC: So do I.

FINE

I never liked Burgess. She's such a fake. She never cared about my sister or me. Maybe if she had, neither of us would have ended up the way we did. I know she isn't responsible or anything, but she clearly didn't help—even though that is pretty much her entire job description. Isn't she there to help kids? Guide them? I suppose it was hard to focus on kids when she was too busy strutting around school in her stupid stilettos and fuchsia lipstick. And those lashes.

I remember having to go see her during school. She thought it would be good to "check in" with me from time to time. It would have been a nice gesture, I guess, if she'd bothered to ask me about the reason I needed to be checked in on in the first place. Each month, I sat through an awkward exchange of niceties followed by a bunch of useless questions about my classes, my friends, and my non-existent future goals. I grunted a few times, which apparently appeased her. She never once mentioned Anna, even though that was the whole reason I was there.

No one expected anything of me in school. If they so much as hinted at me improving my grades, one simple reminder of what I'd been through would stop them in their tracks. It was pretty powerful stuff, being the sister of "that girl." Teachers would let me get away with anything. And I did. I never did my homework, and I skipped first period on a regular basis. I cheated off the smart kids for most math tests and didn't even try to hide it. They let me, of course. They didn't tell the teacher or rat me out to the principal. They were passing me no matter what, probably just to make sure they didn't have to see my face any longer than necessary.

I even got away with getting high at school. The first time, I was a freshman, and two older girls offered me a joint in the girl's bathroom. I was high for the rest of the day, but only my chemistry teacher noticed. He made me stay after class and tried intimidating me. I remember him threatening me with detention and calling my mom, but once I mentioned my sister—he retracted it all. "Just be careful," he said. So I was. I made sure I only smoked behind the bleachers during study hall.

What's funny is I used to get pretty good grades in middle school. The school would send home those letters about being on the honor roll, along with a gift certificate for a free burrito at Chuy's. It felt pretty good to hear my mom get all excited about it and compare me to Anna. Sometimes she would even take us out for dinner, and the three of us would eat our weight in chips and salsa. After Anna disappeared, I didn't really feel like being smart anymore. What was the point, anyway? Anna was smart and it didn't make a difference. Anyway, it was hard to keep my focus on the French Revolution or algebraic equations. My mind was constantly on Anna, and when it wasn't, I was fixated on the next fun thing to distract me from thinking about her.

Unlike Anna, I didn't worry about what bad grades would mean for me down the road or what kind of extracurriculars colleges would like to see on my application. I wasn't concerned about the impact of drugs on my body. I didn't care, and no one else seemed to care either.

Ms. Burgess clearly didn't. She didn't take an interest in my future, if I was even going to have one of those. She knew I didn't apply to colleges and that I had no identified trade in mind. She didn't ask what I was planning to do after graduation, if I graduated. She just ran through a bunch of standard questions and told me she had some resources if I needed them. Resources for what, exactly? She was a mouthpiece rattling off a script handed down from some other mouthpiece, none of whom knew anything about real teenagers. I was a box she had to check off her to-do list. She knew it, and I knew it.

Apparently, Anna knew it too.

Text Exchange Between Anna Williams and Piper Abbot, January 24, 2012

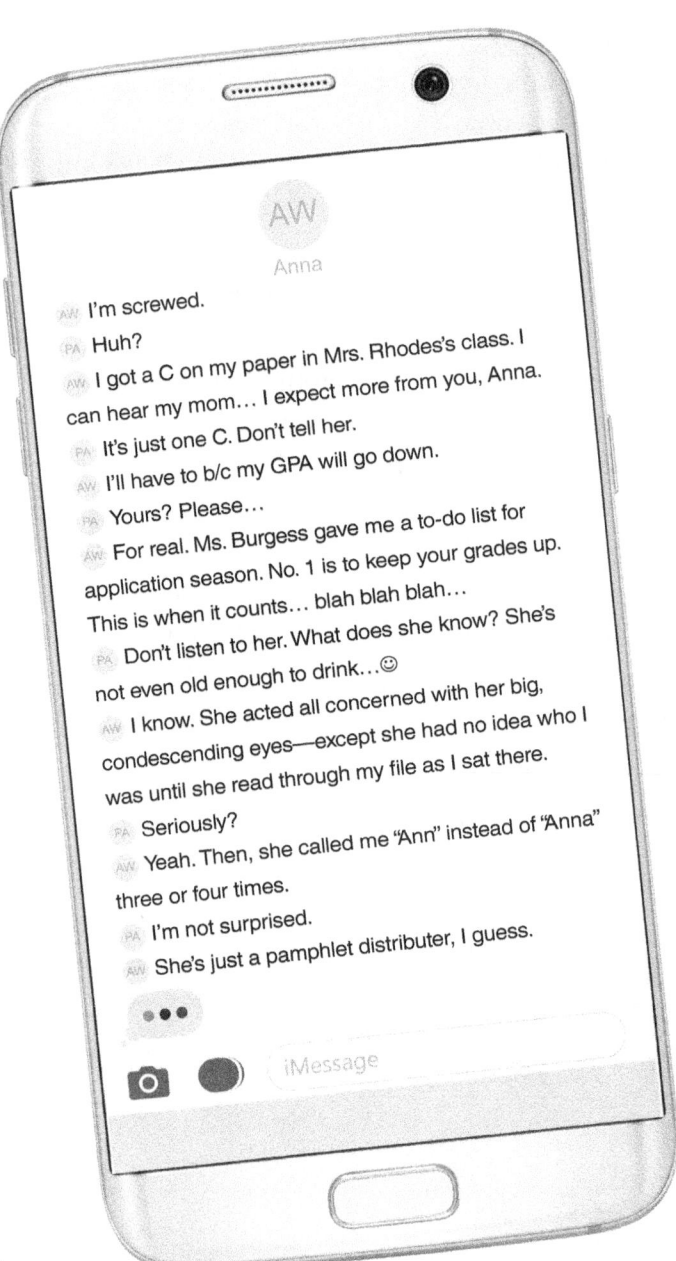

AW Anna

AW I'm screwed.

PA Huh?

AW I got a C on my paper in Mrs. Rhodes's class. I can hear my mom... I expect more from you, Anna.

PA It's just one C. Don't tell her.

AW I'll have to b/c my GPA will go down.

PA Yours? Please...

AW For real. Ms. Burgess gave me a to-do list for application season. No. 1 is to keep your grades up. This is when it counts... blah blah blah...

PA Don't listen to her. What does she know? She's not even old enough to drink...☺

AW I know. She acted all concerned with her big, condescending eyes—except she had no idea who I was until she read through my file as I sat there.

PA Seriously?

AW Yeah. Then, she called me "Ann" instead of "Anna" three or four times.

PA I'm not surprised.

AW She's just a pamphlet distributer, I guess.

● ● ●

iMessage

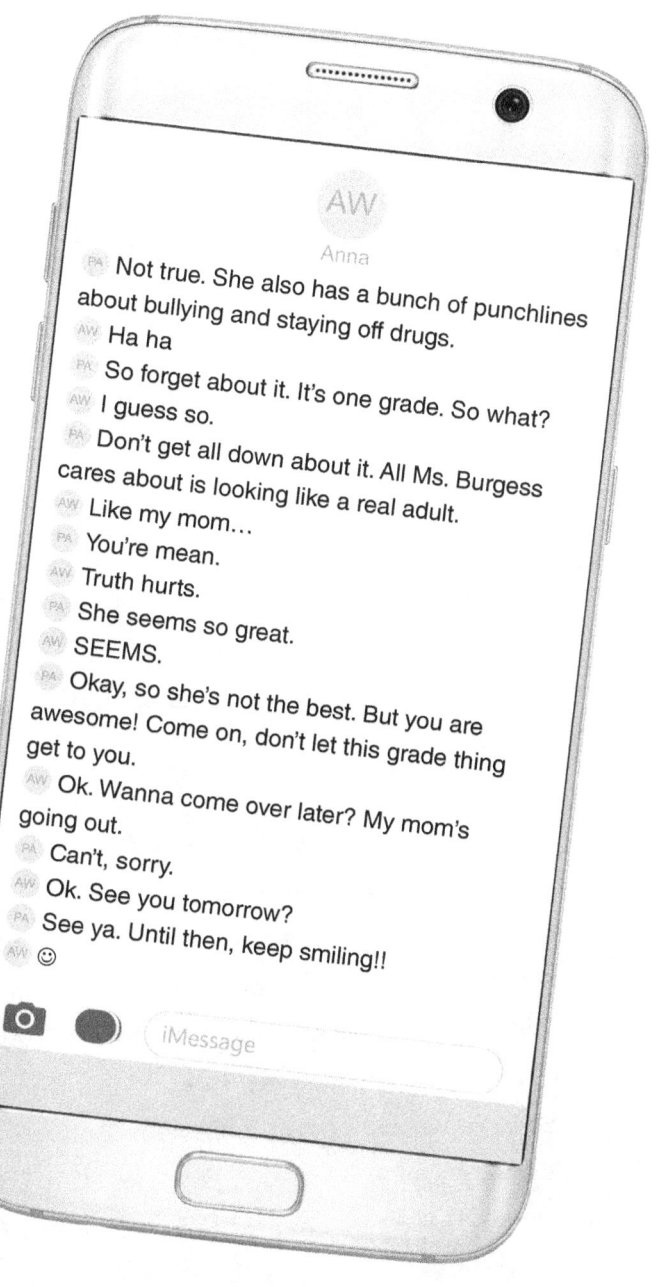

Anna

PA Not true. She also has a bunch of punchlines about bullying and staying off drugs.

AW Ha ha

PA So forget about it. It's one grade. So what?

AW I guess so.

PA Don't get all down about it. All Ms. Burgess cares about is looking like a real adult.

AW Like my mom…

PA You're mean.

AW Truth hurts.

PA She seems so great.

AW SEEMS.

PA Okay, so she's not the best. But you are awesome! Come on, don't let this grade thing get to you.

AW Ok. Wanna come over later? My mom's going out.

PA Can't, sorry.

AW Ok. See you tomorrow?

PA See ya. Until then, keep smiling!!

AW ☺

iMessage

January 20, 2012

I AM SO F-in MAD.

Maddie—my so-called "best friend"—went behind my back and posted stuff online about me. Like really private stuff. No one can take their eyes off their phones for even a minute, so everyone saw it within about sixty seconds. I'm completely mortified.

I called her up and got mad about it, and she said I was overreacting. Just get over it, Anna. It's no big deal, Anna. Let it go already. Let it go? Already? It just happened. She totally stabbed me in the back and acted like it was no big deal.

It's like elementary school all over again. We were playing jump rope, and we got in a big fight over her cheating—because she cheated. She got mad, said all kinds of mean things, and then walked away, leaving me crying in the driveway. Two days went by and we didn't speak. Then we went back to playing jump rope.

So here we are again, only we're in high school. Same rules apply. Girls can say and do all sorts of nasty things to each other, but we're all expected to get over it. Smile, die a little inside, and move on to the next moment—if you want to have friends. Make the mistake of demanding a friend to acknowledge that they hurt you and watch how fast your friendship disappears. It's like the code of girls is to never own up to anything. Ever. !⚡!!

Maddie posted these embarrassing videos of me. Now everyone has seen me goofing around in my bra and panties, acting like I was a model with some terrible British accent. Kids at school keep coming up to me and saying stuff. Austin and his friends had a field day during chemistry, pointing and snickering. Sophia and Nada announced to everyone that modeling was clearly not in my future—for, like, so many reasons. Then Juan and probably thirty more people kept saying, "'Ello, gov'nor?" I think it was better when I was invisible.

I can't believe she would post those things online. That was totally private stuff, the kind of nonsense you share with friends—not the world. She knows that, but she put it out there anyway to humiliate me. Then I heard from Piper that Maddie has been saying stuff behind my back. She called me a poser and loser, and even shared a bunch of stuff I told her in private with Kayla. She denied it, but I know she did it because NO ONE else would know the things she said.

Then, to top it all off, she just sent me a text

asking, "How are you?" She's acting like it's not a big deal, like she didn't just stab me in the back. I don't get it. Maddie was my best friend for so long. How could she do this to me? I know she hated me doing cheer, but what's the big deal? I just wanted to try something new. She said she understood to my face, but apparently, she didn't really understand.

I'm so pissed off and I don't know what to do. I can't confront her again because she'll just get defensive and say that I'm the one who hasn't been there for her. What did I expect her to do? She was just saying the truth, right? She was just posting stuff that we did together—you know, fun nostalgia. Yeah right. Even the truth is supposed to be private sometimes. Just goes to show I can't trust anyone. Not even my supposed best friend, who is no longer even my friend.

INTERVIEW WITH MACKLEMORE
HIGH STUDENT MADDIE LE

Monday, April 23, 2012, 8:15 a.m.
Transcribed from Digital Recording

JC: Officer John Christiansen

ML: Maddie Le

US: Unknown Speaker

JC: Begin recording. Thank you for
        meeting with me, Maddie. I am here to
        talk with you about your friend Anna.

ML: I know.

JC: Okay, so I'm sure you've heard that
        she didn't come home from school on
        Friday.

ML: Yes, everyone knows that by now. We
        all know why you're here.

JC: Right. Well, then you know I need to
        ask you some questions. Answer as
        honestly as you can.

ML: Okay.

JC: Good. How about you start by telling
        me how you and Anna know one another.

ML: We've been friends since elementary
        school. One day we just started
        having lunch together and walking
        the track at recess, talking

about all kinds of things. We had
sleepovers at each other's houses,
and our moms would always end up
yelling at us to go to bed.

JC: It sounds like you are very close
with Anna.

ML: We've been best friends since we were
nine.

JC: Do you have any classes with her?

ML: World History.

JC: How is she in that class?

ML: Perfect. Anna is the perfect student,
you know? She raises her hand, does
all the homework, that kind of thing.

JC: What about at home. What do you know
about her home life?

ML: Umm. Well, her parents are divorced
and she lives with her mom and
sister, Katie.

JC: Does she get along with her parents?

ML: She has a strange relationship with
her dad. They used to be really
tight, but then she didn't want
anything to do with him. He's hardly
ever around anyway.

JC: What about her mom?

ML: Her mom is always preoccupied. She's
one of those moms who always keeps
the house clean no matter what. It's
like you could eat off the floor,
except there's no food in the house

to fall on the floor in the first place. There's a bunch of frozen meals in the freezer and pasta in the cabinet.

JC: Did she ever share anything with you about being abused or otherwise mistreated?

ML: No.

JC: Nothing at all? Maybe something that seemed odd?

ML: Well. She did accidentally see her mom cheating. Anna was really upset. I felt really bad for her, and she spent the night that night. She cried for a while after she thought I was asleep, and I wanted to tell her I was awake, but I didn't. She never wanted to talk about it after that. I don't blame her.

JC: Okay. How does she act at school?

ML: Teachers call on her when they know no one else is prepared or when they are tired of the know-it-alls going on tirades, but otherwise they pretty much leave her alone. She isn't the favorite or the problem—just perfectly in the middle.

JC: How do you think that fits into her being a cheerleader?

ML: That's exactly what I wanted to know. She didn't even tell me she was interested in it. I found out after

she was picked for the squad. I was
so mad that she didn't tell me. Why
wouldn't she share that? I told her
I was pissed off at her for keeping
me in the dark about the whole thing,
but she said she just had this sudden
urge to do it. She just knew she
had to change things. I was like,
'Shouldn't your supposed best friend
know about that?' and she was like,
'I just wanted to try something new.'

JC: So you aren't a fan of Anna being a
        cheerleader?

ML: Are you serious? I'm so not into
        cheerleading. I don't understand
        walking around in a boring tennis
        outfit shouting out stupid chants to a
        crowd assembled for someone else. I'm
        not an athletic supporter.

JC: Your point is well noted, but go on
        about Anna, please.

ML: Can I get some water?

JC: Sure, let me ask the office ladies.

[Sound of a door latch clicking]

JC: Excuse me. Would it be possible to
        get a glass of water?

US: Of course, Officer. I'll bring in some
        water right away.

JC: Thanks.

[Muffled voices, footsteps]

JC: Here you go.

ML: Thanks. All this talking, I guess.

JC: So what happened to your friendship
       after Anna joined the squad?

ML: I still don't understand what
       happened. After that, it was
       cheerleading practice and
       cheerleading get-togethers and
       cheerleading blah, blah, blah. I was
       done with it. I missed my friend, you
       know? I guess she didn't miss me,
       because she was so busy with her new
       friends. Like, all of the time.

JC: Why do you think she changed so
       suddenly? Did something happen?

ML: I don't know. We were going into
       junior year where everything is so
       important. That's the final push to
       get your grades up, ace your SATs,
       drive yourself crazy with clubs and
       sports to show how well-rounded and
       exhausted you are. People start
       freaking out, so I guess that's
       what Anna did. She freaked out. She
       dropped all her extracurriculars—and
       me—and started to cheer.

       [Sarcastic high-pitched voice]

ML: Yay! Whoo-hoo!

JC: Did she do anything else different at
       that time?

ML: She was working at Sub Station. Her
       mom made a big deal about her earning
       her own money and told her she had to

get a part-time job, which is funny
since her mom gets a big fat alimony
check every month. Whatever. Anyway,
I went with her to apply to random
places. No one was hiring at the
time, except this sandwich shop and
Bath and Body Works. She interviewed
with both, but Sub Station hired her
first. I was surprised she took the
job, considering how bad that area
is. Last week there was a shooting
not far from her work. My mom would
never let me work down there.

JC: That must have taken up a lot of her
time, too.

ML: Yeah, I guess. She works on weekends
and one weekday afternoon. She had
to figure out gas money and spending
money for clothes since her mom
didn't like to buy those for her, so
it was kind of a necessity. I visited
her while she was working a few
times. It's a weird place.

JC: Why was it weird?

ML: Let's just say it's not the kind of
place where you'd think a girl like
Anna would work. Damien, a guy I knew
before he dropped out, works there
as an assistant manager. I heard he
went to juvie and that's why he quit
school. He's a nice guy and all, but
I heard he is a hardcore deal—

[Deep inhale]

ML: I don't know why I said that.
        Sometimes I say things before I
        think. I'm working on that. I don't
        even know—

JC: Relax, Maddie. I am only looking for
        information that helps me find Anna.

ML: Oh, good. That's a relief. The thing
        is you'd never guess it based on his
        looks. People would just assume it
        was that other guy. Max, I think.

JC: Who is Max?

ML: He works there too. He has a ton of
        tattoos on his arms and neck, along
        with some serious piercing on his
        face. I think his brother works at
        the tattoo parlor near Sub Station,
        so he gets them for practically free.
        He looks every bit like a scary drug
        dealer, but he doesn't do anything.
        I mean, he probably drinks, but
        everyone does.

JC: Does Anna hang out with these people
        a lot?

ML: I don't know. Maybe. I haven't seen
        much of her for the past six months.

JC: Your friendship has changed a lot
        recently, huh?

ML: Yeah. I thought we would always
        be friends, and I wish I knew what
        happened between us. I tried asking
        her how she was doing a couple of
        times. She blew me off, put up her

happy armor, and pretended like we were fine. She knew we weren't, but I didn't have it in me to fight with her. I was too hurt.

JC: What do you mean by her 'happy armor'?

ML: You know, the face we all put on to please everyone else. Everyone does it. Like when your mom and dad are fighting and you walk in unexpectedly, then suddenly they're all smiles and super concerned with your needs. Or when you're forced to go to class after some girl drama has you in tears and your teacher asks if everything is okay, so you slap on that face to make sure she stops asking questions that'll make you cry. That armor.

JC: I get it. She didn't want to seem affected by what was happening with your friendship.

ML: I guess. I tried asking if she was okay, but she blew me off with 'I'm fine.' Then she just dropped me. I was so angry with her. In fact, I would still be angry if she wasn't missing and scaring the crap out of me. I can't believe she's gone. What could have happened?

JC: That's what I'm trying to find out. Now, let me back up a bit. Do you know if she does drugs?

ML: No, she would never do drugs.

JC: What about alcohol?

ML: No, at least she never would with me.
       She probably drinks at those parties
       her cheer squad throws.

JC: Have you noticed any suicidal
       behavior?

ML: No.

JC: Any self-harming tendencies?

ML: No.

JC: Did you know she got a tattoo?

ML: No! She wouldn't.

[Slight pause]

ML: Did she?

JC: Does she have a boyfriend?

ML: I guess she was dating Jacob Hunt
       for a couple of weeks. I only know
       because dating gossip spreads like
       wildfire around here. Plus, she was
       an unlikely choice for him. I mean,
       Jacob is one of the cutest guys in
       school. He's on the football team,
       he makes decent grades, and everyone
       likes him. He's annoying that way.

JC: Why was it unlikely?

ML: I guess it wasn't unlikely for
       the new Anna. When she joined
       cheerleading, she was invited to all
       those football/cheerleader parties
       and started to get to know a whole

new group of people. But when we
hung out, she would never have been
noticed by him. Like, ever.

JC: How long did they date?

ML: A couple of weeks. Then it was
        suddenly over. I have no idea why,
        other than the probability that Jacob
        got bored with her.

[Sound of bell ringing loudly]

JC: You don't need to worry about getting
        to class. Principle Eggers cleared
        everything with your teachers.

ML: Okay. That totally startled me.

JC: Can you continue telling me about
        what happened between Anna and Jacob?

ML: Oh yeah. So Jacob Hunt has a waiting
        list of girls. She may have just been
        one in the queue. The Anna I know
        wouldn't have been able to talk to
        Jacob, let alone date him, so I have
        no idea how that whole thing happened.

JC: I see. Do you know if she was upset
        by the breakup?

ML: Probably.

JC: You don't really know, do you?

ML: Not really, but I would bet she was
        devastated.

JC: How come?

ML: I don't know. Anna has always
        wanted a boy to make some huge
        gesture, like when Austin runs off

the football field and kisses Sam
in front of the whole school in A
Cinderella Story. Or when King Ben
does that ridiculous dance for Mal
in Descendants. Jacob isn't the type
to do that kind of thing.

JC: Okay, let's move on. Do you think
she's depressed?

ML: I don't know. Anna is more emotional
than other kids. I don't know if
others just don't have that side,
or if it's buried so deep you can't
reach it.

JC: So she's sensitive? Or do you think
she has mental health issues?

[Pause]

ML: I think she just feels what everyone
else should feel but avoids feeling.

[Lapse in time[

JC: I understand you and she had a
falling out. Can you tell me what
happened?

ML: Yeah. She got mad about some things
I posted. I mean, we all live on our
phones, so we post pics and updates
all the time. She was just being
sensitive.

JC: Did you put things online to upset
Anna?

ML: No, of course not. I'm not a mean
girl, if that's what you are saying.

JC: Anna's diary mentions something about
        you posting things she considered
        private. Do you know what she could
        mean?

ML: Well... I mean, it's not like that. We
        all get upset from time to time and
        post things. It doesn't mean anything.
        It's just where we vent sometimes.

JC: Did you post a video of her in her
        underwear?

ML: Yeah, but it wasn't that bad. People
        wear bikinis to the beach. It was the
        same thing, except lacy. She wears a
        cheerleading outfit, so it's not like
        she's not used to showing her skin.

JC: Did she think it was bad?

ML: Well, yeah.

JC: Did she get any unwanted attention
        from the video?

ML: Yeah.

[Sniffling sounds]

JC: It's alright, Maddie.

[Sound of tissues being pulled from a box]

JC: Here.

ML: Thanks. I don't usually cry. I just...

[Sniffling sounds, nose blowing]

JC: She told you she was upset about the
        posts, right?

ML: Yes, which I knew would lead to a fight,
        but she didn't even fight with me.

JC: You thought she would fight with you
        and then you would make up? Even
        after the things you said?

ML: I guess. I mean, no. I don't know. I
        was just so mad at her.

JC: She didn't fight with you like you
        expected?

ML: No. She just blew me off.

JC: Do you think she didn't react in her
        usual manner because she was more
        hurt than she let on?

ML: I don't know. She's usually the one
        who gets really upset about stuff,
        so I was surprised that she acted so
        okay about it. She was fine with it,
        like she didn't care, which is why I
        was so mad at her—

    [Sharp inhale]

JC: What is it?

ML: Oh my God. She put me on the outside
        and I never realized it. She gave
        me the fake routine about how 'fine'
        she's doing, and I bought it. She
        probably thought I was just like the
        rest of the losers who pretend they
        care.

JC: Does Anna feel like nobody cares
        about her?

ML: Officer Christiansen, you don't
        think people put on a show for you?
        When you come in to ask questions,

you don't think people put on an
act about how caring and innocent
they are? Do you really think they
all cared about Anna before she
disappeared? Do you really think
that they put much effort into
noticing she was alive at all, let
alone caring about her, until it
went viral? Now that it's all over
the internet and TV, and cameras
are stalking our school, people are
suddenly her best friend and very
concerned about her. It's so obvious.

JC: Alright, well—

ML: I was the one who cared about her.
Oh, God. What have I done? I was a
horrible friend to her and now she's
missing. It's because of me, isn't it?
I humiliated my best friend and now
she's gone.

JC: Maddie, you cannot claim
responsibility for Anna's
disappearance.

[Sniffles, whimpering sounds]

JC: It's alright, Maddie. It's alright.

[Rubbing and patting sounds]

JC: Is there anything else you think I
should know?

[Pause]

ML: Officer... you are going to find her,
right?

JC: I'm going to do everything in my
power. Alright, unless you have
anything else you want to say, you
better get back to class.

ML: No, I think I said everything.

[Sniffles, pause]

ML: I am sorry, you know.

JC: I know, Maddie. If you think of
anything else that might help us find
her, call me.

ML: Okay.

Text Exchanges between
Anna Williams and Maddie Le

February 2, 2012

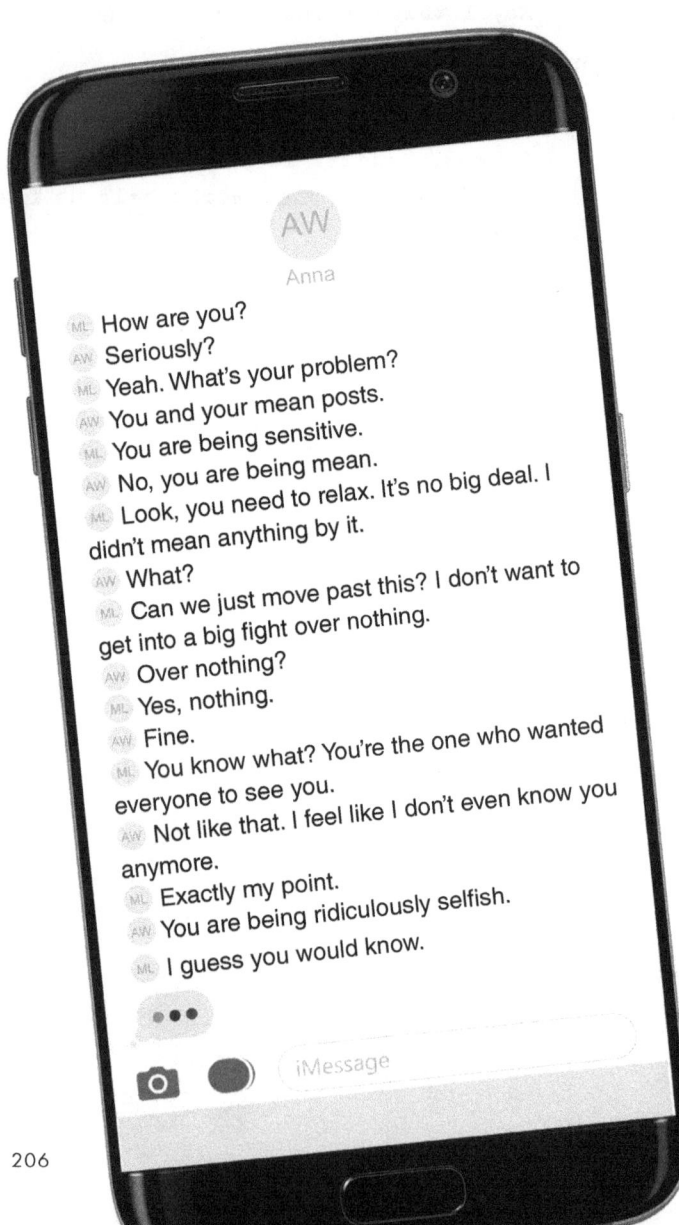

AW

Anna

ML How are you?
AW Seriously?
ML Yeah. What's your problem?
AW You and your mean posts.
ML You are being sensitive.
AW No, you are being mean.
ML Look, you need to relax. It's no big deal. I didn't mean anything by it.
AW What?
ML Can we just move past this? I don't want to get into a big fight over nothing.
AW Over nothing?
ML Yes, nothing.
AW Fine.
ML You know what? You're the one who wanted everyone to see you.
AW Not like that. I feel like I don't even know you anymore.
ML Exactly my point.
AW You are being ridiculously selfish.
ML I guess you would know.

iMessage

March 29, 2012

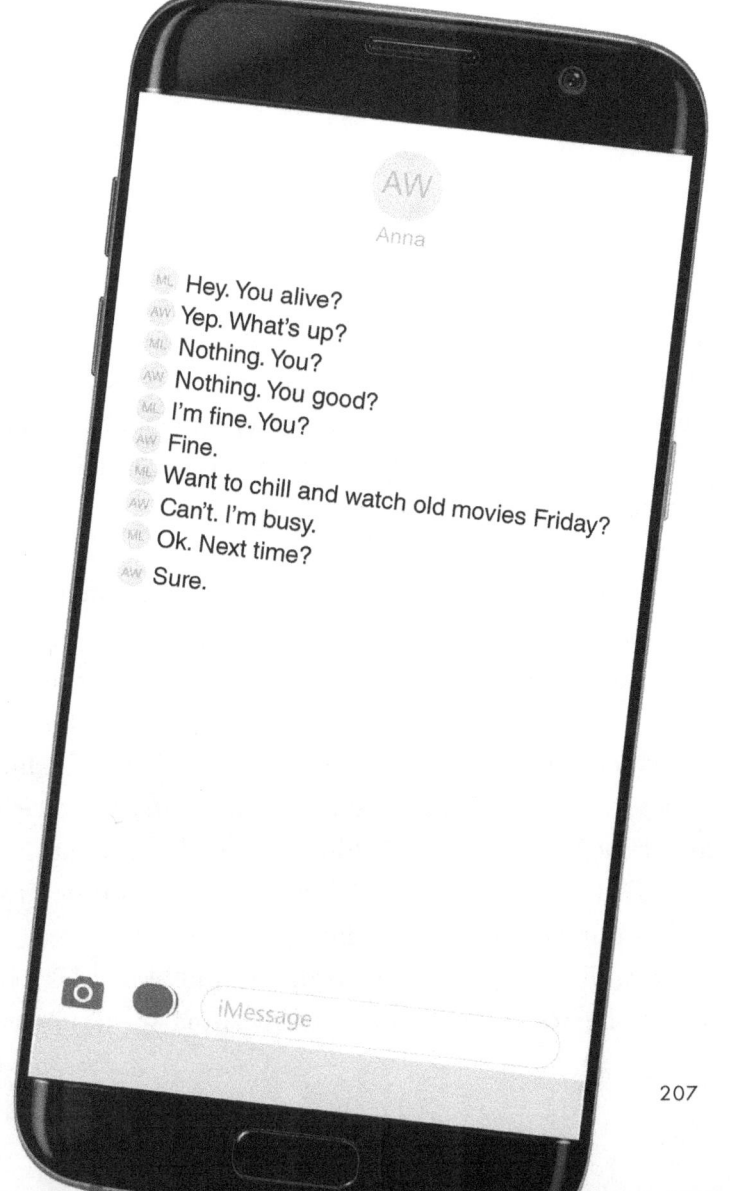

AW
Anna

ML Hey. You alive?
AW Yep. What's up?
ML Nothing. You?
AW Nothing. You good?
ML I'm fine. You?
AW Fine.
ML Want to chill and watch old movies Friday?
AW Can't. I'm busy.
ML Ok. Next time?
AW Sure.

iMessage

I was supposed to be at the Nelsons' twenty minutes ago, but I can't stop circling around the neighborhood. They asked me to come over for dinner and I couldn't say no. They've been so nice to me, especially after I drove my car off the road with their son in the passenger seat. I keep steering my Focus down their street, but I can't seem to slow down and pull in the driveway. I'm too riled up over this whole Maddie thing, and I'm afraid I won't be able to keep it together in front of them.

Reading Maddie's interview was just too much. That girl was at our house all the time growing up. I mean, she and Anna were best friends for nine years. Maddie was Anna's Josie. Nine years of sleepovers, trips to the mall, and late-night phone calls. Nine years of debating Harry Styles versus Joe Jonas, Taylor Swift versus Katy Perry, and how Miley Cyrus would reinvent herself next. Nine long years of thinking you know someone, and then they stab you in the back. And why?

Maddie always needed Anna around as a sidekick of sorts. She couldn't handle it when Anna wasn't focused entirely on her—she always wanted all the attention. I think what really got to her was the fact that Anna didn't just go out and get some new friends, she chose a group that Maddie despised.

I totally understood Maddie at first. After all, I was the little sister left behind every time Anna went off with Piper and the team, so I knew exactly how she felt. Then Maddie pulled this stunt and everything changed. As upset as Maddie felt, she had no right to do what she did. She had no right to take her grudge against Anna into a public arena. Everyone knows how damaging this kind of mean girl crap can be. She did it on purpose because she was jealous, and she got exactly what she wanted. She got everyone to make Anna into a joke.

I remember her coming to the house after Anna went missing, acting so innocent and concerned. She even had the nerve to pretend like the two of them were thick as thieves up until that very Friday. I knew everything by then, so she wasn't fooling me. I gave her a piece of my mind that day. I really laid into her with twelve-year-old insults that would make a grown man cower. I didn't care. She deserved it. Even Josie thought so.

I fumble around for my phone, then thinking better of it, I call out to Siri, "Call Josie."

Ring. Ring. Ring.

"Katie!"

"I'm so glad you picked up."

"Why? What's up?"

"Sorry to bother you. I know you're busy being all European and everything."

"Spill it."

I find myself rehashing everything I read in the file. After offering just the right amount of disgust about my mom and concern about my dad—without being too judgmental—she waits for me to talk myself out.

"Oh, and you should have read the interview with Maddie. Remember her?"

"How could I forget?" Josie asks incredulously. "You know, I didn't tell you this, but I saw her a few days before we left. She's a stylist at Chic. My mom and I went in to get our nails done for the trip, and I saw her putting highlights in for someone."

"Thanks for the warning. I'll be sure to avoid that place."

She laughs, which melts my frustration away. I'm so grateful I have Josie in my life, even if she has decided to live far away from me for the next four years. I don't know what I'd do without her. I really don't.

"Hey, Josie?"

"What?"

"Never mind."

"You know I can't do that."

I hesitate, but only for a second. She and I both know I have to say whatever comes into my head.

"We're not going to end up like Anna and Maddie, are we?"

"Never. You've got me for life, whether you like it or not. And if you do something to piss me off, I'll tell you in person. Then you can apologize and make me chocolate chip cookies, which better be warm and topped with ice cream, and then I'll forgive you. Same for you. Deal?"

"Deal."

Feeling better after talking to Josie, I finally make it to Jack's house. I'm standing on the Nelsons' doorstep when I see Sheila's face smiling at me through the windows framing the door. She flings open the door and invites me inside.

"Hi, Katie! It's nice to see you, sweetheart."

"Hi there. I hope you like spaghetti." Jack's dad, Eric, smiles.

"I do, thanks."

After navigating the rows of shoes stacked against the wall of the entryway, I walk through the living room on my way to the kitchen. Papers are sprawled all over the couch, blankets are strewn across the armchair, and a book has been left open face-down on the coffee table with a pair of reading glasses set on top. As always, the Nelson house never puts style before living.

"Here," says Jack, pulling out the chair next to him and smiling. Man, those dimples.

Sheila's spaghetti smells amazing and tastes even better. Mom and I usually eat out or grab a bite to eat at the kitchen counter. It's not the same as passing warm rolls across a worn-out wooden table with a candle lit in the middle of it.

"I'm so glad you could join us," Sheila says.

"Thanks for having me."

"Anytime," Jack's dad chimes in.

I glance at Jack, who offers an impish grin.

"I'm glad your mom is going to be home soon. She's coming in tomorrow, right?" Sheila asks. It dawns on me that she's the snitch who told my mom about the accident.

"Yeah. I think their flight lands around midnight."

"The flight from Hawaii is exhausting. Remember how tired we were, honey?" Sheila asks her husband, who nods in agreement before clearing his throat.

"Enough about that. Tell us about what's going on in your life, Katie," Eric says, fixing his eyes on me.

"Oh, not much."

I figure it's best to keep it vague, mysterious even. Why spoil his preconceived notions about me? Whatever he thinks I'm about to do has to be better than the truth.

"What are your plans now that you're officially a high school graduate?"

"I'm not really sure yet. I'll probably take a year off to travel, find myself or something." I laugh, too awkwardly.

Jack, seeming to notice his parents' questioning eyes, pipes up, "I think that's great. I have a lot of college friends who took a gap year, and it made all the difference. They were totally able to focus on a major right away. It took me until my junior year before I had any idea what I wanted to do."

"That is true. I was sure Jack would have been an engineer like me," Eric says.

"You mean, you hoped," Jack says, eyeing his father with some seriousness.

"Well..."

"I think it's wonderful that you found your own path.

I'm hoping you can build your father and me a very nice retirement home." Sheila looks at Jack lovingly.

⁓

After dinner, Jack and I sit on the patio together as he catches me up on his college days. He tells me stories about classes he took, professors who invited him to their homes, and places he visited. I admit I'm jealous, and a little bit angry thinking about the fact that Anna should be the one telling me all about college. She should be the one with all these stories. But I can't hold that against him, at least not for long.

"So now you're going to design buildings, huh?"

"That's the plan."

"Do you always have a plan? Wait, don't answer that. I already know the answer!" I laugh, pushing him playfully.

"Do you have a problem with making plans?" he asks, pushing me back with a huge smile on his face.

"No. I mean, not everyone can be spontaneous."

"Oh, really? You don't think I'm spontaneous, huh?" he says, exaggerating how offended he feels.

"Umm, no. Definitely not. I don't think you have a spontaneous bone in your body."

"I can be spontaneous."

"Sure, you can!" I say teasingly. "I'm sure you switch up your Cheerios for Honey Nut once in a while."

Jack leans over, close enough that I can see the flecks of gold in his blue-green eyes. His eyes dart around, taking in my eyes and my lips and my eyes again. I feel like he can see through me, and it takes my breath away. Before

I can say a word, I feel his lips on mine. I melt into him until he pulls away, leaving me feeling incomplete.

"See. I can be spontaneous."

I smile, but I'm too jumbled up from his kiss to act normal. I try to shake it off, acting like it was no big deal. I don't think I'm a very good actress, though. Jack, on the other hand, seems relaxed and quite pleased with himself.

"Do you mind if I ask you something?" Jack asks tentatively.

"Sure," I say.

"What do you want to do next?"

"Oh, come on. Didn't I just dodge that question inside?"

"You dodged having to answer it for my parents. But now you have to deal with me."

"Oh really?" I force myself to look upset, but fail. My mind is still spinning from his kiss. "Fine. You want to know what I'm up to? Nothing. Absolutely nothing."

"You must have something you want to do."

"Not really. Not everyone is destined for greatness like you, Jack," I say, my words dripping with sarcasm.

Jack smiles at me, his dimples showing.

"What?"

"You're cute," he says sweetly.

I'm not sure if he means I'm cute like a child or cute like a girl he'd like to date. Am I amusing to him?

"So whether you're destined for greatness or not, you've got that going for you."

"Gee, thanks."

He moves closer to me, making my heart beat in my

chest. I wonder if he's going to kiss me again. I kind of hope he does.

"It's okay, you know. You'll find your way."

The way he's looking at me makes me believe him. I decide he's definitely not looking at me like I'm a child.

"Life is not a ticking time bomb you have to figure out how to dismantle before it blows up." Jack leans forward, and I feel his eyes disarming me. "It's just life."

I find myself smiling like a goofball as I drive home. It's funny. Nothing has changed, yet it feels different. In this moment, I'm not filled with dread. I'm not hopeless about my future. I'm actually happy. There's something about Jack that makes me feel all girly and stupid. He's adorable, charming, and funny—not to mention an incredibly good kisser. With those ocean eyes and those dimples, who wouldn't be madly in love with him?

But it's more than that. He makes me feel something I haven't felt in a long time. I think it's hope.

February 15, 2012

Yaaaassss!! I'm so excited!! Jacob Hunt asked me out after school today. He is so cute. I mean, he is really, really cute. He has brown hair that looks perfectly messed up all the time. It's slightly too long, just long enough to make him have to shake his head to move it out of his dark eyes. Man, those eyes... If I'm not careful, he catches me staring, and I have to pretend like I'm searching for someone just behind him and then wave slightly to no one in particular, just to make sure he doesn't think I'm actually looking at him. Sometimes he thinks I'm waving to him and gives a slight nod back. When he does that, I melt.

He is seriously the closest thing to a movie star I have ever seen up close. Well, running into Jennifer Anniston at the market doesn't really count. Neither does the time I saw Orlando Bloom on the set where my dad was working. I mean, Jacob is a gorgeous man-boy who should really be on screen. He has the perfect jawline and cheekbones for it. Like a model. But better because I get to see him up close. And now I get to see him on a date!!

I guess it isn't really serious or anything,

since we are going to a party at Danté's house, but still. I'm going with him. He is picking me up. We are going there TOGETHER. So that is awesome.

I have so much to do before this weekend. Let me see. I need to make a list.

1. What do I say to him? I'm totally nervous. Piper said to be myself, but what does that even mean? Should I talk about music and movies? Should I talk about stuff at school? Do I keep it light and easy or dive right into deeper topics so he can really get to know me? I don't want to be a downer, so I should keep it fun. What is fun to him? I have no idea. OMG I have no idea what he likes. I know nothing about football. I can ask about his family, but that seems lame. Oh no, I'm having a complete meltdown now... and the party isn't for three days. I can't just stand there silently gawking at his beautiful face. I have to come up with something to talk about, something that makes me seem intriguing and likable.

2. What do I wear? I have nothing cute enough for Jacob Hunt. I better go shopping. Maybe Piper can help me out.

3. What should I do about kissing and sex and all that? I better figure out what guys like Jacob want from a girl. I mean, am I supposed to let him do stuff, or am I supposed to do

stuff to him? On TV, everyone is doing it, and if they aren't, they are definitely doing something... so what do I do? What if I'm too shy? What if he wants to do something really kinky? What if he does something I've never heard of before? I'll have to ask Piper about all that later.

Okay, that's it for now. I'm going to go running. I have to burn some calories. I'm way too fat. I can't stand the way I look when I sit down because all my belly fat hangs over my jeans. I try to sit up really tall so it doesn't happen, but it always does. Now that I'm stuck wearing these tight-fitting shirts and dresses that show every little problem, I can't hide my flaws. I hate it.

Just the other day, the girls were like, "Anna, you aren't going to eat those crackers, are you? Those are loaded with carbs, and you know how fat carbs make you." So I put down the crackers, only to eat them in the car on the way home. I was hungry! Seriously, when did eating become so hard to do? I can't eat anything anymore. I eat mac'n'cheese with Katie, but that is it. The rest is off-limits. Salads, juices, carrots, turkey, and eggs are about all I can eat most of the time. Man, I miss Cheetos.

That's probably why I binge on pasta and then force myself to run. It's too hard to eat like a bird! I can't starve myself. It's so much easier to just give in to my hunger and then deal with it afterwards. Running burns tons of calories, so I'm going to run until I can't run anymore. Maybe by Saturday, I'll have lost these last five pounds.

I'm going to look so hot that Jacob will be so happy he asked me out. Everyone will take notice of the amazing girl I am because, after all, Jacob Hunt did choose me. They will all wonder why they overlooked me before. Maddie will apologize and realize that I just needed to branch out a bit in order to spread my dragonfly wings and discover my true self. Piper will be ecstatic.

Who knows? Maybe Jacob will be my boyfriend before long and even be my first time. Maybe he will make all my romantic comedy dreams come true. Hey—it could happen.

I'm so happy. I can't wait until Saturday.

INTERVIEW WITH MACKLEMORE
HIGH STUDENT PIPER ABBOT

Monday, April 23, 2012, 9:30 a.m.
Transcribed from Digital Recording

JC: Officer John Christiansen

PA: Piper Abbot

US: Unknown Speaker

JC: Begin recording. Thank you for meeting with me, Piper. I assume you know what I am here to talk with you about.

PA: Yes, I do.

[Door clicks shut, metal clanging of chairs]

JC: Can I ask you some questions?

PA: Yes.

JC: Let's start with you telling me about your friendship with Anna.

PA: I've known Anna for a really long time, but we just became good friends this past year when she joined the squad. We're really close.

JC: Can you tell me about the kinds of things you do together?

PA: Sure. We practice together, but I'm sure you could have guessed that. She was new, so we had a lot of ground

to cover. Practice takes up a lot of
our time as it is, especially before
games and when the competition season
begins. It's totally fun, though.

JC: Do you spend time with Anna outside
        of cheerleading?

PA: Oh yeah. The whole squad is pretty
        much inseparable. We hang out all the
        time. We get together at each other's
        houses and have spa parties or watch
        movies. We talk a lot! We shop or go
        to parties. It's all pretty typical
        high school stuff.

JC: Can you tell me about student
        council?

PA: Oh, sure. I convinced Anna to run
        with me for student body president
        and vice president. I thought it
        would be super fun to plan our prom,
        so that seemed like the best way
        to get involved. Anna's so smart
        and all the teachers like her, so
        I figured her brains and likability
        with my popularity was a winning
        combination. I was right, too. We're
        a perfect match.

        [Chewing sounds, popping of gum]

JC: Is it a lot of work?

PA: Yeah, but it's actually a lot of fun
        too. We do much more than just plan
        parties, although we are currently
        planning prom. We have to handle all

sorts of things like pep rallies, fundraisers, and yearbooks. We have to meet with our teacher advisor once a month to make sure everything's running smoothly. We also have to address things that happen at school that involve the student body.

[Sound of knocking, opening of the door]

US: Excuse me, Officer. I hate to interrupt, but Mrs. Rhodes—one of the teachers Mrs. Eggers suggested you meet with—can meet with you in her classroom when you are finished here. Will that work for your schedule?

JC: Yes, that's fine. Thank you for telling me.

US: Not a problem. Sorry for the interruption.

[Sound of the door closing, papers shuffling]

JC: Sorry about that, Piper. Let's get back to what we were talking about. Let's see, what kind of things do you address in student council?

PA: Whatever comes up, I guess. Anna keeps pushing us to make a campaign about bullying over social media, eating disorders, or safe sex. She always has some serious issue she thinks needs attention, but we all know that's a bit too touchy. I mean, what a buzzkill, right?

JC: You don't think those issues should
be addressed?

PA: We like to stick to reminding
students not to text during class
and the consequences of destructive
pranks. I think we can all agree
that spray painting the lockers isn't
in anyone's interest.

[Popping of gum]

JC: Does Anna think there are certain
issues that need to be addressed?

PA: I don't know. I mean, I guess she
does. She brings up depressing
subjects a lot. Like depression!

[Popping of gum]

JC: Is she concerned about anyone in
particular? Does she seem depressed
herself?

PA: I don't know. She can be kind of
moody sometimes. She's usually fun
and outgoing, but then she can get
really bipolar on you. She just kind
of plummets into this doomsday kind
of mood. I keep reminding her that
she's just a teenager and she has
plenty of time to save the world.

JC: How does she act when she gets in
these moods?

PA: When she's being all mental, she
talks about how it's so important
for people to be understood and
seen and all that. She'll go on a

very uninteresting rant about how the media is screwing up everyone's self-esteem and view of sex. If she doesn't wind it up pretty quickly, I tell her to get it together. I'm her friend, after all. If anyone were to see her acting like that, they would run away from her. Fast.

[Popping of gum]

JC: Your friends don't want to talk about those issues?

PA: I mean, it's not that other kids don't care about all these issues. They just don't like to focus on them. What's the point? We can't do anything about any of it. Are we going to make girls eat? Are we going to change how huge advertising companies and magazines portray women and transgendered people and sex? Am I going to make everyone be nice to each other? Uh, no.

[Puff of laughter]

JC: You feel powerless to change these things?

PA: Yeah, totally. Plus, it's such a huge downer. My mom's always saying, 'This is the time of your life.' She constantly reminds me that I'm only going to be young once, so I might as well enjoy it. So I do. I just ignore all that other deep, dark downer stuff and focus on the positive.

We have to keep everyone happy and hopeful, you know? That's what cheer's all about—keeping everyone focused on the bright side of things. Right?

JC: Okay, so—

PA: When Anna's in her usual place, she's really good at it. I taught her everything I know, and she's a quick learner. She got the routines down fast, and when we get going, there's this light in her eyes. She totally shines. That's why I always try to keep her spirits up. She deserves to be happy.

[Popping of gum]

JC: Do you think she's happy?

PA: Most of the time, yes! She's usually smiling and offering to help out with whatever needs to be done. She's there for any of the girls if they're having a hard time, offering hugs and encouragement. Like I said, she has this huge positive side. The other part slips out once in a while, but not for long. Although, that's how the whole Jacob thing happened.

JC: The whole Jacob thing?

PA: The whole dating the hottest guy in school thing. You know, the Jacob thing.

JC: Ah. Tell me about that.

PA: Well, Anna was feeling really down

one day, probably over the whole
Maddie situation.

[Popping of gum]

JC: Okay, back up. Tell me about the
        Maddie situation first.

PA: Oh, this girl Maddie—who used to be
        friends with Anna—posted a video of
        her and started spreading rumors.
        She said some mean things and, as
        her friend, I had to tell Anna what
        I heard. I felt bad because it really
        hurt Anna.

JC: What was the video?

PA: Just a video of Anna messing around.
        It wasn't anything scandalous, but it
        was definitely not what anyone would
        ever want posted. Trust me, it was
        embarrassing for sure.

JC: So you want to help her feel better?

PA: Yeah. I thought if I fixed her up
        with someone that would make her
        feel really amazing, she'd forget
        about the whole Maddie thing. I was
        afraid she was sinking into another
        doomsday episode.

JC: Does that happen a lot?

PA: Kind of. Maybe. I don't know. Anyway,
        so I talked to Jacob and asked
        him to ask her out. He didn't get
        it at first, but I got him to come
        around. I told him all about how
        great she is and how smoking hot her

body is beneath her frumpy looking
sweatshirts, which I have finally
gotten her to stop wearing. I just
pointed out how great she looked in
her cheerleading outfit—a soft spot
for him—and he caved.

[Popping of gum]

JC: Then what happened?

PA: He asked her out just after school
         the next day. I was there when he did
         it, but Anna had no idea I gave him
         the idea. He was sweet about it, and
         she turned as red as Taylor Swift's
         lipstick. She didn't quite say yes,
         so I said it for her.

JC: When was the date?

PA: Friday night. They went out with a big
         group of us. It was so much fun. We
         hung out at Danté's house, which is
         the place to be since his parents are
         always out of town. When he throws a
         party, you better turn up. Plus, they
         keep things within reach. I mean,
         well... Can we forget I said that?

JC: What happened that night?

PA: I don't know, really. All I know is
         we all sat around listening to music
         and dancing. I was amazed at how
         much Anna knew about every single
         song that came on. She was like my
         own music app, telling me all about
         the singers and bands. It was fun.

[Popping of gum]

JC: Did Anna spend any time alone with
        Jacob?

PA: Not at first, but then they slipped
        off by themselves for a while. Anna
        was kind of sweet the way she kept
        her distance as they walked off, but
        I saw him put his arm around her and
        pull her close. That was all I saw.

JC: Did Anna tell you what happened
        afterwards?

PA: Anna said they kissed and it was
        magical, like butterflies and
        rainbows. I was really happy for her.
        After that, they talked at school and
        I think they were texting a lot. She
        loosened up so much. I knew Jacob
        was just the guy she needed to bring
        her out of her sweatshirt shell. He's
        gorgeous and charming, the whole
        package.

JC: Did they go out again?

PA: They went out by themselves the next
        weekend. I think they went to see a
        movie, but I can't remember which one.

JC: Did the date go well?

PA: I don't know. I figured they were
        really into each other at that point.
        I even felt proud that I had set it
        up. Then, that night I get this weird
        message from Anna, and it seemed
        like she'd had a bad night. I asked

her about it later, but she just said
something like, 'I'm overreacting.
Seriously, I'm fine. Never mind.' That
was it.

JC: Do you—

PA: Officer, do you mind if I throw out my
        gum?

JC: Please do.

[Sliding of chair, thump in trash]

PA: Thanks.

JC: No, thank you. Alright, where were
        we? Oh. Do you have any idea what
        happened between Jacob and Anna after
        that?

PA: That's just it. No one knows. Neither
        of them said a word about it. They
        kept it to themselves. After that
        weekend, they just went their
        separate ways. I guess it just wasn't
        a good fit. I had planned to set her
        up with someone else. We were going
        to go out as a group, but I told her
        I had someone in mind. There's this
        boy, Jayden, and I thought he would
        be much more her speed. He's shy and
        all. But then—

JC: But then... what?

PA: Well, she found out that I had
        encouraged Jacob to ask her out, and
        she flipped out. Apparently, Emma has
        a big mouth as well as a big butt.

JC: Anna was upset that you asked Jacob
        to go out with her?

PA: Yes, but it isn't like I held a gun
        to his head and forced him to do it.
        I just gave him the idea. I did it
        because I thought it would be nice. I
        wasn't trying to hurt her.

JC: But she was hurt.

PA: Yeah. She was really upset and
        wouldn't answer my calls or texts.

JC: Did you eventually talk to her about
        it?

PA: I tried. I said I was sorry and that
        I was just trying to make her happy.
        She said it was fine, but after that,
        she gave me the cold shoulder. She
        was suddenly too busy to hang out.

    [Sniffling]

PA: I thought I'd have another chance,
        but now this has happened. Oh, God.
        I almost forgot she wasn't here. Oh,
        God.

    [Whimpering sounds and quick, staccato
    breathing]

JC: Are you alright, Piper?

PA: I'm fine. It's just that I've been
        thinking about myself this whole
        time, caught up in all the drama
        of my life as if it even matters. I
        can't believe this is happening at
        all. I really can't. Oh, look. Now

I'm crying. My mascara is running
all over. Eww. I'm so sorry. I'm not
usually so emotional.

JC: It's alright. This is an incredibly
        hard situation, and it's normal for
        you to feel this way. Just take a
        deep breath.

PA: I just can't stop crying. I don't
        know what could have happened to
        her. I mean, is it even possible
        that someone could have taken her?
        That just doesn't happen. It doesn't
        happen to girls like her in a town
        like ours. We're safe here. My
        parents always told me that nothing
        bad could happen to me. They said
        they would protect me. They promised.
        What about Anna? What if you don't
        find her? Oh, God. What if you do?
        What if she isn't alive? Oh, God. Oh,
        God. Oh, God.

[High pitched crying sounds, lapse in time]

JC: Alright, now. Calm down. I know this
        is scary, but there's no reason to
        jump to conclusions like that. Let's
        just take it one step at a time. Okay?

PA: Okay. I'll try.

[Sniffling sounds]

JC: Are there any other boys, besides
        Jacob, Anna's interested in?

PA: Umm, she thought Sam was cute. She
        also flirted with Aiden a lot, but

nothing serious. She talks to that guy
Jack sometimes, but he's not her type.

JC: Okay, what about—

PA: Oh, and she mentioned some older guy
at her work being cute. At first, I
was like 'Qoooh, older guy, huh?'
Then, she said he was twenty-six and
I kind of felt weird. I mean, twenty-
two would be super-hot, but twenty-
six is a lot older. I mean, not old
man old, but old enough to be kind of
gross. No offense, Officer.

JC: None taken. What was his name?

PA: Joey, I think. Or maybe Jonah? I'm not
sure.

JC: Did she give you any more information
about him?

PA: Not really. Sometimes it's just fun
to obsess about a guy we haven't
known since third grade.

JC: Can you tell me if Anna drinks
alcohol or does any drugs?

PA: Ummm.

JC: You can be honest, Piper. I'm only
interested in finding Anna, and that
is all.

PA: Well, everyone has a little something
at a party—including Anna.

JC: What are we talking about? Does she
have one beer? Does she try hard
alcohol?

[Tapping sounds from a finger drumming on the table]

JC: Piper?

PA: I know she's had a beer or two at parties. Maybe some vodka. I'm not sure.

JC: Are there drugs at these parties?

PA: Usually, just pot. Someone always brings the harder stuff, but most of us don't ever try it. Anna never does. She's always worried about getting caught and what will happen to her if she does get caught. She worries too much.

JC: Do you think she worried about how she looked?

PA: Not any more than the rest of us. She was into looking good. She did her makeup and always had lip gloss on. She used to wear these hideous baggy clothes, but not anymore. She has a great figure for almost everything, too. Actually, now that she lost some of that pudge, she fits into everything.

JC: Did Anna recently lose some weight? Is that what you mean by pudge?

PA: Yeah. She dropped ten pounds or maybe fifteen. I'm not sure, but you can tell. She looks amazing. She is totally hot now. She said she likes to run and that made the pounds just

melt off her. I would run, but I hate
to sweat. So I just diet with her.

JC: What kind of diet?

PA: You know, just watching what you eat.
Trying to eat less and stop filling up
on carbs. Nothing crazy.

JC: Over the past few months, has she
said anything suspicious or out of
character?

PA: Not really.

JC: Do you know about her tattoo?

PA: No! She got one? I had no idea! We
talked about it, but she never seemed
like she would actually do it. I
figured I would be the one to get one
first.

JC: Okay, Piper—I think I'm done with my
questions. You don't need to worry
about this anymore. But if you
think of anything else you think is
important, take my card and call me.
Okay?

PA: Okay.

Uggh, Piper is so annoying. She's even worse than I remember.

"Hey there. How's it going?"

Startled, I turn my head to see Christiansen standing in the doorway. Man, this guy will not give me any space. What is his deal?

"Fine," I say.

"Alright, well, I'm going to head out soon," Christiansen says, his hands in his pockets. "You want to come back tomorrow?"

"Yeah," I say.

I look up to see it's already six. How did that much time just pass? I organize the pile of papers in front of me and close the folder. When I look up, he's still standing in the doorway.

"I just wanted to say that, for what it's worth, I'm sorry," Christiansen says. "You don't know this, but I have two daughters. Just like you and your sister. When Anna went missing, all I could think about was 'What if this happened to one of my little girls?'"

I stare at him coldly.

"I guess that's why I was so interested in what your sister was going through before she disappeared. Didn't anyone know what was really going on? I was convinced someone must have known something."

Is he messing with me right now? That's exactly what I've been saying. Someone must have known something, right? I mean, how in the world did none of us know what was going on with Anna? Even this guy knows that's weird.

"Anyway, I guess I just wanted you to know that."

I want to punch him in the face. I really do. After all these years, he's standing here acting like some kind of caring father figure. Where was he when I needed him to find my sister, huh? Oh, that's right. He was at home with his two little girls, probably throwing them in the air or reading them bedtime stories. How dare he say he gets it? How could he? His daughters are still here.

"Okay."

I'm about to push past him when he steps aside and gestures for me to proceed. His eyes are understanding and kind, and I feel bad for being so angry. Maybe he did try his best to find Anna. It's not easy to find someone who seems like they're hiding in plain sight. I'm not sure what to think of this guy anymore. I'm not sure what to think about anyone, actually.

I don't know why I thought I would be able to find answers here. All I'm finding are more and more questions.

FINE

The last orange and pink streaks of sunlight fade into the darkening horizon as Jack and I sit at the edge of the ocean. It's a beautiful night, clear and warm with just a slight breeze blowing in over the water. With every wave that crashes down, a salty mist settles over us like a blanket. It feels especially good to be alive right now.

I look over at Jack, who is dragging a piece of driftwood through the sand. In his hoodie and bare feet, he looks more like a meditative surfer than a brainy architect in training. Seeming not to notice me staring at him, he continues to drag the smooth wood in circles. We're both lost in thought. After a while, Jack stops. He lifts his stick and points it towards the sky.

"You can actually see Draco, the dragon, tonight. See?"

I look up unenthusiastically.

"I bet you didn't know that next to that blue and white star—that group of stars there—is part of Hercules."

"Huh," I say, squinting my eyes to make out the shape of the Roman god.

"Turns out that semester I took astronomy was pretty useful."

I look over at Jack, suddenly curious.

"Why are you doing this?"

"I think everyone should know some basic constellations." Jack answers the wrong question, on purpose. "Want to put your toes in?"

"I never go in. Ever."

Jack nods, dropping the topic. We sit quietly for several minutes, but I can't keep my thoughts to myself for long.

"Don't you have better things to do than babysit me? Or am I part of a community service project or something?"

"You are a tough nut to crack," Jack laughs to himself. "I'm here because I want to be. And because you're letting me."

"I was fine before, you know? I don't need you," I say, asserting my independence with attitude.

"I know," he says matter-of-factly.

There's something about the way Jack looks at me. I feel like he understands me in a way nobody else does, not even Josie. I'm so used to protecting myself, keeping people at arm's length, but it's exhausting. With Jack, I feel like I can let my guard down and just be.

"I'm not a nut," I say, smiling.

"Well…" he teases, nudging his shoulder into mine.

I push myself closer to him, letting my head fall on his shoulder. The scent of the ocean mixes with his cologne, creating a smell I don't ever want to live without. I inhale deeply, allowing myself to relax into him. I'm comfortable, yet excited. I'm scared, but happy. I'm where I want to be.

February 20, 2012

   Today I came home after school to grab my Sub Station shirt. I usually take it with me in the morning so I can go straight to work after school, but I didn't get it in the dryer in time. Anyway, when I walked in, I heard my mom in the kitchen gossiping with her friend, Lidia, except this time it was about me. She was telling Lidia all about my date with Jacob—as if it was her news to tell—and how surprised she was that a boy like him would be interested in me.

   I hovered for a minute, wondering if she would follow it up with "Just kidding!" but no. I was so hurt. How could she?

FILE CONTROL NO. 23167
MISSING PERSON – ANNA WILLIAMS
Note to File completed by Officer Christiansen on April 23,
2012, 11:25 a.m.

Records
- Anna's school files have been obtained. After a
  brief review of her file, there appears to be nothing of import in it. She was an above-average
  student with no disciplinary actions.
- Records from Anna's pediatrician were obtained.
  Other than her last checkup in August, where she
  was reportedly healthy, she has not received any
  recent medical attention. She is not taking any
  medication. After a thorough review of these files
  by our team, there is no indication of any physical
  conditions or illnesses, nor any suspicion that
  she is affected by mental illness. According to
  the pediatrician's records, Anna Williams was a
  healthy young woman.
- Records from Anna's dentist were obtained for
  identification purposes. Copies were emailed to
  the clearinghouse. Anna has not had her fingerprints taken for employment purposes or any
  other reason, so these are not available.
- Inquiries and requests for any records regarding
  Anna have been made to area hospitals, prisons, homeless shelters, coroner's offices, urgent
  care centers, and planned parenthood facilities.
  Our record search only included the past five

years and, as of now, there is no indication that Anna received treatment at any medical facilities located within a two-hour radius during the past five years. All facilities have been asked to keep a lookout for Anna.

- Anna's social media accounts are being monitored for any activity. If she makes any contact with friends or family through social media, our department will be made aware of it immediately.

Security Camera Footage

- Footage from security cameras at Macklemore High School and her place of employment, Sub Station, have been obtained and are being reviewed by our team.
- At this time, we have learned that the school's camera shows Anna walking down the pathway that leads to the parking lot where her car is parked at approximately 3:20 p.m. There is no camera footage with a view of the parking lot where Anna parked her car.
- Any further information of interest gained from the security cameras will be included in this file as appropriate.

I can hear my mom making coffee in the kitchen, jazz music playing in the background. Our normal routine has resumed, and I can't say I hate it. It's nice to have her back. I drag myself out from under the covers and pull my hair back into a ponytail before shuffling into the kitchen to greet her.

"Well, there you are. I didn't hear you come in last night."

"Welcome back, Mom," I say, wrapping my arms around her waist.

I let her go, then sit down on the barstool. With my elbows on the counter and my chin in my hands, I watch my mom as she puts two English muffins in the toaster. In her white silk robe and silver jewelry, she matches the décor perfectly. She's the picture of trendiness, right down to her Coach slippers and the expensive oven she never uses.

She pulls out a butter knife and some jam, her movements fluid and familiar. She notices me staring and pauses, placing her hand on her hip.

"Something bothering you?"

I want to force my mouth to say, "No." I want to tell her that everything is fine.

"Umm," I hesitate.

My mom stares me down and says, "Umm... what?"

I have to come clean. I have to just lay it all out there. I take a deep breath and let the words spill out, bracing myself for her reaction.

"I've been looking at the missing person's file for Anna."

"You what?" my mom says incredulously. "Why in the world would you do a thing like that?"

"Because I miss her!" I retort.

"Well, I miss her too. That doesn't mean—"

My mom is about to put a lid on this discussion, and me.

"You act like she never existed! You moved us out of our house and packed away all her things. Did you ever stop to think how I might feel about any of that?"

"How dare you? I am her mother. You have no idea how it feels to lose your own child."

My face flushes and my hands start shaking. I know this is the end of the conversation, the part where I apologize for hurting her and promise to never bring it up again. I know what I'm supposed to do, but I just can't seem to do it.

"No, Mom, but I do know what it's like to lose my sister and my best friend."

My mom doesn't say anything. Her eyes linger on me for a moment, agitated yet cold, before turning around to open the jam jar. She starts spreading jam on the English muffins with force and determination, ignoring me entirely.

"You can't pretend like it never happened."

She slides the knife over the bread again and again, ripping the muffin into shreds.

"Mom! Look at me. You can't ignore this anymore. Any of it."

My mom twists the lid on the jar and shoves it onto a shelf in the fridge. She tosses the knife into the sink, where it clangs loudly—her way of saying that the discussion is finished. I can feel my anger rising, threatening to erupt. I can't go on like this anymore.

"I know Anna was unhappy. I know you and her fought all the time and that she felt like she was never good enough for you. And I know all about your affair and dad's blackouts and—"

"Stop it, Katie!" my mom screams.

An awful silence settles over us. As it does, my fury drains away. I feel terrible about saying all those things. I wish I knew how to keep my mouth shut. I wish I could just move on and pretend like everything is fine. I wish I could be more like Anna.

I've never seen my mom like this before. She's leaning over the sink, her head hanging limply. Her hair falls all over the place. She doesn't move.

"I'm sorry," I say softly, unsure if it's enough.

I hear her inhale sharply, then her head flips up. There are tears in her eyes.

She runs her fingers under her eyelids, ensuring her mascara hasn't smudged. Then she sits down next to me at the counter. Side by side, we stare out past the space in front of us and into another time.

"Why are you doing this?"

"I just don't understand what happened, Mom. I feel like the most important person in my life was ripped away from me and I have no idea why. I just thought if I knew more about what happened... I don't know. Maybe I could start making sense of things. Of me."

"There's no sense to be made, Katie."

"The file has all kinds of things in it about—"

"You can't go believing everything you read. That incompetent detective spent a few weeks poking around in our business, scribbling notes and making guesses. He doesn't know our family and, besides, he never brought Anna back. So what good is he—or his file?" she says venomously. "Anyway, does it really matter anymore? Whatever answers you find aren't going to change the last six years, are they?"

"I guess not. It's just—"

"I think your time would be better spent thinking about your future, don't you?" my mom says as she stands up. "September is going to be here before you know it. There's nothing back there for us, Katie."

My chest deflates as I rest my face on the counter. I can't believe she's going to turn all of this around on me. I can't believe she's going to avoid talking about Anna, yet again, and then remind me I'm being evicted in two months. I'm so glad I didn't tell her about losing my job. She'd have a field day with that one.

After she leaves the room and I hear her shower turn on, I search through my bag for my mint container. I take it over to the junk drawer and rummage through a mishmash of vitamins, batteries, and business cards. Finally, I spot her prescription bottles. I shake out a few of each and put them in my mint container, except for one that goes directly down my throat. Then, I shove one of the forgotten English muffins in my mouth.

February 25, 2012

I am such an idiot. What was I thinking? I totally humiliated myself tonight and I don't even understand why. I am such an idiot! We had such a great time at the party last week, and he even gave me my first kiss, which was perfect, by the way. It was just like I thought it would be. I felt his kiss spread like fire from my lips all the way down to my toes. It was pure magic. And now I've ruined everything.

The whole time we were out tonight, I kept thinking about what he wanted from me. It was our second date, and I figured he was expecting something. We only kissed at Danté's party. Everyone does more than that. So I couldn't stop worrying about what I should do. I couldn't just be in the moment. I couldn't just act like a normal person and have fun. Oh no, I had to be all smiles and laughter on the surface while my insides churned like lava. I ruined everything. I know it.

It wasn't too bad during the movie, probably because we were in the dark. He held my hand and we shared popcorn. I can't even remember what the movie was about... I was too busy obsessing over Jacob and whether he liked me... and what was next... and whether my boobs were big enough.

Afterwards, he took me to hang out with his friends. I could tell they were looking at me funny. At first, all I could think of was the stupid things Maddie posted and how these guys had already made up their minds about me. And then it occurred to me that I looked ridiculous.

I was wearing a skin-tight sleeveless dress that hugged every part of my terrified body. I was sucked in as far as I could be without losing consciousness. My hair was fully blown out with loose curls bouncing all around my face like I was a model for hair products. Oh, and my face. I had caked on layers of makeup and even applied a pair of fake eyelashes to add drama to my look. Those stupid things bothered me so much I kept winking like I was having a seizure. To top it all off, I wore three-inch wedges that, instead of making me seem chic and tall, made me walk like I was on stilts. I wasn't sexy. I was a dork dressing up for Halloween. I should have just written "trying too hard" across my forehead and posted my own picture online.

I felt so weird about my outfit that I became mute. Other than smiling and laughing like a hyena, I was completely silent. It was horrible. When I realized I was not speaking at all, I tried to say things, but they came out stupid. I said things like, "What do you guys do for fun?" and "What teacher do you have for English?" They looked at me as if I was an alien. It was a complete Dirty Dancing moment—and not the one where he plucks her out from the table and says, "No one puts Baby in a corner." The one where she says, "I carried a watermelon."

I could tell he was losing interest in me and that he thought I was a complete loser. It was so obvious the way he looked at me. His friends were definitely freezing me out in this cooler-than-thou way, which made it even worse. It was like I couldn't figure out the code. I was supposed to say something, do something, or be something to fit in with them. It was torture standing there, acting like I was having a good time and trying to be some version of me that they would like.

I failed, obviously. That became clear when Jacob said we should head out. He handled it really casually, telling his friends that we had to split. They couldn't have cared less that I was leaving. I felt like I was exploding inside. Here I was with Jacob Hunt, the most gorgeous boy at our school, and I was screwing everything up. I wanted him to like me so badly.

I know it was silly, but I wanted to be inside

a John Green book. I wanted him to fall for me, despite the odds. I wanted him to see into my soul and say, "I see you, and you are beautiful." I wanted him to take me into his arms and kiss me underneath the stars, slow dance with no music at all, and say that he will never be the same now that he knows me. For days, I had built up this date in my head to be the beginning of a love story, where the popular jock falls madly in love with the shy, quirky girl he has grown up alongside, but never really knew... until one glorious night when the planets aligned and two hearts melted into one.

Obviously, I have seen one too many movies and read too many books because that was not happening at all. I don't even know what was happening. All I knew was that I had to do something, and talking was clearly not getting me anywhere. I couldn't let him lose interest in me after only two dates.

When he pulled the car in front of my house, he put his Mustang in park and ran his fingers through his devastatingly thick hair with an air of disappointment. I could feel him slipping away as he gazed out the windshield instead of at me. The gentle letdown was already forming on his lips. I was already flustered, but in that moment,

I went into a full panic attack and did the first thing that came to me. I plunged right down there. You know... there.

He seemed cool with it, so I guess I was doing the right thing. It didn't feel right, though. I started going out of my mind. I was so confused and overwhelmed, and suddenly, I couldn't do it anymore. I jerked away from him and started crying like a child. Uggggh. I was absolutely mortified.

He was really sweet. He held me and told me it was okay, but I know he was lying. I could just imagine him telling his friends all about it and how they would laugh at me. They already thought I was a complete disaster as it was. I made him promise not to tell, but who knows if he will or not? I can't trust him to keep this a secret. I'm the worst. I'm the absolute worst. I want to die. I just want to die.

I probably don't have any business with a guy like Jacob anyway. I wish I could run away to a place where someone understands me. Like Dorothy wishing she could fly over the rainbow, I wish I could fly away from here so my troubles could melt like lemon drops—or whatever she says.

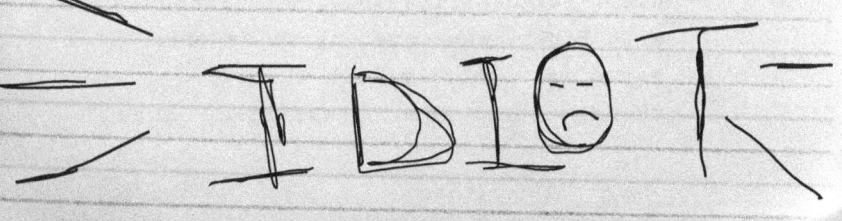

INTERVIEW WITH MACKLEMORE
HIGH STUDENT, JACOB HUNT

Monday, April 23, 2012, 12:10 p.m.
Transcribed from Digital Recording

JC: Officer John Christiansen

JH: Jacob Hunt

JC: Begin recording. Hello, Jacob. Thank you for meeting with me.

JH: Hey.

JC: Do you know why you are here?

JH: Yeah, I know. You're the guy asking all the questions about Anna, right?

JC: Right.

JH: Well, I didn't do anything.

JC: I am not saying that you did. I'm just here to ask everyone some questions so that we can find out what happened and bring Anna back.

JH: Okay, but I'm telling the truth.

JC: Alright. How about you tell me your truth?

JH: Okay. It goes like this. I'm friends with Piper, who comes up to me one day after school to ask what I thought about Anna. I was like, 'Anna

who?' She said there was a new girl
on the squad named Anna. I figured
out who she was and knew her from
growing up and all that, but I didn't
know her, know her. You know?

JC: I do.

JH: So I was like, 'I don't know what I
think about her. I don't even know
her.' Piper started saying how great
she was and how pretty she is now.
She asked me if I would take her out.
I said I didn't know if it was a good
idea and all, but Piper is the kind
of girl who is hard to say no to. So
I said I would.

JC: You asked her out?

JH: Yeah, I asked her to go to this party
together. We get there, and Anna is
totally not into me. Like, at all.
She barely looks at me, stares at her
feet, and keeps like three feet of
distance between us.

JC: Was she nervous?

JH: Yeah, I guess. I'm thinking, what am
I doing with this girl? So I figure I
should take her outside away from the
party to make her more comfortable.
I take her to the backyard, and we
sit around the patio table talking.
By the end of the night, things were
going great, and I kissed her.

JC: Then what happened?

JH: We texted and talked a little at school. Then I asked her out the following weekend. We went to the movies and grabbed burritos afterward. I took her to Chuy's, where most of the guys hang out on Saturday. I thought she'd have fun, but she started acting weird.

JC: Why do you think she acted weird?

JH: I think it was because Piper dressed her for the night. She seemed really uncomfortable.

JC: Did she relax eventually?

JH: Not really. That's why I decided to take her out of there. I figured we could have some alone time to talk like we did at Danté's party. Except, everything changed.

JC: How so?

JH: When I pulled in to park in front of her house, she leaned over to go... you know... downtown. I did not see that coming. Usually, I'm the one pushing things along, but this girl was ready to go. Then, out of nowhere, she started crying.

JC: Why?

JH: I don't know. I told her we didn't have to do anything she didn't want to do. I put my arm around her and told her it was no big deal, trying to calm her down and all that.

JC: Did she calm down?

JH: Yeah, she finally did. I didn't know
        what to do except hold her. After a
        few minutes, she said she had to go.
        She said thanks for a great time and
        then told me we probably shouldn't
        see each other again. I told her it
        wasn't a big deal, but if that's what
        she wanted.

JC: Did you talk to Anna after that?

JH: No, not really. We said 'hi' when
        we saw each other, but that's about
        it. It was awkward, especially when
        people asked what happened. I wasn't
        going to tell them what went on, but
        it made it even more weird.

JC: At any point, did she tell you
        anything about her home life or her
        personal life?

JH: Not really. We just had a good time
        hanging out. We didn't get into that
        stuff.

JC: Alright. Do you know if she drinks or
        does drugs?

JH: I think she had a drink or two. No
        drugs that I know about. She's not
        like that.

JC: Okay, Jacob. That's all I need from
        you right now.

JH: Okay, good.

JC: If you think of anything else, call

me. Here's my card.

JH: Okay. Hey, Officer Christiansen? You
don't think something bad happened to
her, do you?

JC: I'm just here to collect information,
not give opinions.

JH: I'm just saying, it would be a shame.
She's kind of a cool girl, I mean,
once you get to know her.

JC: I agree.

Text Exchange between
Jacob Hunt and Anna Williams

February 26, 2012

JH Hey, you ok?

AW I'm fine. Sorry about Sat.

JH It's cool.

AW Not really—epic fail. Total embarrassment.

JH Do you wanna talk about it?

AW No. I'm fine, really.

JH Ok.

AW Thanks, though.

JH Anytime. We good?

AW Yaass!!

JH Cool.

AW Cool.

March 1, 2012

I have been avoiding Jacob at school, which hopefully I won't have to do anymore. I've also avoided Piper's questions enough that she's dropped it for the most part. After the whole thing with Maddie, I don't know how much more I can take.

It's taken all of my strength to go to class and act like I'm fine, when I'm having a complete breakdown inside. Maybe now that I texted Jacob and made him feel better, I can walk right past him and say "hi" as if I never humiliated myself in front of him.

That is, if I can get out of bed. I'm getting that sinking feeling again, the one where I feel way too tired to move. It's like I swallowed a ton of rocks. I feel like the walls are closing in and my arms are too difficult to lift. I just want to lie in the bed all day with the curtains closed.

It's like the world is brightly colored for everyone else, but for me it's in black and white. Everything is hazy and it seems like nothing will ever get better. Sometimes I get a glimpse of this beautiful world filled with possibilities, and I want to go after it at full speed, but the feeling never stays. I always end up sinking down, down, down to this horrible sinkhole where the world is awful and scary and people suck.

I snuck more of my mom's happy pills, but they haven't done much yet. I feel relaxed, but not happy. I think I'll take a couple more to do the trick. Maybe by tomorrow, I'll be ready to face the world again.

Oh shoot. I forgot tomorrow is our student council meeting. I am so tired of being Piper's assistant. It's like she talks and talks while I do all the work. I have to make all these great ideas just happen, but no one knows how much work it is to do it all. I have to organize everything, shop for decorations and snacks or whatever, and then presto! Piper is a genius. I love her, but this is getting really tiring.

Forget tomorrow. Let's think about Thursday. Thursday I work after school. Shayna and Damien always make me laugh, which is good. Maybe my favorite customer will be there. Maybe he'll tell me how pretty I am again... Maybe he will sing to me while standing on top of the tables. A girl can hope.

But today, I listen to music from under the covers.

Oh, Anna.

I wish I could remember more about what happened during those months before she disappeared. So much was happening in her life. This whole thing with Jacob was more intense than I remember, and it was going on at the same time as her fight with Maddie. Throw in Piper and whatever her intentions were, and I can't imagine what Anna was thinking or feeling.

I feel awful, like I should have been there for her more. I knew she was sad sometimes. I knew she was moody over stuff, but I never asked her about it. If I did, I'm sure I didn't listen enough to her answers. Or maybe I let her fool me with her fake "I'm fine" routine. I was such a terrible sister. I always came to her with my problems, asking her to help me with this or that. I was so selfish. If only I had tried harder to let her know how much I loved her, how much I cared. Maybe things would be different.

It makes me livid to think that a bunch of ridiculous teenage drama could have pushed my sister over the edge. If these mean girls had anything to do with her disappearance, I can't even begin to feel the rage welling up inside of me. You see this crap online all the time. Kids are depressed and suicidal because their entire social life is destroyed over a couple pictures or a few nasty words. It's wrong and we all know it, but somehow it keeps happening. It's almost like a nature documentary where some animal is turning on its own kind, battling to the death over some stupid stature in the pack.

I never would have thought these stupid girls could get to her. She always saw through their ridiculousness. Anna was strong, the strongest person I know. She always held it together. She always seemed totally in control. She had straight A's and never missed cheer practice. She had an after-school job and took care of everything around our house. Without her, none of us would have had clean clothes to wear.

I thought she was impenetrable, a human in Teflon form. Clearly, she wasn't. She was depressed. Did my mom not notice? Did she and Anna ever talk about this? Probably not... I wouldn't. But if I was as sad as Anna, I really hope I would have. My mom sent me to that therapist, so maybe she could have sent Anna to talk to someone.

I just can't understand how she was able to keep all these feelings inside of her without any of us knowing. I suppose they are just feelings. Feelings get the better of me all the time, except I wind up screaming them out to whoever will listen. I have no filter.

What scares me the most is how crazy Anna seems to have been acting back then—and I had no idea. She had those fits after talking to my dad, which is totally weirding me out. She was having nightmares, and her writing is so depressed—saying she wanted to run away or sleep forever. Was she serious? Was she exaggerating, or was she actually suicidal? And how many of my mom's pills was she taking? Is it even possible that Anna had a drug problem?

There's no way. I take my mom's pills all the time. I've had nightmares for six years, and I constantly fantasize about running away. I'm not going to kill myself or end up a homeless drug addict.

INTERVIEW WITH MACKLEMORE
HIGH STUDENT, JACK NELSON

Monday, April 23, 2012, 12:45 p.m.
Transcribed from Digital Recording

JC: Officer John Christiansen

JN: Jack Nelson

JC: Begin recording. Hello, Jack. I'm here to ask you a few questions about Anna. Is that alright?

JN: Yes, sir.

JC: I'm Officer Christiansen. As you probably know by now, I spoke with your mother already, and now I'm hoping to talk with you. About Anna.

JN: Yes, sir.

JC: You can call me John if it makes you more comfortable.

JN: No, sir.

JC: Okay, let's get started.

JN: Okay, sir.

JC: Stop calling me sir.

JN: Oh, okay.

JC: Alright. How about you start by telling me about how you know Anna. I understand you are neighbors?

JN: Yes. We've been neighbors since we were little. She moved in when I was five or six, I think. We basically grew up together. We rode the bus together to the same school, and we spent time going back and forth between each other's houses. I guess we were more like brother and sister for a while.

JC: Can you tell me what she was like when she was little?

JN: I'm not sure how to answer that. We liked to run around outside and play tag. We played house and orphan and all sorts of pretend games. I don't know what you want me to say, exactly.

JC: Well, how's her home life?

JN: It was okay, I guess. Things were pretty normal before her parents divorced. She was close with her dad. They did things together all the time, which made me kind of jealous since my dad worked a lot. Her mom has always been, I don't know, kind of out there.

JC: What do you mean 'out there'?

JN: Mrs. Williams is nice and all, but she doesn't really seem like a mom most of the time. I think that's why Anna always wanted to be with her dad.

JC: I understand that changed at some point. Anna's relationship with her dad.

FINE

JN: Yeah, Anna just started hating him
        one day.

JC: Did she ever talk about what happened
        between her and her dad?

JN: No. She acted like she wanted to talk
        sometimes, but then she would clam
        up and say she was fine. I knew she
        wasn't fine, though.

JC: How did you know?

JN: I just knew.

JC: Her parents split up around that
        time, right?

JN: Yeah.

JC: Did she have a hard time with the
        divorce?

JN: I don't really remember. I think she
        was just glad the fighting stopped.

JC: You mean, her parents fighting?

JN: She would say things like, 'There
        they go again' or 'I just can't take
        it anymore.' I would ask her about
        it, but she wouldn't say anything
        else. The only time she let loose
        about her feelings was after her
        mom... Well, her mom...

JC: I know about her mother's infidelity.
        Is that what you are referring to?

[Coughing sounds]

JC: Do you want some water, Jack?

JN: No, I'm fine.

JC: Were you referring to what happened
        between Anna's mother and another
        man?

JN: Yes. I didn't know if... Well, anyway,
        I remember the day it happened.

JC: Tell me what happened that day.

JN: We both got off the bus together and
        ran to our own houses. Then, she
        came running out her front door and
        headed straight for the row of trees
        at the end of our block. We always
        played there as kids.

JC: What did you do?

JN: I didn't know what to do, so I just
        sat down next to her.

[Pause]

JC: Do you think there is anyone who
        would want to hurt her?

JN: No. No one.

JC: Do you think she would ever hurt
        herself?

JN: No. Well... no.

JC: Why did you hesitate?

[Heavy breathing, tapping of fingers on the
table]

JC: Jack, why did you hesitate?

JN: No reason.

JC: Listen, Jack. Every bit of
        information is important, no matter
        what it is. I can't do my job if I

don't know absolutely everything. If
you care about Anna, you need to tell
me everything.

[Fingers tapping]

JN: Okay.

[Deep exhale]

JN: I guess I hesitated because she's
        been acting kind of funny. It's just
        that, well, she's been doing things
        she wouldn't normally do.

JC: Like what?

JN: Like partying with a new crowd. She
        got a tattoo on her side that her mom
        definitely doesn't know about.

JC: Anything else?

JN: Sometimes she seems all over the
        place, acting like she's high or
        something. I don't know.

JC: Was she on drugs?

JN: No, I don't think so.

JC: Does she do drugs?

JN: No.

JC: What about alcohol?

JN: No.

JC: Did she exhibit any other odd
        behaviors?

JN: She seemed to stop eating altogether.
        She was skinny, not scary skinny, but
        really thin. One night she and Katie
        had dinner at my house, and she kept

moving her food around her plate.
I half joked about her becoming
anorexic or something. She got all
defensive and told me to mind my own
business.

JC: Did you ever mention your concern
over her eating habits or the tattoo
to anyone else, like your mother or
Anna's mother?

JN: No. Anna would kill me. She's a
different person around me. I think
that was because we've known each
other for so long and we couldn't
pretend we hadn't seen each other
changing out of our swimsuits as
kids. That kind of history makes
it impossible to hide some of
your quirks. If I'd told anyone,
especially her mother, she would have
hated me forever. I'm pretty sure
she actually said, 'Tell anyone and
you're dead.' I wouldn't betray her
trust like that.

JC: Do you know if she ever engaged in
self-harming behaviors?

JN: Like cutting or something?

JC: Yes.

JN: No.

JC: What sorts of things do you and Anna
talk about?

JN: We talk about all kinds of stuff.

JC: Do you spend time together at school?

JN: No. She shies away from me at school,
        but she's been doing that since
        eighth grade. She and Maddie were
        always together, but when Maddie was
        too busy with soccer or art classes,
        Anna hung out with me after school.
        She didn't like to go home, and my
        house was pretty much a second home
        to her and Katie. That was before
        cheerleading, though. Now she's with
        Piper twenty-four/seven.

JC: Does she talk about her father?

JN: Sometimes. She talked about how she
        missed him, but she hated him. She
        struggled with that a lot.

JC: Why does Anna hate him?

JN: I don't really know. It probably had
        to do with his drinking.

JC: Did she ever mention if he, or anyone
        else, had ever hurt her?

JN: No.

JC: Did Anna ever share what happened
        with Jacob Hunt with you?

JN: No. We haven't talked that much
        lately.

JC: Did it surprise you that she was
        dating him?

JN: Not really. It seemed only natural
        that she would pair off with some
        football player. It's the same plot in
        every teen movie, and she's seen all

of them, so why wouldn't every girl
want to transform themselves into the
hot cheerleader with the quarterback
boyfriend?

JC: Did you talk to her about her
        transformation?

JN: I made some sarcastic comment once,
        which didn't go over well.

JC: How so?

JN: I don't know, I guess I hit a nerve.
        She was really sensitive after the
        whole Maddie thing. You know, being a
        poser and all that.

JC: Do you think she's depressed?

JN: I don't know. Maybe. It's hard to know
        because she usually acts so happy. I
        know she was sad sometimes, though.
        I think she feels like she has to
        be what everyone else wants her to
        be. We all do sometimes. But for her,
        it was all the time. That's a lot to
        carry around, so I think she just
        gets heavy with all the pretending.
        When we hang out, or when we used to,
        she's just herself.

    [Sigh, clears throat]

JN: I don't know if that answers your
        question or not. I guess I'm trying to
        say that I don't think she's depressed.
        I think she's just sad sometimes...
        for good reason, and maybe for other
        reasons I don't even know.

JC: Did you see her this past Friday at
      school?

JN: I saw her in passing. She seemed
      normal.

JC: Did you see her after school?

JN: No. We have history together with Mr.
      Jones last period, but we usually go
      our separate ways after. On Friday,
      I took the bus since I don't have a
      car yet. Sometimes she'll give me a
      ride if she doesn't have cheerleading
      or after-school stuff to do, but not
      often.

JC: So you didn't see her walking to her
      car?

JN: No, I saw her walking towards the
      back parking lot. Mr. Jones's class
      is near the back lot, but I was
      heading to the front of the school
      where the buses park. I nodded to her
      and she smiled. That was it.

JC: Is there anything that you haven't
      told me that you would like to?

JN: No. Except... Well, there is nothing
      wrong with Anna. She's just like the
      rest of us, you know?

JC: What do you mean exactly?

JN: You don't know how it is for
      teenagers these days. All of us grew
      up in this bubble where everything's
      safe and sound. Then one day, you
      reach this magical age—or if you're

<blockquote>

unlucky, something bad happens first—
and the bubble bursts.

</blockquote>

JC: The bubble bursts?

JN: Yeah. All of a sudden, the world
comes flooding in. There's war,
mass shootings, constant violence,
sexual weirdos, unstable economies,
no jobs, healthcare crises, lying
politicians, terrifying illnesses,
epidemics, racism, transgender
issues... you get the point. All
sorts of issues come on our radar,
and we're expected to embrace it as a
part of our world overnight. Parents
and teachers just expect you to roll
with it like it's always been a part
of life, except it hasn't.

JC: So do you think Anna felt the same
way?

JN: I know she did. She felt it more than
most of us for some reason. It's a
lot of pressure.

JC: What do you mean by pressure?

JN: The pressure to be these perfect,
well-rounded adults who are ready
for whatever the world has in store
for us—except no one knows what the
world will be like by the time we're
running it.

JC: Has she been really stressed out?

JN: Yeah. She's definitely stressed. She has
the added pressure of cheerleading and

student council, but otherwise, we all
know what it's like.

JC: Okay, I think that's all I need from
you. You can go back to class.

JN: Okay. Thanks.

Email exchange between Anna Williams
and Jack Nelson Dated January 14, 2012

- -

To: Jack Nelson
From: Anna Williams
Date: January 14, 2012, 11:54 p.m.
Subject: Midnight Ramblings

I can't sleep, so I'm going to harass you with the crazy thoughts that are keeping me up tonight. Lucky you! So here it is. Why is college important to anyone anymore? Before you roll your eyes, I am being totally serious. I don't see how four more years of learning is going to do me any good. It would be different if I knew what I wanted to do. You want to be some astronaut space engineer or whatever, so it makes sense for you to go. But me? I have no freaking idea. I might end up at Sub Station forever.

I know, I know, it doesn't ever hurt to be educated. I get that, but being educated doesn't exactly pay the bills. We have seen enough kids get stuck in the crevasse between graduation day and actually living life on their own, right? Kim down the street is still living with her parents and she's twenty-six. No privacy, no independence, and no plans. College didn't get her into her own apartment. I can't pay for college in the first place, let alone life afterwards with all those student loans. You probably don't have to worry about that, do you? Your folks are probably paying for everything, right? I'm sure they are, don't answer that. You know my mom won't. She'll tell everyone that I got into these great schools, but she won't help me actually go to one of them.

So I have no idea what I want to do and no way to pay for anything without tons of grants and scholarships. So why bother?

To: Anna Williams
From: Jack Nelson
Date: January 15, 2012, 12:14 a.m.
Subject: Midnight Ramblings

Lucky you – I am still up. Why are you torturing yourself over this right now? You don't have to worry about this for months. You just need to show up at school, get decent grades, and take it a day at a time. You'll figure it out. And if you don't, I'll help you. Seriously, Anna, people find ways to get through college and you will, too. Plus, you're so smart, you'll probably get a free ride.

To: Jack Nelson
From: Anna Williams
Date: January 15, 2012, 12:20 a.m.
Subject: Midnight Ramblings

That's just it. If I don't study hard and get good grades, I won't get into the college of my choice, which means

I won't be able to focus on that one specific major they are known for, which means I will never get that exact opportunity, which means I will forever regret my life choices. And I'll lose any scholarship money I get. That's the reasoning as far as I can see. One bad test and that particular path in life is doomed. It's stupid.

- -

To: Anna Williams
From: Jack Nelson
Date: January 15, 2012, 12:26 a.m.
Subject: Midnight Ramblings

You need to breathe. It's not all that bad. You just need to focus on what you like. What do you care about? What makes you happy? Don't forget, you can always be a Dallas Cheerleader. Or a party planner. ;)

- -

To: Jack Nelson
From: Anna Williams
Date: January 15, 2012, 12:34 a.m.
Subject: Midnight Ramblings

Umm, no.
I don't know what I like. Or what I care about. Sometimes I think I'm never going to amount to anything. Other times I feel like I'm meant to do something amazing like joining the Peace Corps or Teach for America. Maybe I could be a social worker and help kids or old people.

Maybe I could work to end poverty or be a civil rights
lawyer. Or maybe my dad can put in a good word for me
or introduce me to someone in the film industry. Owning
a bakery could be fun. I'd probably like being a mom to a
bunch of kids, but that doesn't pay. Actually, cheerleading
and party planning doesn't sound too bad either.
What color is my parachute? Rainbow.

To: Anna Williams
From: Jack Nelson
Date: January 15, 2012, 12:41 a.m.
Subject: Midnight Ramblings

Well, Miss Sarcasm, that book was actually very helpful.
I'll tell my mom you're glad she loaned it to you.
Look, you like lots of stuff. Maybe that's your problem.
You're too colorful inside. Maybe you should wear that on
the outside—it might be a nice change from your cheerleading outfit. You don't need to choose one color for the
rest of your life, you know? You can just try different ones
out and see what happens.

To: Jack Nelson
From: Anna Williams
Date: January 15, 2012, 1:00 a.m.
Subject: Midnight Ramblings

I guess you're right. I just wish it didn't feel so intense. I
just need to relax about the whole thing. Thanks, Jack.
I'm glad you were up.

FILE CONTROL NO. 23167
MISSING PERSON – ANNA WILLIAMS
Note to File completed by Officer Christiansen on April 23, 2012, 2:15 p.m.

PREMISES SEARCH

A thorough search of Macklemore High School was conducted on April 23, 2012. All known spaces were searched, including all classrooms, dumpsters, restrooms, hallways, custodian closets, media rooms, library, cafeteria, auditorium, outdoor quad area, and resource buildings. No evidence was found in any of these locations. Officers expanded the search to include the surrounding areas, including the fields and trees directly surrounding the school and the neighborhood adjacent. As of this report, there has been no sign of Anna Williams.

Officers are joining forces with community volunteers in a search for Anna Williams. Lidia Stephenson, a friend of the Williams family, has enlisted the assistance of the Rotary Club, the Lions Club, the Buena Vida YMCA, and a variety of other community groups and individuals to assist in searching for Anna Williams. The community members have been working in small groups in the neighborhoods near Anna's home and school. Officers have been instructed to coordinate with Lidia Stephenson to avoid duplication and streamline their efforts.

A complete search of Anna's car was completed. The black Honda Civic she drove to school that day does not appear to have been tampered with in any way. All items inside the car, and the car itself, are undisturbed. The doors were locked and a search of the vehicle revealed nothing suspicious. Items found in the vehicle include chewing gum, an empty cardboard coffee cup, a phone charger, two flavored lip balms, several hair ties, a Sub Station polo shirt, an empty can of Red Bull, two school library books, a stuffed bear, a string of beads hanging from the rearview mirror, and a pair of running shoes.

Anna's locker was searched as well. Binders, books, and folders were recovered and looked through for any scribbling, notes, or other clues. Nothing of import was found. In addition to school supplies like pens, highlighters, etc., we recovered a shirt for cheerleading, lipstick, foundation compact, and a Starbucks Double Shot. The keys for the Honda Civic and Anna's cell phone were not recovered.

INTERVIEW WITH MACKLEMORE HIGH
ENGLISH TEACHER APRIL RHODES

Monday, April 23, 2012, 3:35 p.m.
Transcribed from Digital Recording

JC: Officer Christiansen

AR: April Rhodes

JC: Hello, Mrs. Rhodes.

AR: Officer Christiansen, it's nice to meet you. I'm glad we could meet this afternoon. I do hope I can be of some help. This whole thing is just so awful.

JC: Let's get started, then.

AR: Yes, let's begin.

JC: Tell me what you know about Anna Williams.

AR: Anna is in my fourth period Honors English class. She is an A student and always hands in excellent work. She is very creative in her writing and a joy to have in class.

JC: What makes her a joy in class?

AR: Well, she's very smart, and I know if I call on her, she'll give me a solid answer. That helps when you have a room full of smart-mouths ready to fire something outlandish if given the opportunity. It also saves me when I can tell that no one is prepared, because Anna is always prepared. She's one of those quiet, polite kids who make it so much easier to teach. She makes you feel like you're doing something worthwhile, you know?

JC: What does she do to make you feel that way?

AR: Oh, I don't know. She always makes a point to thank me after class. She pays attention when I speak, and I can tell she's been listening when I read her assignments. I swear half the class doesn't hear a word I'm saying most of the time.

JC: Have you spent any time with Anna one-on-one?

AR: No. We did meet after school to discuss letters of recommendation for college. I asked her specific questions so I could make the letter read more personally, which colleges like. I asked about her hobbies and interests so that I knew what to plug in. She was very helpful and appreciative.

JC: Has she shown any signs of distress?

AR: Honestly, I haven't seen any change in her. She seems a bit stressed out, but so many teens do, now.

JC: Does she seem troubled?

AR: No, not that I noticed.

JC: Does she seem to have lost a lot of weight?

AR: Well, now that you mention it... she does seem thin. Much thinner than at the beginning of the year.

JC: Does she ever act out?

AR: No, never. I've never had to tell her to stop talking, scold her about missed assignments, or anything else. She is really a top-notch student.

JC: Have you noticed any change in her behavior lately? Perhaps a change in her clothes or her friends?

AR: I don't generally pay attention to any of that. I'm concerned with how well they know Shakespeare and E.E. Cummings, not what the current fashion trends happen to be or what groups are popular now.

JC: Has her work been consistent?

AR: Yes. Her work has been fine, except one paper I had to give her a C on. That was unusual, though.

JC: Has she—

AR: I spoke with Anna after class about that paper, actually. I wanted to be sure that she wasn't falling into any bad habits. Sometimes students will suddenly slack off as they head into

their senior year, and I do my best
to keep them on track.

JC: How did she respond?

AR: She was embarrassed, I think. She
didn't say much at all, but it was
clearly upsetting for her.

JC: Other than that C paper, has she been
handing in things on time and doing
acceptable work?

AR: Well, now that you mention it, her
work has changed a bit in the last
few months. She's usually so deep and
poetic, but not lately. You should
see her personal statement, though.
Now that was something.

JC: What's that?

AR: Every year I have the students write
their personal statement for college
applications as an assignment. I
think it helps them put their best
foot forward.

JC: Oh. Can I have a copy of it?

AR: Of course.

JC: Is there anything else you want to
add?

AR: I wish there was. I just want Anna
to be found and brought back home.
She has such a bright future waiting
for her.

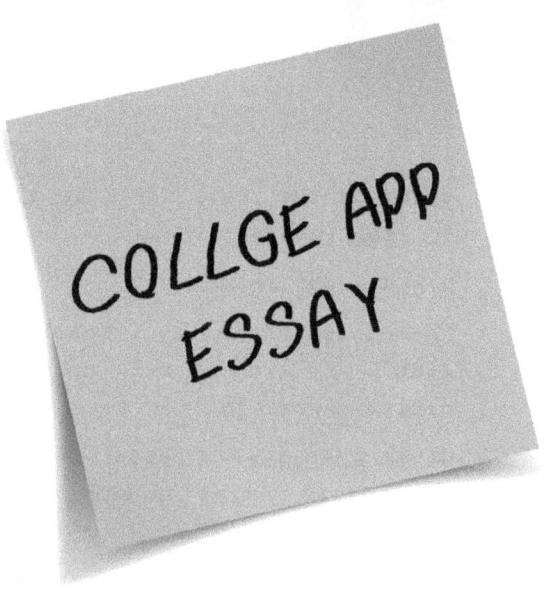

PERSONAL STATEMENT—ROUGH DRAFT

Mrs. Rhodes

English, p. 4

3/5/2012

People always talk about teenagers being angry, hard-to-control aliens who are impossible to understand. We're just a bunch of raw emotion without any clue as to how to harness it, making us prone to outbursts and exasperation. We're no picnic to be around, because one moment we're on top of the world and in touch with our greater purpose, and the next we're sobbing over running out of shampoo. We are a bunch of drama queens, highly sensitive to unfairness and hypocrisy. We have eye-rolling attitude. We think we're invincible superheroes and hold unrealistic expectations. People say these things like it's a bad thing to be a teenager, but it's not.

I think we're trying to figure things out, just like everyone else. We're discovering who we are and what we believe. Our brains are questioning the world around us, the people in charge, and why any of it matters. Everyone struggles with good versus evil, fate versus free will, and God/Allah/ Great Spirit/Whatever You Call the Divine Creator or Creatively Inspired Evolution Expert versus absolute chaos. Most people have stopped grappling with these enormous ideas, but teenagers are submerged in them. Whether in history class or at a football game, we are in it knee-deep.

Teenagers are thinking about all of these things, trying to understand why the world is so crazy. Our eyes are being opened to war, racism, and poverty. We're learning about complicated issues of climate change, technology, and all kinds of other things that are wholly out of our control. We're wondering why the adults in charge haven't found a way to solve any of it. And while we contemplate all this, we're trying to have some fun and make some memories.

The truth is, everything is complicated. That's why we're all stressed out and anxious. Gone are the days when we can look at our parents for answers and know, for certain, that they have them. There are no clear answers. We're all just guessing and hoping to make the right moves. No one likes to admit that they don't know what they are doing. No one likes to admit that everything is complicated and just a breath away from being out of control. I think that's why no one likes teenagers—we embody that.

However, teenagers also embody the excitement of living in the moment, even if it is a complicated one. Teenagers are used to swinging from one extreme to another. We are bold and daring, and we would rather think about what can be, not what can't. We are angry at the greed and selfishness of those in power, angry enough to want to do something about it. We have unrealistic expectations that life can be more fair, more kind, and more equal for all.

More than that, we are just crazy enough to dream up ideas that everyone else tells us are a waste of time. We don't listen when people tell us something can't be done. We are insubordinate renegades, ready to make the world a better place. Or at least a more interesting one.

I am proud to be a teenager, but that's not all I am. I'm also a philosopher, a cheerleader, a student body leader, a part-time sub builder, a writer, a movie fanatic, a sister, and a daughter. I'm happy to be complicated, and I'm eager to talk about the things that should matter and do something about them. I'm a stubborn dreamer and, today more than ever, that is something to invest in.

As you consider applicants for admission to your school, I hope you will see that I am exactly the kind of student who will use my education to make the world a better place. With the right support, my life could make a difference. Invest in me and let's see what an average teenager can do.

My sister had so much going for her. She was all those things—a philosopher and cheerleader and writer. She was seriously going places in her life. She could have been anything she wanted to be. The girl who wrote that college essay is the real Anna. That's the Anna I knew.

Anna was so close to getting out of our house and our town. Only one more year and all those jerks at school would have been a distant memory. There's no way she would have made it seventeen years and then give up just as the finish line came in sight. She would never run away when she was close. Maybe she could have done something reckless, but I still don't believe that. She would never put herself in danger.

I close the file. I don't know how I thought I could finish it before my mom got back. Tomorrow, it will be one week since I opened this can of worms. There's not much more to go through, which leaves me feeling conflicted. On one hand, I want more and more. On the other hand, I'm not sure I do. Either way, it will have to wait until tomorrow, because Jack is meeting me for dinner.

I find Jack seated at a tall table near the window of the restaurant. I thought I had been to all the places in Buena Vida, but this one is new. It's got less of a beachy vibe and more of a sporty one. I see Jack's got his eyes on a baseball game. I make my way towards him, and when he sees me, he gets up to greet me. What a gentleman.

"There you are," he says as he hugs me. "You found the place alright?"

"I'm here, aren't I?"

"Yes, you are," Jack grins. "Can I get you a drink? Diet Coke, maybe?"

Hearing his voice is a little uncomfortable after reading about how close he was with my sister. Maybe my crush on him is a little weird. Maybe I'm interpreting his kindness as flirting when it's really just his way of being close to his old best friend, Anna. Or maybe I think too much and should just let him order me a Diet Coke.

"Yeah, that would be great. Thanks."

By the time our dinner comes, we're talking like old friends. We laugh about our childhood adventures, and even though Anna's intertwined in all of them, it doesn't make me sad. It's nice to talk freely about all the good times we had together. I love that Jack and I can share that.

"I'm glad we're hanging out," Jack says timidly.

"Me, too," I say brightly.

Jack reaches his hand across the table and places it on mine. Feeling a rush of excitement flush my cheeks, I do my best to act casual. Like I'm not dancing on the inside.

We eventually order our food and move on to talking about things we want to do, like skydiving or learning to parasail. Jack's afraid of heights, so he says he'll stick to learning guitar and hiking the Pacific Crest Trail. I tell him both suit him. I'm having so much fun that I almost forget how messed up life is for a minute.

Then everything comes to a screeching halt.

"I was thinking. Maybe you should go to community college in the fall."

"What?" I ask skeptically. "Why are you bringing that up?"

"I know you're trying to figure out what to do next, and I just thought it would be a good step, that's all."

"Why is that?"

"For starters, you're really smart. You could do a lot. College is kind of essential these days, so maybe you could go for a couple years and transfer to a four-year university. By then, you'll probably have a better idea of what you want to do."

"I can't go to community college and work enough hours to pay for an apartment."

"Your mom might let you stay if you're going to school. I'm sure my mom can talk to her. She's very convincing."

"Don't bring Sheila into this."

"Well. What do you think?"

I take a sip of my Diet Coke, mulling over his suggestion. I won't lie. Part of me wouldn't mind having a do-over with the whole school thing. Plus, I'm not exactly on the fast-track to making money. Any job I get now isn't going to be much better than The Smoothie Spot, and it paid hardly enough for gas. I'm not sure my mom would let me stay, but she might.

As I think about it, a strange feeling comes over me. I suddenly feel really defensive and angry.

"Why do you care?" I ask suspiciously.

"What do you mean? I care about you and I want you to be happy."

My face sours as I look at him. His dimples suddenly don't look so cute.

"You feel sorry for me."

"Huh?"

"That's why you're hanging out with me. You feel sorry for me."

"Hang on a minute," Jack says, his brow furrowing.

"Poor little Katie can't get her life together. I'll swoop in and help her because I'm the Almighty Jack Nelson."

"That's not what I'm saying."

"Isn't it?" I say, feeling myself getting more and more upset.

"I just thought it was something to consider, that's all," Jack says quietly.

"Not everyone is like you, Jack. Maybe not everyone is destined to be successful in life. Maybe some of us are just trying to survive."

I can't help but think that Jack has no idea what it's like. His parents are annoyingly sweet, some kind of alien species from another planet. He's always been smart and level-headed. People always expected great things from him, and it was easy for him to comply. Whether he's an engineer like his dad or an architect doesn't matter. He's going to be somebody either way. How could he possibly understand what it's like for the rest of us? He doesn't even understand the fact that sometimes life really is a ticking time bomb. Sometimes there isn't time to figure it all out.

I didn't have time to figure out my sister before it was too late. My sister was stressed about being what everyone wanted her to be. She thought she had to be popular, skinny, smart, and pleasing in order to survive high school. She thought she had to be the strong sister-of-the-year, the perfect daughter, and a college-bound success story in order to survive the world. She twisted herself up like a pretzel. Everyone's expectations, including Jack's, seem like they paved the way for my sister's disappearance—all before I had time to disarm the bomb I didn't even know was there.

"You feel bad that you didn't do more to help her. I know all about how crazy she was feeling back then. I read her diary. I read what you told Officer Christiansen. There were signs that she was struggling, and you—along with everyone else—missed them. It kills you, doesn't it? And now you want to clear your conscience by saving another Williams girl. Am I right?"

As soon as the words leave me, I regret them. Jack's gorgeous eyes are boring a hole into mine. I can see I've hurt him. I suddenly feel really bad, yet at the same time, protective of myself. I want to say I'm sorry, but instead, I cross my arms and lock eyes with him.

"I told you. I'm fine. I don't need to be saved."

Jack looks away from me, shaking his head.

"You keep these walls up like they're going to protect

you. You're just like Anna that way. Her walls were happy and cheerful, yours are angry and defensive, but they do the same thing—shut people out. The good people, not just the bad."

Jack gets up, pulls out a couple of twenty-dollar bills from his pocket, and places them on the table. He shakes his head and then turns his eyes towards me.

"I don't want to save you, Katie. I want to be there for you. There's a difference."

As I watch him leave the restaurant, I feel myself crying. It seems like crying is my new hobby, one I'd like to give up. I reach for Anna's dragonfly pendant and squeeze it between my fingers. I've always wanted to be just like her. I guess I am, in more ways than I thought.

I honestly don't know why I acted that way to Jack. Why did I push him away? He's been nothing but nice to me. So what if he suggests that I go to community college? It's not like that's a bad thing. He's looking out for me. I guess I'm not used to that. Or maybe I'm just not sure who to trust. I don't even know anymore.

I wait another few minutes to give him time to drive away, then I slip out to my car feeling absolutely miserable.

April 10, 2012

I can't believe I actually tried to reach out to Maddie at school. She basically blew me off, acting like we were strangers. Then I tried to make an appointment with Mrs. Burgess, since her job is to guide kids like me, but she was booked until Friday. I felt like asking the front office if there was a priority list for kids who have a pocket full of their mom's pills and a death wish, but my sarcasm is for my ears only. Instead, I politely accepted an appointment for lunchtime on Friday, which I'm sure I will cancel beforehand.

I tried talking to Piper, but she's no use these days. She's all about fun, and the biggest problem she seems to have is deciding what to do on the weekend. I guess that's not fair. She does worry about stuff, but not like I do. She's going to go into her dad's business if her acting pursuits don't work out, so there isn't much pressure when it comes to grades or planning. She takes an acting class once a week, and that stresses her out. Her looks stress her out, too. She's obsessing over them constantly, always telling me that she's going to get her boobs done as soon as she graduates. Her boobs are fine, but she doesn't think so. I try to remind her how beautiful she is and stop her from worrying about it so much, but it doesn't work. After all, if she isn't pretty enough as she is— what in the world does that make me? Who told her she wasn't perfect anyway?

I bet it comes from all the stuff we see on TV and online. It's like every model or celebrity in the world is pumped with fillers, implants, and other stuff. There are ads for waxing, surgical lifts, and diet plans everywhere. I know everyone says to love our bodies and take care of them by eating well and exercising, but what their artificial bodies are really saying is eat celery, work out until you're thin, get plastic surgery, and look like a magazine cover.

Anyway... Piper and I are dieting together. She has this great plan to eat only celery and apples during the day, followed by a bowl of broth at night. If we get hungry, we drink a ton of water to fill us up and send each other pictures of really fat people or really gorgeous people for encouragement. It's like a carrot and a stick approach. I lost another three pounds already, which is great since I'm almost down to a size zero. Okay, two. Alright, I'm not quite there, but I'm trying. Apparently, I'll feel a lot better if I can just lose some more weight.

We all know that's a lie. I hope it will help, but I'm not stupid. I know I am way too messed up these days to think a diet will help me feel better. I can't just go get a manicure and change my world. I'm dark and troubled. Maddie understood that, or at least she used to. She used to be the one person I could talk to about stuff.

I like Piper and all, but it's not the same. I've known Maddie since third grade. We've shared a lot since then. She was there during my parents' divorce and all that chaos. At least at one time, Maddie knew my whole self. Piper and I are new, and I'm still trying to be my whole self around Piper. Still, Maddie didn't let me change. The thing is, I didn't want to lose my friend—I just wanted to find myself. Now, I feel like I am nowhere near finding myself, and I haven't a friend, either.

I'm being dramatic. That's all it is, right? Drama. When I'm old or dead, there will be moments no one even remembers. I'm not sure if that makes me feel better or worse. On one hand, my feelings are so insignificant that they will be forgotten in a second. On the other hand, these feelings may actually pass one day and finally leave me in peace.

Where's my fairy godmother at a time like this? It seems like everyone should get a fairy godmother of some kind. There should be a crazy aunt who steps in or a kind teacher who takes interest in a kid in need, standing in as a support for them during hard times. Maybe it's a coach or a pastor or a neighbor. Do people even do that anymore?

April 12, 2012

OMG. Shayna and I got so high yesterday. I wasn't just buzzed like usual—I was full-on stoned. I don't even know how I got home. I didn't plan on it, but like Shayna says, you can't plan everything! Thankfully, my mom was out and Katie was at a friend's house. I'm not sure I could have hidden it as well as last time.

I love how it makes me feel, like I haven't a care in the world. For once, my brain is still and empty. I can just sit around, looking up at the ceiling and contemplating life. I don't fret about deadlines and assignments. I don't worry about my mom or Piper or Maddie or Jacob or the squad. I could care less what any of them think about me when I'm high. It's awesome.

Who knew I could feel like this? Maybe I'll see if I can score some of my own so I don't have to worry about getting it from Shayna or anyone.

I look around the office, which has become more familiar over the past week. It's not as bad as I thought at first, but I won't be sad when I don't have to come back. There's something stale about the whole place, and I don't like it. Maybe I'm just in a bad mood after my fight with Jack last night or the cold shoulder I'm getting from my mom. Maybe it's because I'm angry over what I just read.

After all the lectures Anna gave me on not doing drugs, this is seriously upsetting. She was the good girl who swore she would never do any drugs or even sip alcohol. Anna had a fit when I said pot wasn't such a big deal, but she was doing it. What a hypocrite! And who the hell is Shayna?

I get that I was twelve, and she felt like she was my mom more than my sister, but that's seriously messed up. She was doing drugs and drinking and getting tattoos. I mean, was that the real Anna? Was the one I knew a total fake? I guess she thought she was protecting me, but it feels more like she was lying to me. About everything. Then again, maybe she was just trying to get by, the same way I am.

I pull out my mint container and look at it with disgust. That's it. I'm not doing this anymore. I empty the tiny round pills into the garbage can and then throw the whole container in, too.

INTERVIEW WITH CO-WORKER, DAMIEN CURTIS

Tuesday, April 24, 2012, 10:00 a.m.
Transcribed from Digital Recording

JC: Officer John Christiansen

DC: Damien Curtis

JC: Begin recording. Can you state your name for the record?

DC: Damien Curtis, assistant manager of Sub Station.

JC: Thank you, Damien. As we talked about just before I turned on the tape, I am here to ask you some questions about Anna Williams. What can you tell me about her?

DC: I don't know, man. I'm not sure what to say.

JC: Well, I understand that you work with Anna here at Sub Station. Is that right?

DC: Yeah. I'm the assistant manager, so I'm here a lot. She works a shift or two over the weekend and one during the week. Thursdays, actually. I see her Thursdays and sometimes during the weekend.

JC: What is she like at work?

DC: I don't know. She's like the rest of us losers, only she cleans up better.

[Stilted laughter]

JC: What do you mean?

DC: Nah, man. I'm just messin' with you. She's great. She works really hard, actually. She makes sure everything is prepped at the beginning of the shift, cleans up when it's slow, and acts like she's every customer's best friend. People like her best, which is not a surprise if you knew the whole crew. She's kind of like our little sister. Anna Banana.

JC: Is that what you call her?

DC: Yeah, we started calling her that on day one.

JC: Does Anna ever talk about her personal life or home life?

DC: I guess so. We get to talking sometimes, especially when it's slow. Like now.

JC: What do you and Anna talk about?

DC: She talks about her little sister and her parents sometimes. She brings up school stuff a lot since none of us are at Macklemore, so it's safer. No ties and all. She asks a lot of questions. She is all kinds of complicated, but she's cute. So we keep her around.

JC: Has she talked about being afraid of anyone?

DC: No, more like how she's afraid of everything. She's on the college grind, you know? Everyone in her life is all about college this and college that. All her grades have to be A's and she has to seem well-rounded. That's why she does charity work here!

JC: So she's worried about getting into college?

DC: Yeah, man. She also worries that if she gets into college, it will be too expensive. Her dad says he'll pay, but Anna doesn't believe it. She's got issues with him, I guess. Anyway, then she worries about leaving her sister. I keep telling her she doesn't need to get worked up over it.

JC: Do you think she would want to take a year off?

DC: Maybe. She could always work here, but she'd be running the place in no time and then I'd have to worry about job security.

[Laughter]

JC: Did she ever—

DC: Look, I'm here because I dropped out. I wasn't exactly a smart kid, at least not with tests and all that crap they want you to learn. I definitely did not get along with all the teachers. Everything was 'do this' or 'do that' and I just couldn't hang. I was bouncing off the walls, literally. They couldn't handle me any more than my mom could. She left when I was five or something, probably because I was such a little twerp. But I'm doing alright, you know, livin' the life. The ladies aren't complaining!

[Loud thud of hand banging on table]

DC: Oh swerve!

JC: Look, you seem like a good guy, but—

DC: I am, thanks. I knew you were cool. Anyway, Anna's got lots of options. She can do whatever she wants.

JC: What else can you tell me about Anna?

DC: Anna, obviously, is the exact opposite of me. She plays by all the rules, and everyone expects great things from her. I know my life ain't all that, but at least I'm not everyone's puppet. That girl has so many strings on her, it's crazy.

JC: Do you mean her parents or teachers?

DC: Yeah, and the world. Anna's the kind of girl who absorbs things like a sponge. Like her tattoo. She wanted a tattoo, but for weeks she kept going on and on about it. What should she get? Where should she put it? What if her mom found out? What if it was a mistake?

What would her grandchildren think? It
was seriously intense.

JC: So she got the tattoo, right?

DC: Oh, yeah. I told her, 'Look, whose life
        is it anyway? Whose body is it? So
        maybe a tattoo will be a regret... but
        maybe living your life for everyone
        else will be a bigger regret.'

JC: Did she get the tattoo with you?

DC: Yeah, I went with her to Max's
        brother's shop. I know all of them,
        so I made sure she was taken care of.
        That girl handled pain like a warrior.
        The rib is tender, but she didn't even
        cry. She just closed her eyes and
        handled it. She's hard-core, man.

JC: She must have a high pain tolerance.

DC: I guess. I think she just has a will
        of steel.

JC: What do you mean?

DC: She's a good girl. The thing is, it
        takes a lot of work to be a good
        girl. You have to harness all the
        crazy inside your head and make sure
        no one sees anything they don't like.
        That takes serious effort.

JC: I see.

DC: Yeah, man. She's got that down. What
        she doesn't have down is being Anna.

JC: What makes you think that?

DC: She doesn't even know who she is half

the time. You ask her if she wants
a puff of a cigarette, and she's all
'yes' and 'no' and 'I shouldn't' and
'maybe' and 'I don't know.' Then you
ask her what kind of milkshake she
wants, and she's like 'chocolate' or
'strawberry' or 'vanilla' or 'Oreo
cookie' or 'whatever you're getting.'
She has no idea what she likes or
what she wants.

JC: So she has a will of steel when it
comes to doing what other people
expect?

DC: Exactly, dude. That's exactly what I'm
saying.

JC: But when it comes to doing what she
wants, she's weak?

DC: Totally. She just wants to jump in
whatever river's flowing by. The thing
is, she's pretty adventurous, even
wild. I think if she could drop the
whole good girl thing, she'd be a
hell of a time. She'd be doing all
kinds of crazy stuff.

JC: Do you think there's a part of her
that wants to act out?

DC: Oh, yeah. She hangs out with me,
doesn't she?

[Loud whooping sounds]

DC: I'm always like, 'Stop living inside
the box, Anna Banana.' She usually
tells me I'm right, but does nothing

about it. Hell, maybe she's doing
something about it right now.

JC: Do you think she could have run
away?

DC: I hope she did! She needed to get
away from all the pressure and
bullsh— I mean, bull. Sorry, Officer.
Anyway, everyone's so concerned with
themselves, usually, but not Anna.
She lets everyone squeeze her dry. I
hope she just snapped and was like,
'I'm outta here.'

JC: Yes, but do you think she would do
it?

DC: I don't know. I think if she was
pushed too far, she would. I'm not
sure it would have been a great idea,
since she has no idea what she's
doing, but then again, that's what
she'd be running from... everyone
telling her what to do and not to do.
So yeah, I think she would.

[Sound of a phone ringing, yelling heard
in the background]

DC: You can handle it! I'm busy over here,
can't you see? Sorry, Officer.

JC: That's alright. Where do you think she
would go? Does she ever talk about
wanting to go any place in particular?

DC: Hmm. She was always talking about
going to Paris. She wanted to sit
at one of those cafés, sipping a

cappuccino with foam in the shape of
a heart. Anna Banana dreamed big.

JC: Did she talk about any other places?

DC: I guess. Every time we talked about
this place or that, she'd chime
in with 'I've never been there—is
it cool?' But, no, man, she didn't
really have specifics.

JC: When is the last time you spoke to
Anna?

DC: At her last shift. She worked
Thursday night.

JC: Do you know if there is anyone who
would want to hurt her?

DC: No. I can't think of anyone.

JC: What about drugs?

DC: She did some pot. She tried ecstasy
one time, but that's all I know.

JC: You're telling me the truth—the whole
truth?

DC: Yeah, man.

JC: You know where she got the drugs?

DC: Well, she knows she could always come
to me. I mean, I could hook her up
with people who do that sort of thing.
I don't do that, of course. I just have
a variety of friends, you see.

JC: I need to know who. They may know
something.

DC: I couldn't say for sure.

JC: I need you to understand that finding
              Anna is more important than whatever
              you think you need to protect.

[Brief pause, background music filters
through]

DC: It was me. Just me.

JC: Okay. Who else does she hang out with
              from work?

DC: Me, Shayna, sometimes Max. She tags
              along with bigger groups sometimes,
              but she really only knows us.

JC: I need you to write down the names of
              every person Anna ever hung out with—
              that you know of. Numbers, where they
              can be found, too.

DC: Alright.

[Lapse of time]

DC: Here.

JC: Thank you. Did Anna come by here on
              Friday?

DC: No. None of us heard from her at all.

JC: Alright, I think we've covered almost
              everything. Thank you for your
              cooperation. Do you have anything
              else you want to add?

DC: No, not really.

JC: Well, if you think of anything, you
              can reach me at this number.

DC: Okay. Hey, I hope you find her.

JC: Me too, Damien.

INTERVIEW WITH CO-WORKER,
SHAYNA RODRIGUEZ

Tuesday, April 24, 2012, 10:48 a.m.
Transcribed from Digital Recording

JC: Officer John Christiansen

SR: Shayna Rodriguez

DC: Damien Curtis

JC: Begin recording. Hello, Shayna. I'm Officer Christiansen.

SR: I know you're here about Anna. What do you want to ask me?

JC: Well, tell me what you know about Anna.

SR: She's cool. We work the same shifts sometimes, so we talk. We hang out once in a while after work, too.

JC: What do the two of you talk about?

SR: Life. We talk about whatever comes up. Customers, lipstick, whatever. It just depends.

JC: Does she talk about her family?

SR: Yeah, she complains about her mom from time to time. In my opinion, she doesn't complain enough, because Anna's mom is a piece.

JC: Do you think Anna is unhappy at home?

SR: I don't know. She seems happy most of the time. Whenever she was down, I didn't have to say anything to cheer her up. I just waited for her to do it herself

JC: Do you think she would ever run away?

SR: No. Well, I don't know. We always talk about going places, but that's just talk. You know, like if I had a billion dollars, the first place I would go is... That kind of talk.

JC: Did she mention any place specific?

SR: She always starts with Paris, and then it would change from New York to Hawaii to Switzerland... or basically any place in the world.

JC: Why does she want to get away?

SR: She feels kind of stuck here. I think that's why she was so stressed out over the whole college thing. I told her, like, don't worry about it. It's just school. Go or don't go. You got time, girl. You're young, and you can do it later if you want to. She said she didn't have any other choice. I was like, girl, you always have a choice.

JC: Did Anna ever do drugs or alcohol around you?

SR: Nah, of course not. She was only seventeen, Officer. That would be illegal.

JC: Look, I'm here on a very strict and
        time-sensitive mission to find Anna
        and bring her home safe. If there is
        anything you know, you need to tell
        me now. We have no time to waste.

SR: Okay, okay, man. She did a little
        something. She was curious, you know?
        She said she wanted to try something,
        so one night after work we went out
        with some of my friends and she
        experimented. She tried a little pot
        once or twice, but that's nothing.

JC: Did she ever try any other drugs?

SR: She might have done a tab of ecstasy.

JC: Did she ever ask you to get some?

SR: Well, yeah.

JC: Did you give her any?

SR: Yeah, I gave her a joint. It was all
        I had.

JC: Did she smoke it with you?

SR: No, she said she wanted to try it
        with kids from school.

JC: Did you have any other conversations
        about drugs?

SR: Well, she did ask me where to get more
        pot. I told her I didn't know. Anna
        Banana is kind of like our little sister
        around here, so we look out for her.

JC: Did she talk to you about friends?

SR: Not really. Some girl Maddie really

pissed her off, but other than that
girl, no.

JC: What about boyfriends?

SR: She had a thing for this guy, Jacob.
She was crushing on him for a while.
Then there's the guy who comes in for
a turkey club.

JC: Who is this person?

SR: I don't really know. We call him
'turkey club' since 'turkey club no
mayo' seemed too long. Hold on.

[Loud shouting of the name Damien]

DC: Why are you yelling?

[Shrieking sound]

SR: Stop sneaking up on people, Damien!
You freaked me out. Listen, what's
the name of the guy who comes in
here on Thursdays for Anna?

DC: Turkey Club.

SR: Be serious. Do you know his name or not?

DC: No, I don't keep tabs on everybody
who comes in here. I just make
sandwiches.

SR: Sorry, Officer. No idea what the guy's
name is.

JC: Wait a minute. Is his name Joey?

SR: Joey! That sounds right.

DC: Sure, why not? Joey, Joe, Joseph. Sounds
like a good name for Turkey Club.

OC: Damien, why didn't you mention this man to me earlier?

DC: I don't know. I didn't think it was a big deal. Girls flirt all the time and it doesn't mean anything.

JC: Except the 'girl' in question is missing. You need to be forthcoming.

DC: I don't know every guy she's got a thing for.

JC: But you do know the guy who comes in here every week and what sandwich he orders.

DC: Alright, alright. I get it. Sorry, man.

JC: What do you know about this guy?

DC: Not much. He mostly talks to Anna, so I don't really know.

JC: Does he seem dangerous?

DC: Nah, man. He seems pretty laid back. I wouldn't be afraid of him... although I would be afraid he'd talk me into something. He's pretty smooth.

JC: Talk you into something like what?

DC: I don't know, like, buying a busted phone or lending him money he won't pay back. He didn't seem like a bad guy, but he was definitely slick.

JC: Do you think he was manipulating Anna somehow?

DC: I don't think so, but I really don't know. I thought it was pretty innocent.

FINE

JC: Do you think they got together
        outside of work?

DC: Nah, I doubt it.

JC: Alright, Damien.

SR: I think Officer Christiansen is done
        with you now, Damien.

DC: I can take a hint, Shayna. Cool your
        jets.

JC: Thank you. If you think of anything
        else—even if you think it doesn't
        matter—call me and I'll decide. And
        if you see that guy in here, you need
        to call me immediately. Got it?

DC: Got it.

JC: Alright, Shayna, how often does he
        come in here?

SR: Every week on Thursday, at least for
        the past month or so. He knows Anna
        Banana will be here then.

JC: He knows her schedule?

SR: Well, yeah. I guess so.

JC: Does Anna talk with him when he
        comes in?

SR: Oh, yeah. At first, he would order his
        turkey club and sit down close to
        the counter so he could talk to her.
        They flirted a little, but nothing
        big. Then he finally asked her to
        come over and sit with him, so we
        were all like, 'Get on over there'
        and all that. She's so shy. Anyway,

they started talking one day, and
he stayed for a couple hours. We had
to pull her back behind the counter
when customers started coming in.

JC: Did she tell you what they talked
        about?

SR: Um, not really. She was into him, but
        she's also shy, so it's hard to get
        anything out of her.

JC: When did this happen?

SR: Probably about three weeks ago? Maybe
        a little more...

JC: Did they continue to talk when he
        came in after that?

SR: Oh yeah. I think he was trying to win
        her over, showing up all the time and
        hoping that she would give him her
        number or go out with him afterwards.
        Damien didn't think so. He thought
        the guy was just enjoying being
        around a cute girl and didn't want to
        eat alone.

JC: Did she give him her number?

SR: I told her not to give out her phone
        number because she had no way of
        knowing if he was some kind of sex
        offender or murderer or something. I
        made her promise, but you never know
        what someone will do when they're
        crushing.

JC: Can you recall anything at all about
        this man?

SR: Let me think. I think he worked
        nearby, she said. But if he did, why
        did he show up here for hours at a
        time? Didn't he have to work? Maybe
        he was in college or something. Maybe
        that's why he had such a flexible
        schedule. Still, it seemed weird for
        him to be into a high school girl.

JC: Do you think she could be with him
        now?

SR: No. She doesn't have his number, for
        starters. Plus, they've only seen
        each other a couple of times when
        she happens to be working. She would
        never run away and, if she did, it
        wouldn't be with some random guy.

JC: What does he look like? Give me as
        much detail as possible.

SR: I'm not sure I could describe him.

JC: How about you tell me how tall he is.

SR: Um, he's average height. Light-
        skinned. Maybe five-eleven or so.

JC: What about his hair?

SR: I think he has light-brown hair, but
        I don't know for sure. It's cut pretty
        short.

JC: What color were his eyes?

SR: Brown. Well, they could be green.
        They were pretty light.

JC: Did he have any tattoos or other
        unique features?

SR: No.

JC: What about his clothes?

SR: Most of the time, he's in jeans, though. And he usually wears a baseball cap pulled way down in front of his face.

      [Sigh from Officer Christiansen]

SR: What? You don't like baseball?

JC: No, no. It's just the cameras won't... Never mind. Please keep going.

SR: What else do you want to know?

JC: How old did he seem to be?

SR: Older than Anna, that's for sure. Maybe in his mid-twenties?

JC: Was he here this past Thursday, the day before Anna went missing?

SR: No. She stayed thirty minutes past her shift hoping he would show up, but he never did.

JC: I need you to really think about this for me. Do you know any more about him? Did Anna share anything at all about this guy? Anything at all?

SR: Let me think. I thought he worked around here, but I don't actually know. He made it sound like he was some up-and-comer or something. He was all kinds of smooth talk, you know?

JC: Did Anna say anything about meeting up with him or going anywhere with him?

SR: No. I told her she was playing hard to get. I think that boy obviously had a thing for her and she was totally into it. She was just shy.

JC: Was she leading him on in any way? Do you think he thought she was?

SR: No. I mean, she's young. That's all. And I don't mean her age. I mean she just doesn't know certain things, so she couldn't have any idea that she was leading him on. I think he knew that. We all knew that.

JC: Did you ever see him driving?

SR: No.

JC: Has he been in here since Anna disappeared?

SR: No.

JC: Listen, I need to know the second this man comes into the shop again. If he comes in, you need to call me immediately.

SR: Yeah, yeah.

JC: Immediately, Shayna.

SR: Alright... I get it. Do you think Turkey Club took her? For real?

JC: I don't know.

[Pause, music filters in from the background]

JC: Is there anything else you can tell me about Anna?

SR: No.

   [Pause]

SR: I really hope she's alright, and
        didn't put herself into some
        situation or something. God, I can't
        imagine what could have happened to
        her.

JC: Okay, I don't have any further
        questions, but I need you to call me
        if you think of anything else.

SR: No problem. Officer?

JC: Yes?

SR: You think she is alright, don't you?
        I mean, you don't think something bad
        happened?

JC: I can't say anything at this time.

SR: Oh man. I hope you find her quick and
        bring her back in one piece.

JC: I'm doing my best.

FILE CONTROL NO. 23167
MISSING PERSON – ANNA WILLIAMS
Note to File completed by Officer Christiansen on April 24,
2012, 12:20 p.m.

NEW INFORMATION
Anna has been seen with an older man who comes into
Sub Station to see her every Thursday for the past month
or so. Her friend, Piper, expressed concern about his interest in Anna given the fact that he is much older than her.
Her co-worker, Shayna, divulged that Anna and this man
spent a lot of time talking and flirting.

Security footage from Sub Station does show the
man entering and eating, talking animatedly with Anna.
However, as suspected, his baseball cap completely hides
his face in all the footage. We were not able to pull any
footage of him wearing a suit, because security footage at
Sub Station is recorded over every two weeks.

At this point, his description has been given to authorities to be on the lookout. Since Anna is seventeen and
there is reason to believe this unknown man could have
abducted her, an Amber Alert has been issued.

WITNESSES
Damien Curtis and Shayna Rodriguez know Anna in an
entirely different light than her friends at school, affec-
tionately looking after her like a younger sister. They both
noted that she experimented with marijuana and ecstasy,
but didn't know that she scored marijuana on her own.
They said she expressed interest in travel, and felt stress

about college. They both confirmed Piper Abbot's observation of a growing chemistry between Anna and this mysterious Joey character—who we haven't been able to locate yet. Is it possible she's with him now?

PHOTO FROM ANNA'S INSTAGRAM ACCOUNT
A selfie taken of Anna Williams and an unidentified male—potentially the suspect "Joey"—was recovered. Anna appears to be at Sub Station wearing her uniform polo shirt. She is smiling directly at the camera, but the male is turned towards her and kissing her cheek. She appears startled, as if he surprised her. He is wearing a baseball cap and what appears to be a t-shirt. The photo is unusually granular, seemingly taken in the dark without a flash. As a result, the male's face is indiscernible.

What! I never once heard about this guy "Joey." No one ever mentioned it back then, and if they did, they never alerted me to the fact that he could have been the one person who knows what happened to Anna. Did they ever find him? Did they question him? I start flipping through the file for names, but I don't see anything that seems relevant. Frustrated, I stop and try to calm my thoughts.

I just don't understand how she could be flirting with some guy and not come home to gush about it to me. She told me everything about Jacob. Okay, maybe not everything, as it turns out. She did share the good parts, though. She talked about his hair, his deep voice, and the way he leaned up against the lockers like he was posing for a photoshoot. She could have mentioned something about this guy who was lighting up her life. Then again, she failed to mention she tried ecstasy! Why did she shut me out?

OMG. This guy took my sister, didn't he? Maybe he was one of those sickos who plots to steal a young girl and hide her away somewhere. Or drags her into some prostitution ring or slavery situation. Oh, god. Tell me that isn't what happened. Tell me she wasn't plucked from Macklemore High School by this guy who had the worst of intentions.

That's it. I'm going to Christiansen. He has to tell me what happened with this guy. Did he find him or what?

I storm out of the office and burst into his unannounced.

"Who the hell is Turkey Club? Where is he? Why don't I know about him?"

Christiansen stands up cautiously. "Hang on a second."

"Hang on? I've been hanging on for six years."

"We searched long and hard for this guy, I assure you. There just wasn't enough to go on and no one ever identified him."

"Weren't there security cameras?" I ask.

"None of them got a good look at him. He had on a baseball cap pulled down over his face, loose clothing."

"Didn't he ever show up at Sub Station again?" I pester.

"No."

My mind is racing. Thoughts spring up, one after another.

"So he was stalking her. She was, like, a target or something."

"I mean, it's possible."

"He was luring her in, telling her what she wanted to hear and making her think he liked her, and then bam! He scooped her up into some trafficking ring or something."

"It's not out of the question, but—"

"That's why her car was still in the parking lot. He

probably told her he'd pick her up that day. Did anyone see an old guy hanging around campus? Did he call her? Did you check her call list?"

"Yes. There were some unidentified callers, but they weren't traceable."

"What are you talking about? Everything is traceable."

"They were burners—prepaid phones used by people trying to stay off radar."

"See! That Joey guy is a criminal! He took her and you know it!"

"Katie, there's just not enough information to support that theory—and the guy never turned up."

"Exactly. He never turned up because he was on the run with my sister. You didn't even try to find him, did you?"

"We conducted a thorough search."

"No you didn't! You didn't ask any of the kids at school if they saw him. You didn't issue a warrant or anything."

"Katie, there are procedures that—"

"You weren't even looking. You just assumed my sister was a mental case who didn't want to be found, huh? Just a runaway teenager... a kid who slipped through the giant cracks in the system. Not your problem. Not anyone's problem."

Christiansen sighs, shoving his hands in his pockets. I wait for him to answer, but he doesn't.

"Convenient, isn't it? How labeling my sister a runaway or a drug addict gets you off the hook for not finding the jackass who took her."

"I know you're upset. You have every right to be."

Christiansen's words feel patronizing. I don't need him

to tell me I have a right to my feelings. Of course, I do.

"That's the hardest part of this job. Kids who go missing are usually dealing with some kind of trauma… at home or elsewhere. Sometimes there are mental health issues we don't know about," Christiansen says, eyeing me cautiously. "By the time we get called in to help, most of the safeguards have failed and it's often too late."

I can't quite feel my face, which has turned to stone.

"Katie, I know you want answers to explain exactly what happened that Friday. Unfortunately, I can't give them to you. All we know is your sister was depressed, self-medicating, and struggling with a lot of emotional issues—which made her vulnerable."

"She sounds like a normal, everyday teenager to me!" I laugh ironically. "It's the plot of every teen movie, Officer. Social pressures in high school, crappy friends who humiliate and betray you, overcoming a broken home, too much pressure to be what everyone wants you to be. Isn't The Breakfast Club from your generation?"

Christiansen's eyebrows go up.

"Seems to me that life sucks for everyone at some point. Maybe if we didn't act like life is some happily-ever-after Disney movie rather than the shit-show it is, you wouldn't be so quick to disregard a girl who was having normal emotions while handling it all. And then you could focus on finding the guy who took her!" I scream.

"Are you finished?" Christiansen says calmly, too calmly.

My hands are shaking. I'm so angry I don't even know what to do with myself. It feels like there are fire ants running through my veins. What am I going to do now? Without thinking, I turn around and run back to the office I've been cooped up in all week.

Fuming, I pack up the file in its box and put it under my arm. Then I run. I hear Christiansen calling after me, his voice concerned but not necessarily angry. I don't look back. I just run as fast as I can to my car, shove the box on the passenger seat, and drive off.

After I circle the block a few times, I feel myself settling down. When I'm finally calm enough to think straight, I steer my Focus in the direction of Sub Station. The neighborhood is just as run-down as it used to be. There are some questionable characters wandering around, graffiti everywhere. And it feels dirty, like the sidewalk is steaming with years of filth. It's hard to imagine this place is ten minutes outside of a place like Buena Vida, that people can live such drastically different lives within miles of one another.

There are bars on the windows of my sister's old workplace. I wonder if they've always been there, or if they are a new addition. I rarely visited her at work because my mom would have had to drive me, so I can't remember. I suppose it doesn't matter. I get out of the car, making sure to lock the doors, and go inside.

The inside looks the same as every other sandwich place on Earth. It's clean and smells like bread and salty meat. I pretend to look up at the brightly colored menu while taking stock of the place. I try to imagine Anna cleaning the tables in her polo shirt or filling the ice in the soda machine. I can't quite picture her here, but knowing she used to walk where I'm standing still feels good.

A girl suddenly appears from the back, her black ponytail swinging out from her Sub Station cap.

"Can I help you?"

"Umm, yeah," I say. "Actually, I was wondering if Shayna or Damien work here?"

"No," she says, slightly annoyed. "You gonna order something?"

"No, thanks," I answer before pushing on, undeterred. "Are you sure? Do you know anyone who worked here six years ago? Maybe someone named Max?"

"I don't know a Max," she says, sighing.

"Hmm. Damien and Shayna don't sound familiar either?"

"No."

"What about your manager?"

"Leo? He's new. Even I've been here longer than him."

"Oh," I mutter, losing hope.

"So, you don't want to order nothing?"

"No, thanks."

Disappointed, I turn to leave. I don't know what I was thinking. Why would those people still be working at the same minimum wage job six years later? Of course they've moved on.

I push the door to leave, then stop in my tracks. My eyes narrow in on the advertisement for the sandwich of the month, which is stuck to the door exactly at my eye level. As if to mock me, giant letters spell out the words.

Turkey Club.

April 17, 2012

OMG. OMG. OMG. I found out today from Ella that Piper begged Jacob Hunt to go out with me. I'm totally mortified.

How could she do this to me? I thought we were friends! I was so upset when I heard that I left school in a hurry and drove straight home, ignoring her texts and calls. I know she will just say that she was helping me out. She is either oblivious to how pathetic it makes me look or she doesn't care. How could she treat me like this? How could she lie to me? I'm just so angry.

And how am I supposed to handle this at school? Does everyone already know? Of course they do. Even if they don't, it's going to be all over the internet in a matter of seconds. Just like last time. People just can't help themselves. How am I going to show up for school tomorrow? I can't face Jacob.

Oh, God, and to think what I did. I not only was being fooled by Piper and Jacob and everyone else who was in on it, but I took it to a whole other level. I did that to a guy who, as it turns out, didn't even like me! He was just being helpful or charitable or whatever. Oh no, what if Jacob told everyone? He probably did. Oh, no. No, no, no, no, no, no. I can't believe I hadn't thought of this before. What am I going to do if the whole school knows what I did?

I have to get a hold of myself. I have to calm down. Deep breaths in and out, Anna. Deep breaths. This too will pass. What doesn't kill me will make me stronger. I won't let them see me cry. I will put on a brave face. Deep breaths. I will get through this somehow. I just need something to calm down. Some pot. Maybe a Xanax or two. Or maybe a whole bottle...

INTERVIEW WITH CARMEN HERNANDEZ, BVPD CRIMINAL PSYCHOLOGIST

Tuesday, April 24, 2012, 5:15 p.m.
Transcribed from Digital Recording

JC: Officer John Christiansen

CH: Carmen Hernandez

JC: Begin recording. Please state your name and occupation.

CH: Carmen Hernandez, criminal psychologist.

JC: Thank you.

CH: Of course.

JC: As you know, I've asked you to look into the case of Anna Williams. Given your expertise, maybe you can add something that will help me put the pieces together.

CH: I'm here to help. Please.

JC: The girl seems depressed, no?

CH: Well, the problem is there are many different symptoms that may present, and every adolescent may present with a different combination of symptoms. I couldn't make a proper diagnosis from the information I have, but it's very possible she suffered from depression.

JC: If she's depressed, then—

CH: Then again, it's just as possible that
          Anna is the normal, albeit emotional,
          teenager everyone says she is.

JC: If she is depressed, is she depressed
          enough to kill herself?

CH: I'm not sure. She definitely has signs
          of suicide ideation.

JC: What is that?

CH: It basically means they think
          about dying in a positive way. For
          instance, if I was talking about how
          nice it would be to kill myself and
          how peaceful I would feel once I'm
          dead, that would be suicide ideation.
          It doesn't necessarily mean they will
          kill themselves. It just means that
          their pain is so intense that they
          don't see a lot of ways to escape
          it, besides escaping their life
          altogether.

JC: I get the idea.

CH: She may be bipolar, as well. She
          seems to have experienced episodes of
          extreme lows that meet the criteria
          for a depression diagnosis. However,
          she also seems to have had periods
          of extreme highs—either euphoric or
          irritable moods—called mania. Or a
          less severe form called hypomania.
          That could indicate she is suffering
          from undiagnosed bipolar disorder.

JC: Bipolar? You think others would notice if she were experiencing such drastic swings.

CH: Those closest to Anna would likely have noticed her behavior being off, but unless they encouraged her to seek treatment by a professional trained to identify this kind of disorder, they wouldn't necessarily know that it was due to being bipolar.

JC: So if Anna's bipolar, would she—

CH: I'm not saying she's bipolar. I'm only saying that's a possibility.

[Sigh]

JC: Look, I'm three days into the investigation and no closer to figuring out what happened to this girl. I need to know where to focus.

CH: Alright, let's go through the possibilities. The most obvious one is suicide. It's the third leading cause of death among teenagers, so it seems like the most likely. Although, if she did, she didn't leave a note. Plus, her body hasn't turned up anywhere.

[Pause]

CH: You know, many adolescents will turn to various outlets for dealing with their emotions—besides suicide. Teens can develop unhealthy relationships with food, resort to self-harming or promiscuity, and turn to drugs or alcohol. Sometimes these behaviors lead to them to get involved in some kind of risky activity that may have led to her disappearance.

JC: There are some concerns about her behavior, but the odds are against it. The statistics say she is a runaway.

CH: Do you think she had a reason to run?

JC: I think she may have thought so.

[Sound of papers crinkling]

CH: Is there anyone, in particular, she may have been running from?

JC: Her relationship with her dad leaves a lot of unanswered questions, but there's nothing to suggest he has anything to do with her disappearance. Other than driving her away, maybe.

CH: What about kidnapping?

JC: We have no real suspects, except there is this one guy. I'm concerned he may have sweet-talked her into leaving school with him.

CH: Do you know anything about him?

JC: No. The guy's either real slick at luring young girls away without leaving a trail, or he's a ghost. I can't get any leads on him.

CH: You think he has something to do with this, don't you?

JC: I can't rule it out.

[Slight pause]

CH: He could've taken her against her will. It's also possible she could have run away with him willingly, only to find herself in the grasp of a sex trafficker, pimp, or murderer. That's if he had anything to do with it at all, which is unclear.

JC: So that leaves me... nowhere.

CH: If I may...

JC: You will anyway. Go ahead.

CH: People are complex creatures. They're driven by their emotions, whether they realize it or not. So to understand people's behavior, we have to look at their emotions. Understanding how they feel when they're sitting right in front of you is a difficult task. Trust me, I know. To figure it out in hindsight is almost impossible.

JC: No kidding.

CH: It's especially difficult when the person purposely tries to conceal their emotions—since that's what drives motives. Which, as you know, point us in the right direction.

JC: It's such a shame—such a seemingly avoidable shame.

[Few seconds of silence]

JC: Carmen, you have been immensely unhelpful.

[Laughter]

CH: I do my best.

JC: Thank you.

CH: I do wish I could've been more helpful, but you didn't give me much to work with.

JC: Don't look at me—I don't create these messes. I'm just the one trying to clean them up.

CH: I know, I know. Good luck with this one.

JC: Thanks. I guess I better get going.

CH: Alright. I'm here if you have any other questions.

JC: Okay, say 'hello' to Ed for me.

CH: I will.

I'm down to the last few pages of this stupid file. I'm going to get through it tonight if it kills me. I can't take it anymore. I just can't. I tiptoe out to the kitchen to fix a cup of tea, hoping it will keep me company long enough to finish. I turn on the stove, then pull out a mug and an Earl Grey tea bag.

I'm starting to feel bad about yelling at Christiansen and taking his file. I know it was wrong, but I couldn't help myself. All I've done lately is yell at people—my dad, my mom, and even Jack. I don't mean to do it, but they give me no choice sometimes.

I feel so alone, like nobody understands me. My mom is living on a different planet and my dad is, well, I can't even go there. Josie is the only one who has any clue, and she's gone, probably forever. A few phone calls and texts are not enough between best friends, especially when she's the only friend I have. I thought Jack might be my friend, or even more, but I blew that.

The worst part is knowing he was right. It's like Anna and I are the same person. We both feel horrible inside and can't figure out what to do about it. The only difference is she swallows her feelings, and I throw mine up onto everyone within reach. I seriously can't help it. I'm just so angry all the time.

I don't understand why life has to be this way. I don't understand why there are never any answers. I thought if I could just find some answers... but that is clearly not going to happen. I'm going to have to learn to live in the unknown.

Maybe I have some kind of mental illness. Depression or anxiety or bipolar or whatever. I know someone would be more than happy to tell me my head is broken in some way or another, although I think what's really broken is my heart. I never would have thought Anna had mental health issues, but maybe she did, and maybe if she had gotten help in time, she would still be here. Maybe I should talk to that therapist again. Just in case.

The kettle whistles and I pour my tea, then head to my bedroom. I set down my tea and crawl on top of my covers. With my legs folded up beneath me, I reach for the next part of the file and continue reading.

"Knock, knock."

I look up to see my mom peeking her head through the crack in my door. I must have woken her.

"Can I come in?"

"Sure."

She emerges in her pajamas without makeup. Stripped of her usual mask of foundation and blush, she seems older, but just as pretty. She approaches me cautiously and sits on the edge of my bed. As she lets out a heavy sigh, her entire frame deflates. I wait for her to say something about the file spread out across my bed.

"Look, Katie. I'm not a perfect mother. I know that."

I look at my mom curiously. I've never seen her like this before. I've certainly never heard her talk like this.

"I was so young when I got married. We had Anna right away, and then a few years later, you. We were happy in the beginning. We really were. Then we moved into the house, your dad started working more—drinking too— and the next thing I knew, we were fighting all the time."

I stay quiet as she considers what to say next. I'm afraid to move or breathe. I don't want to scare her off.

"Those years happened so fast, really. I guess I just couldn't face things. It was easier to distract myself with things I could control, things that could be fixed. I just wanted everything to be perfect," she says, her voice quivering.

A tear rolls down my mom's cheek, followed quickly by a river of them. She brushes them away, irritably. I know how much she hates to cry, probably more than me.

"There are so many things I wish I could go back and do differently, especially with Anna. But I can't. It's too late," she says through her tears. "I don't want it to be too late with you, Katie."

I can't stand seeing her this way, so I reach out to hug her. She clutches me tighter than ever. I let her embrace comfort me. She may be crazy and sorely lacking parenting skills at times, but she's my mom. I don't want it to be too late for us, either.

When I decided to look into the file, I thought I

wanted to know more about what happened to Anna. I thought I wanted to know the truth about everything that went down six years ago. But maybe what I really wanted was to find a way out of the shadow Anna's disappearance cast over our lives. I didn't want to drown in all that darkness.

I suppose there are a lot of ways out of a bad situation—running, numbing, ignoring, pretending, and even dying. After all I've been reading, I don't really like any of those options. There's got to be a better way out.

"Mom?"

"What?" she asks, bracing herself for more of my questions.

"I was thinking. Maybe I could do the whole community college thing."

"Really?" my mom says with surprise. "That's great."

"Yeah?"

"Yeah. It's the first time I've heard you talk seriously about anything regarding your future. I'm thrilled."

"I figure if I work hard over the summer, I could pay for tuition and books and all that. But, umm, do you think I could stay here a little longer, instead of moving out right away?" I ask tentatively, hoping the window she opened for me hasn't shut yet.

She mulls it over quietly. The longer she takes, the more I think she's going to say no.

"I think we can figure something out," she says, smiling softly.

I squeeze her tightly, excited and relieved and worried all at the same time. I don't want to let go. I want to savor this moment, this moment where we are not fighting or faking or being sarcastic. We are just a mother and a daughter who need each other. When we finally let go, I see that her eyes are glossy.

"Thanks, Mom."

After one more hug and a promise to talk more about it tomorrow, she gets up to leave. As I watch her move across the room, I notice the bathrobe she's wearing. She hasn't worn it in years. It's probably the oldest thing she owns, and it looks it. The hem is coming undone, and the color has faded from vintage rose to a pale pink. I remember she wore it every Christmas morning when we unwrapped presents, and she practically lived in it for a year after Anna went missing. Seeing her in it makes me want to curl up on her lap and watch TV until the sun comes up.

"I love you, Mom."

She turns around, her face open and vulnerable.

"Love you too."

When she leaves, I sit motionless for a few moments. Then I let my body fall back into the pillow and stare up at the light on the ceiling.

Note to File completed by Officer Christiansen on April 25, 2012, 7:30 p.m.

POTENTIAL THEORIES

Foul Play – Could have been abducted by "Joey" suspect she met at Sub Station. She could have left with him voluntarily at first, perhaps excited to see him at her school and willing to take a drive. She could have been taken by some unknown suspect as well. Given her more wild behavior as of late, she may have found her way into an unsafe area and in the hands of dangerous individuals. If that is the case, she could have been kidnapped, dragged into sex trafficking, prostitution, or any number of other dangerous activities that are keeping her from returning home.

Runaway – Could have deliberately run away. Social strife, academic pressure, and an unhappy home life all factor into this theory. She constantly talked about getting away. Plus, she has money from her paychecks somewhere. However, why would she leave her sister? Why not wait for college? Did she really feel that was her only option when so many other things were going so well in her life? Plus, where would she go without her car? And why didn't she pack a bag?

Suicide – Possibility. Anna exhibited signs of depression and loneliness, even talking about suicide ideation in her diary, yet she shared it with nobody. There's evidence of extreme mood swings and erratic, even risky, behavior. If she did take her own life, she would have run off to do it remotely and probably would have covered her tracks to protect her sister. Anna was a normal girl most of the time with pretty typical problems, none of which would seem to support this theory. She is outgoing, smart, and has a lot of options.

Unknown Circumstances – In light of Anna's experimentation with drug use and her tendency to hide it, it is possible Anna could have disappeared somewhere and accidentally overdosed. Her excessive dieting and exercise could also have led to an unforeseen health complication while she was in an unknown location.

Email Exchange between Anna Williams
and Jack Nelson, Dated April 18, 2012

To: Jack Nelson
From: Anna Williams
Date: April 18, 2012, 4:41 p.m.
Subject: Thanks

Hey,
I just wanted to say thanks for being a good friend to me. I
know I'm not easy to deal with, but you've always been good to
me. So thanks. Seriously.

- -

To: Anna Williams
From: Jack Nelson
Date: April 18, 2012, 5:21 p.m.
Subject: Re: Thanks

Hey back. You're welcome. What's gotten into you?

- -

To: Jack Nelson
From: Anna Williams
Date: April 18, 2012, 5:24 p.m.
Subject: Re: Thanks

Nothing. Just saying what I should have said a long time ago.
You're a really good person, Jack Nelson. I wish more people
were like you.

- -

To: Anna Williams
From: Jack Nelson
Date: April 18, 2012, 5:30 p.m.
Subject: Re: Thanks

You need help with chem? Is that what this is all about? I can help you free of charge, no compliments necessary.

- -

To: Jack Nelson
From: Anna Williams
Date: April 18, 2012, 5:34 p.m.
Subject: Re: Thanks

You really are oblivious sometimes, aren't you?
For your information, I mean it. You're different and special in the best of ways. You are going to make some girl really happy one day.

- -

To: Anna Williams
From: Jack Nelson
Date: April 18, 2012, 5:37 p.m.
Subject: Re: Thanks

Is 'some girl' code for Anna Williams? Hmmm? JK
And thanks.
To: Anna Williams
From: Jack Nelson
Date: April 18, 2012, 6: 56 p.m.
Subject: Re: Thanks

Hey—I was just kidding. You don't have to get all silent on me...

- -

Jack opens the door to his parents' house, surprised to see me.

"Apology burrito?" I ask, handing him a brown paper sack.

I need to say something else, but I've gone mute. I stand there awkwardly, nodding my head and shifting my weight from one foot to the other.

"Thanks," he says coldly, taking a step back into his house.

"Wait!" I yell, startling myself. "I'm sorry. I'm really sorry. I shouldn't have said all those things. I don't know why I did. I guess I had just read all that stuff about—anyway, I freaked out a little. Then I started wondering how you actually felt about me and whether or not I was some kind of charity case. I know, I know. I'm a freak. I had no right to yell at you, and I'm really sorry. It's just I thought we were friends or maybe more than friends. Whatever. I know you're probably done with me now and I totally understand if you are. It's just I liked having you in my life, and I haven't felt that way about a lot of people. I definitely don't go around telling most people that, and—"

My eyes have been darting all over the place during my rambling apology. When they finally land on Jack, I stop talking. He's grinning at me with those dimples, and I'm really confused.

"What? Why are you looking at me like that?"

"I told you. You're cute."

I feel my cheeks burning.

"I can be mad at you, you know. That doesn't mean I'm going anywhere."

"Oh," I say. "So you're still mad?"

"Nah. How could I still be mad after an epic apology like that?"

"Good," I say, letting the air and stress drain out of my body. Then it dawns on me that I just told him I liked him, or something like that. I made it weird, I just know it. "I didn't mean what I said about being more than friends or anything, by the way. I don't know why I said that."

"Oh?"

"Unless..."

He grins at me again, thoroughly entertained.

"How about we split this burrito and take it from there."

Jack closes the front door and steps out onto the porch. He plops down on the top step and motions for me to join him. He pulls out the burrito, rips it in two, and hands me half. We eat quietly, sitting side by side, completely at ease together even after our fight. His leg feels warm pressed against mine, and I like how close he is to me.

"Did you finish the file?" he asks, completely out of the blue.

"Almost," I answer. "I don't know if reading it has helped anything."

Jack nods his head slowly. "You know when you're a kid and you fall off your bike? You go running to your mom crying, and she kisses it better? Don't you wish every problem was like that?"

"You know our moms are very different, right?" I say.

"You get my point."

"I do."

"I don't think anyone knows what really happened to Anna," Jack says solemnly. "We just know it shouldn't have."

"You're right," I say with a sigh. "I just miss her. It feels wrong to still be here when she's not."

"I get it, but don't forget that your life is precious, too. If you really want to honor Anna, and keep her with you, don't let how she left overshadow the amazing person she was when she was around. Don't let the ugliness of this world block out its beauty."

I nod, soaking up his words and the sunshine all around. I notice the flowers in his front yard are in full bloom, surrounded by bugs delighting in their colors and fragrance. I notice the faraway sound of children playing, birds chirping, and cars passing by. I notice the smell of jasmine in the wind. And I notice the willow tree, our willow tree, and the way its branches hover protectively over the secrets hidden in its shade.

April 19, 2012

I bet no one would notice or care if I disappeared. I could probably just evaporate into thin air without raising an eyebrow. Think about it—people kill themselves all the time. And the reaction is always the same.

At first, it's a huge shock because no one believes that things could ever be so bad that suicide is a viable alternative to living. How could it be that bad? How come they didn't ask for help? How come they couldn't see beyond this one moment to a brighter future? Why weren't they able to hang in there just a little longer?

Then everyone feels pity. Oh, that is such a shame. What a waste of a life. So much potential down the drain. If they had only come to me or talked to someone. Such a sad, sad story. Didn't they know it gets better?

After that, sadness seeps in. Any genuine feelings for the person rise up, and their loss is felt. They light candles and place flowers in familiar places, maybe the place they found them. They hold vigils. They miss the person, but no one really knows how to miss someone who left them on purpose.

So eventually, everyone silently decides that the person was haunted, mentally ill, or weak. They must be, because normal people get on with life one way or another. Normal people show up for life, even if they suck at it. They may do meth, cheat, steal, drink, hurt people, or whatever—but they don't throw in the towel. Suicide is for quitters. And it's selfish, too. Well, unless you're suffering a terminal illness or something people can relate to.

Then people will talk about doing more to prevent it, but no one has any idea how to do that. They set up 5K walks to raise awareness and give out t-shirts. They do studies and research, make goals and demand verifiable evidence, and issue a statement everyone can circulate on social media. They get removed, detached, and official.

What they don't do is look that person in the eyes to see their pain. They never talk to them about what's really going on. They never ask them how they are really doing and listen to the answer... and worse, they usually don't believe the answer.

People wait until it's too late to lament the fact that they had no label or red flag to put them on alert that this was a person at risk—that this was a person who needed them. They think to themselves, "If only we had known..." But that's the wrong perspective entirely. They should be thinking, "If only we had looked..." "If only we had cared..."

Of course, they won't look. To look is to see the pain—the same pain that's unbearable for the person who commits suicide. We can't get on with things and be happy and talk about the latest episode of Game of Thrones if we're saddled with that kind of torment. That's too much. Better to write a check, give a speech, or add the problem to the list of other social concerns we really should pay more attention to.

But that means that we go about our lives never looking at each other. We never see a whole person. We never tolerate the good and the bad in people... we banish the ugliness. We banish wrinkles with creams, we hide our fat in Spanx, we post only smiling faces online, we boast of positivity, and never let on that we have been inflicted with even the slightest bug of sadness, anger, bitterness, or pain. Because if you have that kind of ugliness forced into your bloodstream, you're contaminated. You're a carrier of unhappiness—and no one wants to catch that. Better to avoid, deny, and look away.

"Children, look away! Everything is fine. Nothing to see here, nothing at all. Just keep walking."

No one wants to open their eyes to the fact that sometimes hope runs dangerously low... and sometimes the balloon pops. But maybe if they did, hopelessness wouldn't win.

I close the file and put it back into the beat-up cardboard box. I let my hand brush over Anna's name one last time and then notice Officer Christiansen's name handwritten on the edge. *Officer John Christiansen.* Seeing his first name makes him seem oddly human.

We've all blamed him for not finding Anna since the very beginning. My mom and dad used to carry on about him like he was a supervillain or something. My parents never talked about all the truths the investigation uncovered—all these secrets Anna kept—just about how inept that stupid detective was. After all, he never did bring back Anna.

I guess blaming Christiansen was far easier than deconstructing the days and weeks and months before Anna's disappearance. We may never know exactly what happened that Friday afternoon, but we all know she was struggling during the time leading up to it.

It's hard not to wonder if one of us could have changed her fate. If my mom had been more in touch and less angry. If my dad had been less absent or drunk or screwed up. If Piper or Maddie or Jacob hadn't done what they did. Or if Shayna and Damien hadn't introduced her to drugs and recklessness. If only someone had known about Joey or found him. If any of us would have noticed she was more than just a little sad.

I suppose her disappearance hit a nerve in everyone. Not only did it make everyone question what they could have done differently, it exposed the cracks in our otherwise perfect lives. A girl like Anna doesn't suddenly disappear. Not at a school like Macklemore with its distinguished reputation and award-winning music department. Not in a middle-class family in a pristinely maintained suburban neighborhood. Not in a town like Buena Vida where the sun is always shining. How could a girl be abducted here? Why would a straight-A cheerleader ever run away? How could a seventeen-year-old girl ever be so reckless with her life?

No one wants to admit that bad things happen. Maybe we're all too willing to believe the show Anna put on for us because it's what we wanted to see. She was right when she said that it's easier to pretend that everything is fine than admit that life isn't all that great sometimes. For everyone.

But she was wrong, too. Because I would have stayed up all night with her, night after night, crying and yelling, if that's what it took to keep her around. I would have stared straight into the sun and gone blind if it would have kept her close to me.

Article from The Buena Vida Sentinel
Dated April 30, 2012

𝔅eunea 𝔙ida 𝔖entinal

ONLINE

—

Local

Body Found
at Starlight Beach

Two runners discovered what appears to be the body of a young girl at Starlight State Beach in Mancino, a seaside community approximately two hours north of Buena Vida, early this morning. The pair were jogging near the surf on their usual path when they came upon the body and immediately alerted authorities. Although the identity of the deceased has not been confirmed, there has been speculation that the body may be that of Anna Williams of Buena Vida. The local seventeen-year-old has been missing for ten days without any progress in uncovering her whereabouts.

APRIL 30, 2012

Article from The Buena Vida Sentinel
Dated May 1, 2012

𝔅eunea 𝔙ida 𝔖entinal
ONLINE

–

Local
Police Confirm Body Found at Starlight is Missing Teen

Officials have confirmed that the body of a Caucasian female found on April 28th in Mancino is, indeed, that of Anna Williams. The seventeen-year-old girl has been missing from Buena Vida since April 20, 2012. Last seen at Macklemore High School in Buena Vida, officials have not been able to determine the reason for her disappearance. A report, completed by the Mancino Coroner's Office and released this morning, stated the cause of death as seawater drowning. However, officials have not commented on whether the drowning occurred due to suicide, an accident, or the result of foul play. The community will be holding a memorial in her honor tomorrow afternoon at Macklemore High School, starting at 5:00.

MAY 1, 2012

To: chernandez@buenavidapd.org
From jchristiansen@buenavidapd.org
Date: May 1, 2012, 11:15 a.m.
Subject: The Anna Williams File

Carmen,

I'm sure you heard that they found Anna Williams's body. Since she is no longer missing, protocol requires that I hand off the whole file to homicide so they can further investigate the circumstances surrounding her death. Therefore, I am emailing to ask that you forward any and all notes or research to me for inclusion in the file. If you don't have anything on her, just let me know.

This case is going to get a lot more press. The news is already asking all the usual questions. Did she kill herself? Was she murdered? If so, was she taken from school, or did she run away and then get pulled into harm's way? Did she overdose? I've already gotten four calls asking when the lab will have her toxicity results back. It's the same circus as usual, so all eyes are on us. If you have anything, please get back to me ASAP.

I know we've been through this a million times before, but this one is really getting to me. I don't know what it is about this girl, but she got under my skin. I'm usually very professional about these cases. I know most of the kids who go missing are never found, and we never find out what happened. I know to keep my emotional distance by now, but there's something about Anna Williams that broke through my walls. I feel like I let her down. I just keep thinking, what kind of world have we made for ourselves where our youngest have lost all hope before they even graduate high school?

—John

My phone buzzes as I enter the police station, carrying the box filled with the documents detailing my sister's last moments. It's Jack wondering where I am. I've decided he really is the sweetest boy in the world, and I'm lucky to know him. Whether we ever share a three-bedroom house with two kids and a Goldendoodle or just spend the rest of our lives as good friends remains to be seen. My fingers are crossed, though. I'll have to call him back in a minute. There's something I need to take care of first.

I nod at the uniformed woman at the front desk. I tell her I am here to return the file. When she waves me on, I nervously make my way down the hall to Officer Christiansen's office. I slowly poke my head inside the door, unsure how he will react. He's pulling on his jacket, turning off his monitor. He's ready to go home. I hover awkwardly until he spots me.

"Hi, Officer Christiansen," I offer politely, then wait for him to scold me.

"Officer, huh?" he chides, picking up my sudden display of respect.

I wasn't expecting him to be so nice. It throws me. Stripped of my defenses, I just stand in the doorway of his office. My eyes are locked on him, which is weird for both of us at this point.

He walks towards me with slow, measured steps, and with each one, his expression morphs from amused to concerned. I hate it. I want to disappear. I want to roll my eyes at him, say something spiteful, and then run out—but my body will not cooperate. Instead, I thrust the box forward.

"Sorry I took this."

"Thank you for returning it," he says, taking the box and placing it on his desk. "Although, if you want, you can keep it. It's my personal file, and I don't have any reason to hang onto it."

"No, thanks."

Officer Christiansen stares at me thoughtfully.

"Do you want me to see about getting the homicide file for you to look at?"

"No!" I erupt, which surprises both of us. "I think I know enough for now."

I try to act natural, but I can't. I'm on fire and frozen at the same time.

"Are you alright?" he asks.

"Yeah, I'm fine."

Oh, my God. In what world am I fine? With every day that passes, I miss her more. It seems impossible to miss someone this much. Sometimes my heart aches so desperately that it seems like everything stops. Yet the world keeps spinning around like she wasn't a part of it for seventeen years. And now all that's left of her life fits into a crumby cardboard box. It's just not fair.

Dammit. I'm going to cry. Again! I can't cry. I have to keep it together. Stop it, Katie.

Officer Christiansen is glancing at the floor, clearly avoiding my trembling lip. He leans back on his heels. Then he lifts his face to look at me, which feels overwhelming. I open my mouth to say something nasty, but I can't. I know if I give breath to my voice, it will betray me.

"You know," he says gently, "it's okay if you're not 'fine.'"

The world stops for a moment. I'm stuck inside my heartbeat, cocooned from the outside world. Officer Christiansen has become a blurry figure that I can't quite decipher. I hear a faint whirring sound and there's a ringing in my ears. Then, without warning, I hear muffled crying. It's me. I'm wailing.

Officer Christiansen reaches towards me and I relent to his protective arms. I become a little girl again, fragile and insecure, but soothed by the warmth of his body. It's like I've gone back to that terrible time all over again, wondering and waiting and hoping this man will bring my sister back to me.

I'm stuck in the darkness, consumed with thoughts that torment me. My beautiful sister will never go to college or get married and have kids. She will never jump up and down in excitement over a new band, gush over some cute guy, or snuggle next to me on her bed while we talk. She'll never go to Paris. I wish I had known more, done more. Anything to undo what happened.

I guess I'm not the only one. Officer Christiansen had the audacity to ask the same questions over and over again. He had the nerve to wonder if there was something we all missed—if there was something we all should have done differently. He didn't buy into the usual runaround everyone gave. He pushed people, pressing them about anything and everything, to find out why my sister felt so desperate. He was probably the only one besides me who cared enough to get to know her, even if it was too late.

"I'm sorry," I finally say, my words muffled against his jacket.

"You have nothing to be sorry for, Katie."

Officer Christiansen guides me to one of the two guest chairs in his office, taking a seat next to me. With our knees practically touching, he leans in sideways and tilts his head toward me.

"It's just that—"

He cuts me off with a brisk shake of his head. "Katie, I get it. You're angry as hell. You've probably got a lot of other emotions in there, too."

He's right. I'm all full up on crappy feelings. I can't name them, but there is a whole volcano of them inside. And he doesn't even know the half of it.

"It's normal, Katie. Any kid who has been through as much as you would be feeling the same way."

I'm not sure why, but I like how he calls me kid now. It feels like he knows me, at least well enough to know I'm still a kid.

"You think I should see a psychiatrist or something, huh? You think I should go on medication or check myself into some place where they can monitor me." I say, scornfully.

"I think if those things would help you, you should

do them," he says diplomatically. "But I also think that there's a pretty strong chance you are a normal, everyday teenager who is having normal emotions about a difficult situation. You know, like in every teen movie."

I can't help but smile, but I try to do it wryly. "I'm not normal."

"Yes, you are."

I want to believe him. I want to believe that what I feel isn't the end of the world or a life sentence. I want to believe I'm not too broken.

"Come to think of it, you were a little hard on Disney movies. Most of those princesses had some pretty hard situations to overcome, you know? Cinderella's dad died and then she became a servant to her step-mother and step-sisters, Sleeping Beauty was put to sleep for a hundred years, and Rapunzel was locked in a tower her whole life. They may have gotten to happily-ever-after in the end, but it wasn't easy," he says.

"So you think I should start singing or hanging out with forest animals?" I joke.

"Like I said, whatever you think will help," Christiansen says, undeterred by my sarcasm.

A puff of laughter escapes from my pursed lips.

"What happened to your sister is hard for anyone to understand. Homicide ruled it inconclusive. No one could put together exactly what happened with any certainty." Officer Christiansen pauses, then sighs. "What I couldn't wrap my head around was how she went missing in the first place. If just one of the people in her life had done something diff—"

We're both quiet for a moment. It's not awkward or uncomfortable, but soothing in the way we're just breathing the same air. We're sharing space together, and in this space, there is room for my sister.

I like hearing him talk about Anna. It's like he knew her, even though he never even met her. Then again, he read her most private thoughts and put the pieces of her life together in a way that no one else ever did. He probably knew more about her than all of us.

"Look. When I go home, my wife is going to ask me how my day went. It's not very often that I get to share something good."

I let my eyes drift towards him, but I don't look directly at him.

"Tonight, I'm going to tell her about this amazing girl who crossed my path six years ago, albeit under the worst of circumstances. She was dealt a raw deal in life, one that most people don't understand or care to talk about really. Then this incredible girl, who had been carrying around so much grief and sorrow, did the most amazing thing. She courageously walked into my office to face the hurt of her past and began to heal it."

I bury my face in my hands. His words are too kind and they feel frightening. I stay hidden in my palms for safety as I let each word sink into my heart.

"Then I will tell her that this girl gave me the most wonderful gift. She trusted me enough to be real, and she let me be there for her the way I wish I could have been there for her sister."

I feel his hand land gently on my shoulder, his eyes

boring a hole into my soul.

"So you have nothing to be sorry about, okay? You're kind of the hero here."

I lift my head and turn my face towards him, letting my skeptical eyes do the talking.

"You'll see. One day, you are going to do all the things you wish Anna could have done. You're going to live a great life. And you'll take her with you."

"You think so?" I ask.

"I know so."

My lungs fill up with air that feels brand new, like crisp mountain air during a snowstorm. It's like I'm breathing for the first time in six years. Meanwhile, a warming sensation travels through my arms and legs and into my heart, forcing all the air out in a heavy, satisfying sigh. I feel keenly aware of how alive I am and how good it feels, even though my eyes are burning and swollen. I've been pretending that I'm fine for so long that I forgot what it feels like to just be. I forgot what it feels like to be in my own skin, feeling my own feelings.

Just like Anna, I've been putting on an act. I've been the tough girl, the girl who doesn't care. I've been pretending because it's expected, and it's easier. But also because I'm scared. I'm terrified of being rejected, teased, or abandoned. I'm afraid of what others will think, and even worse, I worry that their bad opinions of me might be right. I'm afraid my sadness and imperfections make me unlovable. When it comes down to it, I think I act like I'm fine because I'm afraid if people know I'm not, I'll get hurt even more.

I think everyone puts on an act. Everyone's scared of showing their true selves, because what if no one likes who we really are deep down? We need people to love us and care for us, especially as kids. We need them to pick us up when we fall and remind us that the world isn't as ugly as it might seem in that moment. We need people to look us in the eye and be honest, even when it hurts. We need people to stick around, even after we show them the worst of ourselves. And we need people to believe in us so that we can believe in ourselves. But what if the people we need don't do any of those things?

People can do a lot of messed up stuff to each other. People lie, cheat, steal, and hurt one another. Even the best people can break our hearts. We all broke Anna's, and she broke ours. It's hard to trust in anything or anyone when that happens. If you get your heart broken enough times, you stop believing in the goodness of people, which means you stop believing in your own.

I guess it's like when Tinkerbell's light grew dimmer and dimmer until it almost went out entirely, simply because not enough children believed in her. When we lose our faith in the goodness of people, we lose the power that belief gives us. We lose our most renewable resource. The world becomes very dark then, dark enough to seem impossible.

I never want the world to get that dark, and I don't think it will as long as there are bright souls like Jack and Sheila and Christiansen in the world. People can be like stars, lighting the path forward when everything seems black and hopeless. They see you through until the light shines again. But you have to believe they are out there, or else you might not look up to see them.

I lean into Officer Christiansen and say, "Thanks."

The next thing I know, I'm in my car, heading towards Jack's house. My radio is blasting and I'm singing along, watching the summer poppies and tall grasses fly by. The morning sun is bright in my eyes, making me squint. I roll down the windows and take in the ocean air. It really is a beautiful world.

I feel Anna with me, smiling and nodding her head in approval. I'm smiling, too, thinking about whether or not she'd like the song on the radio right now. I decide I like it and turn up the volume, letting my body move along to the rhythm. I'm lighter somehow, not so angry. I guess I'm figuring out a way to live with Anna's ghost, rather than fighting it.

For the first time in a long time, it matters to me that I'm still here. I'm not sure my life is precious, but I have one, and that must mean something. I'm starting to think that if I'm taking up space on the planet, I might as well do something while I'm here. Maybe I'll really do the college thing. Maybe I'll become a teacher or a counselor. Who knows? I'm only eighteen and, like Jack says, I've got time to figure things out.

Resources

National Runaway Safeline:
(800) RUNAWAY

National Center for Missing and Exploited Children:
www.missingkids.org

National Suicide Prevention Lifeline:
(800) 273-8255

National Alliance on Mental Illness:
www.nami.org

Prevent Child Abuse America:
www.preventchildabuse.org

SAMHSA National Helpline for individuals facing
mental or substance use disorders:
(800) 622-4357

NACoA Voice for the Children, Teens of Alcoholic Parents:
www.nacoa.org

National Eating Disorders Association Helpline:
(800) 931-2237 or text 741741

Anxiety and Depression Association of America:
www.adaa.org

Substance Abuse Resources for Young Adults:
www.aolescentheath.org

You are not alone.

Acknowledgements

A heartfelt thank you to all of the people who made this book possible, especially:

Calee Allen, Isabelle Murphy, Gail La Carbonara, Sarah Mae, and Book Bin Diver Beta Readers for your invaluable feedback and editorial contributions;

Alan and Ian with the Book Designers for brilliantly bringing my vision to the page; and

Kimberly Brower for first believing in this book.

A special thanks to Greg Murphy, the emissary of dreams. Without his steadfast support, his investment in Katie and Anna, and his willingness to read yet another version, this book would still be an idea.

About the Author

AmyLea lives in California with her husband and three children. When she's not writing, she enjoys music, nature, and dancing in her car with the windows down. For more, you can visit her website at www.amyleamurphy.com.

CPSIA information can be obtained
at www.ICGtesting.com
Printed in the USA
FSHW020204030221
78286FS